Singularity

Singularity

KATHRYN CASEY

St. Martin's Minotaur ✖ New York

This is a work of fiction. All of the characters, organizations, and events portrayed in this novel are either products of the author's imagination or are used fictitiously.

www.minotaurbooks.com

Library of Congress Cataloging-in-Publication Data

Casey, Kathryn.
  Singularity / Kathryn Casey.—1st ed.
    p.   cm.
  ISBN-13: 978-0-312-37950-6
  ISBN-10: 0-312-37950-1
  1. Texas Rangers—Fiction. 2. Criminal profilers—Fiction.
3. Single mothers—Fiction. 4. Texas—Fiction.
5. Murder—Fiction. I. Title.
  PS3603.A8635S56   2008
  813'.6—dc22   2008012484

First Edition: July 2008

10 9 8 7 6 5 4 3 2 1

In memory of Joan Lippolis,
who left too soon

Singularity

One

Consciousness crept through him, as gradually as night yields to daybreak. His eyes adjusted, shade by shade, dark giving way to a gray haze. Gathered beneath his head, his backpack played pillow to the bed of coarse, tan sand. The young man's bones ached from a night of half-sleep and disturbed dreams, thoughts that toyed with his exhaustion and left his brow layered in thick sweat. It always began that way, as a hollow anxiety that built, until it left him jagged and edgy, as lethal as the eight-inch blade on the hunting knife he carried inside a leather sheath, tucked flush against his back.

Where am I? he wondered, scanning the emerging landscape.

Overhead, a sheet of gray-white clouds tented the sky, and a warm, early spring breeze cooled his skin. The salted fragrance of ocean filled his nostrils and stirred his memory, just as streaks of sun painted the pewter waves of the Gulf of Mexico gold.

Ah, that's right. Galveston, he remembered.

As the sun crawled above the watery horizon, he left the beach behind and entered the nearly deserted streets of old Galveston, where he surveyed the empty avenue before him. A brightly painted arch, patterned with jacquard and exuberant flowers, crowned the aged pavement, illuminated by the burgeoning morning. Seagulls squawked urgently overhead.

He paused, considering a boxy, brown brick building with five rows of tall thin windows, a former warehouse where more than a hundred years earlier cargos of Texas cotton waited to be loaded aboard ocean-bound ships to supply English sweatshops. A sign across the top of the building read NEWLY CONVERTED, LOFT APARTMENTS. He scanned the aged structure, checked the address stenciled in gold above the glass door, and noted that the lobby was well lit, inviting, while nearly all the apartments remained shrouded in darkness.

It won't be long, he thought.

"Give it to me. Give it to me," someone mumbled. The young man turned back to the Victorian storefronts that lined the street and eyed a disheveled old man wrapped in an oily, stained wool coat sleeping on a makeshift bed against a doorway. Above the vagrant's rumpled figure, a window displayed gaudy Mardi Gras costumes—yellow-, purple-, and green-feathered masks on wands, all with empty eyes.

The young man scowled as the old man muttered, twitching and trembling. From the look of him, the drunk would soon die from the alcohol that ate away at his mind and his body.

"You're not worth killing," the young man whispered, a small laugh escaping his lips.

Drawn by the bright display inside, he gazed into the store window, and his expressionless image stared back from far inside the glass, a bland, characterless, ordinary face framed by hair the color of ripened wheat but with extraordinary eyes—ice blue, sharp, and resolutely cold.

Dead quiet moments passed, and he waited, nearly motionless, until something unseen pricked his senses, filling him with a visceral anticipation, a sensation he'd grown to welcome as the first sign of impending release.

"It's time," he whispered.

Moments later, a woman rounded the corner and walked toward him: slim and athletic in neon pink running shorts and a sweat-stained white T-shirt, short blond wisps escaping from under her white baseball cap.

He drank her in: the tilt of her head as she wiped her brow with the corner of a thin, light blue towel draped about her neck. She had a lovely neck, long and white. The image of his blade tracing above her collarbone, slicing through her soft, yielding flesh flashed through his mind. He imagined the perfume of her fear, as the seeds of arousal trembled deep within him.

I'm here, he thought. *I'm here for you.*

The woman walked hurriedly past him but then glanced back. At first, a warm smile. Then her lips froze, pulled taut and anxious. Instantly, she turned away and quickened her pace, sprinting across the street, toward the converted warehouse, and disappearing inside the lobby's welcoming golden light.

Outside on the street, the young man smiled.

Two

I glanced at the clock on my office wall when the message from the captain hit my desk at 1:07 that Friday afternoon. The governor's office had called, and my services were requested in Galveston. Some bigwig was dead, not of natural causes, and the island's police chief wanted assistance. At the time, nothing appeared out of the ordinary. Later I'd wonder why the little hairs on the back of my neck didn't stand up or I didn't hear a bell go off. Seems like there should have been some kind of warning, a heads-up that my life was about to throttle into high gear, and that nothing I'd encountered in my years in law enforcement would prepare me for the task ahead, that maybe this time I'd met my match.

Texas Rangers aren't supposed to be caught unawares. There's a saying that dates back to the bad old days when the West was wild and rangers were commissioned for $1.25 a day to fight Indians and war with Mexico: "The Texas Ranger can ride like a Mexican, trail like an Indian, shoot like a Tennessean, and fight like the very devil."

Whoever said that wasn't insulting Mexicans, Native Americans, or Tennesseans. But can anyone really be prepared to battle the devil?

The evil that invaded my life the moment I hung up the telephone, packed my Colt .45 semiautomatic with the worn staghorn grip inside my holster, grabbed my navy blue jacket, and rushed out the office door would soon threaten all that I held dear, everything I believed in, even my very life.

So I ask, shouldn't God have given me a warning, rung that damn bell? But then, in hindsight's twenty-twenty, it's evident that the Almighty wasn't entirely to blame.

The truth? I wasn't listening.

Most people don't really understand Texas. It's a cliché that it's big, so people rarely consider how big. Texas contains more land than Illinois, Indiana, Iowa, Michigan, and Wisconsin combined. We rangers are kind of a lone-star Scotland Yard, under the auspices of the Texas Department of Public Safety and reporting directly to the governor. Our jurisdiction encompasses the entire state, from the panhandle to the Rio Grande, from El Paso to Corpus Christi, including the bulk of the U.S.–Mexico border. In all, 118 rangers cover 163,696 square miles of mountains, valleys, and forests, ranch lands, little towns, and big cities. Still, we're a reclusive bunch. We enter an investigation only when invited by local authorities, when a case exceeds a department's resources, when it crosses jurisdictions, or, as in this case, when from the get-go the local police know it's bound to make headlines and hold their feet to the fire. We're counted on to put the fire out by solving the case quickly and quietly.

As for me, I'm the rangers' only criminal profiler. A police department anywhere in Texas needs a profile to narrow down a list of suspects, I'm the one they call. I work out of Ranger Company A, based in my hometown, Houston, a brash city, part cowboy, part wildcatter, part gray pinstripe and Italian loafers. Like Texas, Houston sprawls.

Just driving across the city takes longer than crossing most of those skinny East Coast states.

Picture a flat, inland Los Angeles covered by trees.

Galveston Island lies southeast of Houston, just off the coastline, in the Gulf of Mexico. With the strobe flashing on the top of my burgundy Chevy Tahoe, I left my westside office that afternoon and sliced on I-10 through downtown's slick mirrored skyscrapers, housing a who's who of oil giants, from Shell and Chevron to Exxon, and then drove south on I-45, the Gulf Freeway, passing the exit where the cars bottle up to tour the Johnson Space Center. An hour later, I'd crossed the causeway into Galveston. I cut across the island and then trailed along the coastline on Seawall Boulevard until I arrived at Playa del Reyes, in English "Beach of the Kings," a swanky colony of multimillion-dollar beach houses that serves as a playground for Houston's big money crowd. The local guys were right; a murder in this zip code wouldn't go unnoticed.

Galveston P.D. squads lined the street in front of a beige stucco mansion on fifteen-foot stilts. The place was enormous, perched on a spur, jutting out over the water, so exposed to the Gulf that it had to be uninsurable. There's that little matter of hurricanes. The most powerful to hit Texas dates back to 1900; even counting Katrina it was the deadliest natural disaster in U.S. history. It nearly leveled Galveston and killed more than six thousand, including ninety orphans from the old St. Mary's Asylum. Some folks in this part of Texas still figure the island is haunted.

On the beach a band of the curious in swimsuits and shorts stared up at the yellow crime-scene tape. TV news cameras whirled, and a clutch of reporters holding spiral-bound notebooks shouted questions as I hurried past. I kept my mouth shut. First, I didn't have anything to tell them. All I knew was that there'd been a double murder, a rather grisly one involving a prominent citizen. Second: rangers scrupulously avoid the press. It's one of our credos. I just wanted to get inside, get busy, and do my job. At the massive front door, I flashed my badge, the traditional silver wagon wheel with the Texas Lone Star in the center.

"Sorry. This is a closed crime scene," the baby-faced officer guarding the door said, as he threw up his arm to keep me out.

I frowned and stared at the kid. Not too bright this one.

It wasn't a totally unexpected reaction. There's an old story from the 1901 oil rush about a riot in an East Texas boomtown. At wit's end, the sheriff telegraphed Austin, begging the governor for rangers to put down the violence. At the railroad station the day his salvation was to arrive, the exhausted lawman waited for a squadron, but only one tall, lean, dusty cowboy wearing a badge exited the train.

"The governor only sent one ranger?" the sheriff gasped.

"The way I hear it," the ranger growled back, "you've only got one riot."

Imagine that sheriff's surprise if instead of that tall drink of water carrying a Winchester, I'd been the lone Texas Ranger on that train.

"Okay, kid," I said, shooting him a warning glance. "We'll do this one more time before I call your sergeant. You want another look at the badge?" I'd had a bad year, the worst of my life, and I'd long since used up all my patience on more important matters. I was about to let the young cop have it when Detective O. L. Nelson, Galveston P.D., popped the door open.

"Boy, don't you know what a Texas Ranger looks like?" Nelson snarled, giving the kid a conspiratorial wink. "This pretty lady is Sarah Armstrong. Lieutenant Armstrong to you. There's a whole cotillion of people inside waiting for her and her alone to solve this heinous crime. Now get your bony butt out of the way and let this famous and learned lady through."

Suddenly the kid was a genius. Obviously, the detective planned to have a little fun with me, so the rookie swooped into an exaggerated bow as he pulled open the door. "Why, right this way, ma'am," the kid crooned, winking back at the detective. "They're waiting for you inside."

These days, women cops are about as common as male nurses, but it's different with Texas Rangers. It's the oldest law-enforcement agency in the country, and change doesn't come quickly when you're dealing with the stuff of legends. I'm one of only two women in what's still a good old boys' club, and, I've got to admit, sometimes it's about as much fun as wearing a flak jacket in Houston in July.

Detective Nelson, a tall, heavyset man with a cocky swagger and a twitch that now and then jerked the right side of his face, placed his hand under my elbow and squired me into the house as smug as a high school senior escorting his date into the gym for the prom.

"Kid's still wet behind the ears," he scoffed, in mock disgust. "He just ain't learned his gentlemanly manners yet."

"Imagine that," I said, stone-faced.

I'd first met Nelson years earlier, and neither of us particularly liked the other.

That summer there'd been a string of carjackings on the island. With Galveston dependent on tourists who flock to the beaches, that didn't sit well with the chamber of commerce types. Frightening headlines rarely do. I don't usually take robbery assignments, but it was busy that week and the request came in when all the other rangers were out. My arrival on the island didn't please Nelson, who'd been working the case for weeks. I disagreed with his theory, that the stolen cars were being trucked to the mainland. Why hide an entire car, when they're easier to transport and more valuable in parts? Once in charge, I focused the search on the Galveston port. On the second day, an unmarked squad spotted the thieves' water-front warehouse.

We borrowed a DEA armored vehicle with a battering ram to raid the place that night. Once we were inside, chaos erupted, as the perps fled like red ants out of an injured hill. In all the commotion, some stupid white kid jumped out from behind a crate and smacked Nelson on the back of the head with a two-by-four. He fell, his gun dropped on the cement floor, and a scrawny black kid with a straggly goatee dove for it. My luck, I just happened to be close enough to plant my .45 on the center of the kid's forehead. I didn't have to say much to convince him to drop the gun.

That night, we arrested four thieves and recovered parts from six stolen cars crated and waiting to be boarded on a ship for Mexico. As far as I was concerned, the case was closed, but Nelson's superiors suspended him for a week without pay for not protecting his weapon. I thought it was tough luck, that given the right circumstances it could happen to anyone. Silly me, I even considered calling to tell him that. Then a week later, I found an envelope with a Galveston postmark and no return address on my desk. Inside was a hand-drawn cartoon of a half-naked woman cop straddling a urinal.

I hung it up with the *Ziggy* and *Bizarro* strips on my office door. It was there for nearly a year before I tore it up and threw it away.

Inside, the beach house looked like a furniture store ad, a place where real people could never live, at least not comfortably. Everything was perfect, from the leather couches and rough, bleached pine tables the color of Galveston's sandy beaches, to the watercolors of waves crashing on dunes.

"Where are they?" I asked.

"This way," said Nelson, visibly relishing being in the lead. He snickered and added with a grin, "Prepare yourself. You ain't seen nothin' like this before."

"Maybe. Maybe not," I said, chewing on the memory of that damn cartoon. "Let's take a look."

Once we reached the master-bedroom wing, sunlight poured

into the room—immense with high ceilings. A wall of windows framed a spectacular view of the Gulf surf. But my eyes were drawn dead center, to the king-size canopy bed. There, on top of the cream satin bedspread, two naked bodies appeared like a life-size statue, motionless figures caught in the act of making love.

The scene was at the same time beautiful and horrifying. For what felt like minutes, I couldn't look away. So much so, that at first I didn't notice the wall above the bed. Then Nelson tapped my shoulder and pointed up to where someone had smeared a thick, vertical four-foot reddish-brown line crossed by a three-foot horizontal bar. I didn't need lab results or my FBI training in profiling to know I was looking at a bloody cross.

"Figured crime-scene photos wouldn't do this justice," someone said behind me. It was the gruff voice of Captain Don Williams, my boss, who walked up beside me. The captain's as unlikely a ranger as I am. He's nearly seven foot, a former University of Texas basketball star, the first black Texas Ranger and the first to make captain. I've always favored the basics, namely black Wranglers, cowboy boots, and a white cotton shirt with a jacket, but like most of the men I work with, the captain dressed Western, from his polished snakeskin boots and silver-belly Stetson, to his gold captain's badge pinned on a dark brown leather vest. "Pretty strange, eh?"

"Sure is," I said.

I'd nearly forgotten Nelson was there until he gloated, "I told you this was one of a kind."

"What do you think?" the captain asked.

I stood for a few minutes, taking it all in. I thought of a museum sculpture I'd once seen, pure white marble cut and polished into two Greek lovers. The victims' upper bodies had that same pale, bloodless sheen, but I nudged down the comforter and saw that the woman's calves and the man's backside were bluish purple, postmortem lividity, gravity pooling blood in the lowest regions of the bodies. That meant they'd been dead for at least six hours. When I brushed the back of my hand against the woman's forearm, she felt cold, and a shiver ran through me. I quickly moved on, but when I glanced his way, Nelson was watching me and he smiled a small, crooked grin. I ignored him and went back to work.

As a profiler, I'm trained to view victims' bodies as evidence, no different from fingerprints and blood splatter. Sometimes that's hard, trying not to think of them as people, I mean. No matter how often I've done it, no matter how engrossing the scene, working around dead bodies, my skin prickles. I think about the horror of their deaths, and my stomach gets unsettled, as if I'd had too much red wine the night before. Especially after all that's happened in my own life. It's made it even harder not to let my mind drift to thoughts of the families left behind, the pain that waits for them.

After my second trip around the bed, I pulled out a steno pad and jotted down notes: the man was spread-eagled, tied to the bed frame with expensive silk ties, most likely out of his closet. A dime-size bullet hole in his forehead, its edges burned and sooty, exposed tissue turned a bright cherry pink from absorption of carbon monoxide, explaining the bloody halo on the pillow.

The woman was on her knees, straddling the dead man. Left to their own devices, dead bodies don't do that, stay upright I mean. From across the room, all I could see was that something tied to her upper body braced her. Up close, I tapped a latex-gloved finger against translucent fishing line, the sturdy, deep-sea kind, anchoring the corpse to the bed's ornate brass canopy. A single length hog-tied the dead woman's ankles, her wrists behind her, and then formed a slipknot around her neck. The killer knew what he was doing; as she struggled, the fishing line cut into her throat, squeezing her airway tighter and tighter. What from across the room appeared to be sexual rapture was in reality a vain attempt to keep her head back and live.

Thinking about how the killer had used the dead rich guy's ties, I asked the captain, "The fishing line from the scene?"

"Looks like it's off a rod and reel in the downstairs storage," he confirmed.

That settled, I climbed a few rungs up on a ladder the Galveston crime-scene guys had positioned and inspected the woman's corpse from a better angle. She had all the outward signs of ligature strangulation, her face bloated and bruised. A line of blood spilled from a gash across her throat. Whether or not he needed to, the killer had finished her off, slitting her throat with a razor-sharp blade.

A dark burgundy river of dried blood on her chest came from slashes cut from collarbone to navel, then breast to breast. Down from the ladder, I gave the man another look. He had the same marking on his chest, mimicking the bloody cross on the wall.

"Who are they?" I asked.

"Meet Edward Travis Lucas the third," Captain Williams said.

He needed to say nothing more. The Lucas family, real estate developers for more than three generations, had their name on half the buildings in Galveston along with a healthy chunk of Houston. In its present condition, I barely recognized the man's plain face framed by graying, mousy brown hair from the frequent photos in the *Houston Chronicle* society columns. I vaguely remembered a wife from those same photos, taken at the poshest parties. The woman I remembered looked nothing like the deceased on the bed. The wife was pretty, petite, and dark-haired. This woman was at least a decade younger than Lucas, tall and slim, with short blond hair. Athletic—from the muscles jutting down her thighs and calves, I guessed a runner.

"Not the wife," I said.

"We found her ID in her purse. The dead woman is Annmarie Knowles, a lawyer at Lucas's Galveston office," the captain said. He picked up a framed photo from the nightstand, of the dead man standing beside the brunette I remembered, surrounded by three apple-cheeked kids. "My guess is this is the wife."

"Does she know?"

"Yeah," said Nelson, reinserting himself into the conversation. "We sent a squad car to tell her an hour ago. Our guys said she took the news with less emotion than the dry-cleaning being late."

"Any leads? Anyone hear or see anything?" I asked.

"Nothing," said the captain.

"This time of year you could fire a bazooka off around here and no one would hear it," explained Nelson. "On weekdays ninety-nine percent of these houses are empty until summer."

"Do we know how the killer got in?"

"No forced entry," Nelson said.

"The killer followed or brought them here? Entered when they did?" the captain asked.

"That would be my guess," I said. "Absent any evidence of a break-in."

"So you figure they knew him?"

I thought about the bodies, about the type of mind that would fantasize about killing in such a ritualized way. "Probably not," I said. "You never know this early in the investigation, but even though he didn't force his way in, I doubt—"

"I'm thinking the guy had a key." Nelson interrupted, pulling up on the worn leather belt that held up his shapeless gray slacks. It was obvious that he hated having me on his case. Despite the cartoon, my sex had little to do with it. Nelson and I both knew why I'd been called in on the carjackings and why I stood across from him now; his boss didn't trust him to solve the tough cases. Every cop has a jacket, a reputation. O. L. Nelson's was that he'd earned a detective's slot based on seniority and little else. He did nothing to challenge that image when he righted his buckle over his bulging waistline and speculated. "I figure Lucas's old lady gave the killer the key, set the whole thing up. The way I've got this thing pegged, this has the look of hired talent."

Then, slowly, as if explaining algebra to a second grader, Nelson looked at me and went on. "Little woman finds out hubby is screwing the hired help. Maybe he talks divorce. Maybe he and the wife have a pre-nup and the old lady figures he'll find a way to leave her high and dry. Bye, bye checkbook. Hello full-time office job. She doesn't like the prospects, so she puts out feelers, a little dough, and poof. Her problem vanishes."

"Why the elaborate staging of the bodies?" I asked. "Why the crosses?"

"Camouflage," he answered. Although I'd posed the question, he flashed the captain a knowing glance. "The guy wants us to think he's some kind of psycho to keep us from connecting the murders to the wife."

"Possible," I said.

"You look doubtful," the captain said.

"Take a look at their hands and feet," I suggested.

Nelson bent down to get a better look at the rash of small cuts on both victims, as the captain shot me a questioning glance.

"This killer's piqueristic, fascinated by knives. The coroner will be the final judge, but from the bleeding, my guess is that they were still alive. The SOB tortured them, most likely using the same weapon he used to slit her throat."

"So?" Nelson said. "He enjoys his work. So what?"

"That knife is his preferred weapon. He carries it with him. When you find him, he'll have the knife on him," I said. "The gun is an afterthought. My guess is he picked it up on the scene like the fishing line and the ties. You might even find it abandoned in the house. He doesn't care about it."

Captain Williams glanced at Nelson.

"We found a 9mm pistol, wiped clean of prints but recently fired, on a table in the den," Nelson said. "We're thinking it's the murder weapon."

"And it belonged to Lucas not the killer?" I speculated.

The captain nodded. "There's also an empty gun box with Lucas's name engraved on it. And this is odd, blood traces around the shower drain."

"He didn't wash the bodies," I said, looking again at the bloody scene and considering the possibilities. "The guy showered?"

"Maybe, but if he did he cleaned up. Not a trace of anything left," the captain said. "This guy was careful."

"To take down two victims at once, he's had practice. He was sure of himself. He didn't run. He watched them, targeted one or both well before the killings, followed them until he knew their habits. He knew they wouldn't be interrupted. He took his time and enjoyed the killing, then afterward . . ." The film playing in my mind wrenched my gut tighter, and I felt suddenly ill.

"So our guy has balls." Nelson shrugged. "So what?"

I visualized them in the room, the terrified couple tied to the bed, begging for their lives, while the shadowy killer lurked in the background.

"What about other physical evidence?" I asked. "Anything we can use from forensics?"

"The maid comes three times a week, even if the family's not around. She was here yesterday, so there aren't many. We'll have a report by the end of the day," said the captain, frowning. "There are so few, my guess is our killer wore gloves."

"Which proves my point," Nelson said, smugly. "He's a pro."

"Think about it," I challenged. "What kind of hit man counts on finding a gun at the scene? He didn't even bring his own rope to tie them up."

For a moment, Nelson appeared to reconsider, but then he smiled. "Maybe the wife told him there'd be a gun and where to find it."

"This isn't about money," I said, turning from Nelson to the captain. "This guy gets off slicing people up. This wasn't personal. It wasn't work. It was about power, control, obsession, and, maybe most of all, pleasure."

The captain took off his hat and scratched his temples, vainly attempting to repair the ear-to-ear indentation the Stetson left behind. Gray had been taking over in the past few years, and I'd noticed he'd started cutting his hair shorter. "You've got to admit, we've got a murdered husband and his mistress, you've got to like the wife at least enough to give her a close look," he said.

"That's all I'm saying, Captain," Nelson said.

I looked at the detective and frowned. This was going to be a long day.

"I'm not suggesting that it's impossible that you're right, Detective. None of us knows enough yet to throw out any theory," I said. "But the captain wanted my impression, and it's that Lucas and this woman had the misfortune of running into a seriously twisted killer, one who enjoys slicing people up."

"So we can agree that this is just your opinion, and that I'm entitled to a different one?" Nelson asked. I couldn't help but consider that perhaps this case wouldn't be a fresh start for us. I might have to live with the prospect that Detective O. L. Nelson and I would never be best friends.

"Of course," I conceded. Eager to avoid further confrontation and to start the investigation that would end all the speculation, I asked. "Where's the wife?"

"At home," said the captain. "She's the one who called the station, asked Galveston P.D. to check out the beach house."

"Another reason to like her for this," Nelson insisted. "She tells us to check the beach house and sure enough, what do we find? Two dead bodies."

I had to remind myself not to groan.

"Captain, I'm finished here. You can let the M.E.'s folks process the bodies. I'm assuming you have the search warrants signed?" I asked Nelson.

"All done," he said.

"Good. Then I'm going to the dead woman's place to take a look." I frowned at Nelson, unhappily considering departmental protocol that dictates we work with the local P.D., and reluctantly added, "Detective, you are, of course, welcome to come along."

Three

Annmarie Knowles lived in a loft apartment in downtown Galveston, ten minutes from the beach house. The building manager said she'd signed the lease a year earlier. She paid her rent on time and kept to herself. It was obvious she thought of it as no more than a temporary setup. She'd done minimal decorating, little furniture beyond a bed, an old dresser, a tomato-red couch and two old tables that could have come from the Salvation Army resale shop. She had one painting on the wall, a small work by Jackson Pollock that looked, at least to my untrained eye, like the real thing. Most likely a gift or loan from Lucas. That meant the relationship must have been serious. You don't trust a masterpiece, even a minor one, to a casual girlfriend.

Annmarie was a good housekeeper. The place was spotless, except for rinsed breakfast dishes stacked in the sink and a well-worn pair of Nike running shoes discarded on the living room floor. The view from her window was of Old Galveston, restaurants, Victorian storefronts, and, a brisk five-minute walk away, the rail yard.

She must have been here just this morning, I thought. Healthy, young people don't expect to die, even today with the papers crowded with the fear of terrorist attacks and headlines about deadly convenience store holdups. Violent, senseless crimes are nearly always a surprise. It's assumed they only happen to others, people who aren't careful, aren't lucky, aren't smart. Not beautiful young lawyers who live in expensive apartments and bed their multimillionaire bosses.

In the kitchen, Annmarie had covered the refrigerator with photos held by magnets attached to papier-mâché fruit, her only personal touch. A green-and-yellow apple gripped a likeness of two young girls, maybe nieces or the daughters of a friend? Nearby, a sprig of bright purple grapes held a sixty-ish couple, who, from the resemblance, I guessed were her parents. Someone would have to find them. Another family introduced to the unrelenting pain of inexplicable loss, another set of parents left to wonder about the horror of their child's final moments, the fear that must have sliced through her as surely as the killer's knife through her throat.

For the next hour, Nelson and I rifled through Annmarie's papers on her desk, her Jimmy Choo, Giuseppe Zanotti, and Miu Miu shoeboxes and the Prada, Michael Kors, and Gucci frocks in her closet. The girl dressed well on a young lawyer's salary. Of course, once the police show up, nothing is sacred. I played the answering machine: one message, a reminder for a hair appointment the next day.

We found nothing apparently tied to the murders.

Questioning the neighbors proved more fruitful. First, we learned Edward Lucas had been a frequent visitor to Knowles's condo. No surprise there. Then I stopped a gray-haired medical-software salesman returning home from a day at the office, as he waited for the elevator. He'd heard about the murders on the car radio during his commute, but until we told him, he didn't know one of the victims had been a woman from his building.

"A couple of mornings ago, something strange did happen," he explained. "I didn't think much of it at the time."

"What's that?" I asked.

"I was on my way to work, say seven or so, maybe earlier."

"And?"

"And, I was walking through the lobby to the garage when that woman you're asking about kind of burst through the door after her run, looking frightened."

"Of what?"

"I remember she was fumbling her keys," he said. "She looked rattled."

"Why?" I asked, again.

"I don't know." He shrugged. "I didn't ask. I didn't know the woman well enough to ask. She just looked, well, scared."

A few minutes later, we learned another bit of information that might prove fruitful, when Nelson and I tracked down Annmarie's immediate neighbor, a real estate woman in her fifties, busy washing clothes in the second-floor laundry room.

"There was shouting in that girl's apartment last night, starting about seven. I thought about calling the building manager, but I knew he'd be gone. His poker night," she said, still annoyed at the memory. "Anyway, I had an early meeting scheduled with an important client and wasn't happy about all the noise. I wanted a quiet dinner and an early night. When the quarrel ended, about eight or so, I looked out my peephole and saw a woman leaving."

"What did she look like?"

"Rather short. Brunette. Expensively dressed."

The description fit Mrs. Lucas down to her undoubtedly French-manicured nails. Nelson puffed up with such self-satisfaction, I considered warning him that the wind might change and leave his face frozen that way.

"Could you hear what they were arguing about?" I asked her.

"I couldn't make out any words," she said. "Just loud voices. Both the women sounded very angry, very upset."

Outside on the street, early evening tourists sat on benches overlooking the water. It's days like this, spring, winter, and fall, that make this part of Texas habitable. In the summer, when the temperatures and humidity hunker down at the mid-nineties, even Gulf breezes can't break the sweat factor. Summers, I wonder how my great-grandmother survived without air-conditioning.

I knew Nelson had been biding his time to get me alone, and on the way to our cars he let loose. There's nothing like a redneck cop with a snout of self-righteousness to build up a head of steam.

"Who do you think Annmarie Knowles had reason to be scared of?" he prodded. "Think maybe the petite, brunette wife of the man she was screwing? The woman she was arguing with last night in her condo?"

I smiled back at him, the sweetest, blandest smile I could muster, the way my mom taught me when I was a kid and Sam Reyerson pulled my ponytail in math class. I'd turn around in my seat, smile at that kid, and presto, the little weasel stopped bothering me and got back to the weekly quiz. At first, Nelson looked puzzled, but pretty soon I got the result I'd hoped for. He shut up.

"You know, you may be right. At the very least Mrs. Lucas has some questions to answer," I said. "Let's have the uniforms bring a spread including her driver's license photo over for Annmarie's neighbor to ID. In the meantime, let's talk to the grieving widow."

Four

As prominent as the Lucas family was in Galveston, many people assumed they lived on the island. They didn't. As the sun set, Nelson and I parked our cars in front of a River Oaks mansion, on six acres surrounded by an eight-foot fence, just west of downtown Houston. The place was white brick, pillared, right out of *Gone with the Wind*. A maid in a black-and-white uniform answered the door and assured us Mrs. Lucas would be with us momentarily. That gave us a chance to scan the front parlor: all antique furniture, oil paintings, and polished wood floors. Nelson gawked at a bronze Remington of an Indian warrior on horseback with his lance drawn on stampeding buffalo. I felt like a small-town tourist in the big city, as I admired the antique Afghan prayer rug.

Moments later, Priscilla Lucas bustled in surrounded by a wave of nervous energy, the kind that instantly makes my curiosity tingle. Her long, dark brown hair was anchored with a gold-and-diamond barrette. She wore a tight white silk shirt over breasts too round and firm not to have been tampered with and black silk slacks that hugged her trim waistline and hips. Even without plastic surgery, she would have looked good, a development that didn't escape Nelson's pop-eyed scrutiny. I studied her face, not flushed, eyes clear. She hadn't been crying.

Unusual for a woman whose husband had just been brutally murdered.

"Please, come with me," she said, leading us to a sunroom off the parlor. "The children are watching a movie. I'm waiting for my father and a grief counselor to arrive. I haven't told them about their father yet. I hope this will be all right."

"Of course," I said.

We barely sat down when Nelson got right to the point: "Mrs. Lucas, we have some questions for you."

"I knew you would," she answered. "You might as well know up front, Edward and I weren't happily married. We were talking to attorneys. The word 'divorce' had been mentioned."

Nelson shot me a knowing glance, but I turned back to the new widow. I was impressed that she was being so open, but then I realized that a woman like Priscilla Lucas isn't used to being questioned by police. She undoubtedly believed her social position placed her above suspicion.

Always a fan of the one-word question, I asked, "Why?"

"Edward was a rather distant man, rather cold. We grew apart," she said, so matter-of-factly I felt sure she'd rehearsed. "And there were the affairs. This one with this young lawyer in his office, Miss Knowles, well it was just the latest in a long string. And—I may as well tell you this because someone else surely will—I've been seeing someone."

For the wife of a murder victim, this seemed a surprising admission, and I saw Nelson straighten up, perching expectantly on the edge of the calico-cushioned couch.

"Who?" I asked.

"A man I met this past fall. We're in love and want to marry.

Edward didn't initially favor a divorce, but I was winning him over to my point of view."

"What does this man do?" Nelson piped in. "Your lover?"

"He's a professor at Rice University," she said, blanching at his characterization. "He teaches French."

"What does a French teacher make?" Nelson asked, as he fingered the thick lip of the swan-shaped Lalique bowl resting on the coffee table. "Forty, maybe fifty or sixty a year, max?"

"I'm sure I wouldn't know," Priscilla answered, eyebrows arched in peeved commas. "Money wouldn't be a concern."

"Counting on the divorce settlement?" Nelson prodded, his implication hanging in the air between us.

"No," she answered, her bow lips pursed. "You, Officer . . ."

"Detective."

"You, Detective, haven't done your homework," she chastised. "I have no need of Edward's money. It's no secret that my maiden name is Barker, as in Barker Oil."

Nelson said nothing, but his gaze hardened. He didn't like being scolded, especially by a woman he judged wasn't coming from any particular moral high ground. Despite her lack of grief over her husband's death, I was beginning to appreciate Priscilla Lucas.

"Mother?"

We all looked up. Standing in the doorway was a young boy, maybe eight or nine. He had his mother's blue eyes. I wondered how long he'd been there and what he'd already heard.

"Travis, really dear, now isn't the time," said Priscilla Lucas, her voice weary yet soft. "Watch the movie with your sisters. I'll be with you as soon as our guests leave."

"Who are they? Why are they here?" he asked, his young brow wrinkled with concern. I thought of my daughter, Maggie, and the night we learned that her father had died. Death was so unfair, especially for the children left behind.

"I'll tell you everything in a few minutes, dear," Mrs. Lucas explained, her voice strained but calm. "Now please, let us finish our discussion."

"Is something wrong?" the boy asked, looking young and scared.

"Travis, I need to have you rejoin your sisters," she repeated. Then she nearly begged, "Please, listen to me and do as I ask. It's important."

The boy sized up Nelson and me one more time. Then, reluctantly, he turned and walked away. Moments passed before any of us spoke. I was still lost in my own memories when Nelson asked Mrs. Lucas, "So, where were you this morning, about nine?"

"You don't think I could do such a monstrous thing?" she demanded, for the first time appearing worried. It must have suddenly dawned on her that we weren't there offering our condolences. The woman looked appalled and at a loss for words, not a good turn of events. Unless Nelson backed off, I had no doubt that at any moment she'd regain her composure and refuse to talk to us without her lawyer. From that point on, we were at the mercy of some well paid suit whose primary agenda would be to keep us away from his wealthy client.

Weary of Nelson's theatrics, I attempted damage control. "Please understand, Mrs. Lucas, that it's nothing personal. In the beginning, we ask everyone even remotely involved in a case that question. What we really need from you are a few facts, to draw a picture of the days leading up to the murders. Let's start with where you were this morning."

"Well, I'm happy to help. Edward and I have three children, after all. I do want you to find his killer," she said, regaining her former placid expression. "I was here, in my home. You can verify that with the maid, the cook, and about six friends. I hosted a meeting that lasted nearly all day. We were planning the fall ballet ball. It has a Venetian nights theme, rather difficult to pull off, I must admit, and

Edward and I are . . ." She paused, hesitated, and then continued, "We *were* chairing. That's why I called him this afternoon. I wanted to ask if that was a good idea, considering our marital situation."

"And you called the police . . ."

"Because I couldn't find my husband," she said bluntly. "Edward is, was, always reachable. When he didn't answer his cell phone and no one in the office could find him, I knew something was wrong. My husband may sneak away for a . . . shall we call it a recreational break? But he runs a substantial business. He does not just disappear for hours without leaving a number."

"Why did you suggest the police check the beach house?" I pushed.

Priscilla Lucas sighed, creases tracing thin lines across her brow. "Edward is a creature of habit. His routines rarely vary. I know, I've always known that he takes them there, his women-of-the-moment," she said, her voice smooth but unable to hide what must have been a long-lived anger.

"Did your husband have any enemies?" I asked.

"Nothing beyond the normal business rivalries."

"Was there any reason for you to fear he'd been injured?"

"Just what I've told you, that I couldn't find him," she said, losing patience. "It may be difficult to believe, but in all the years we've been married, this is the first time I haven't been able to locate Edward for any substantial period of time. That and I had a feeling, call it a premonition, that something was wrong."

"Mrs. Lucas, does your husband own a gun?" I asked, wondering if she would admit knowing about the handgun at the beach house or have reason to deny it.

"Yes," she said, without hesitation. "Edward owns more than one. We argued about them often. I've never liked guns. I've always been afraid the children might find them. But Edward has a locked cabinet in our bedroom here at the house with two pistols, and he kept another at the beach house, in a box in the nightstand next to our bed. Why do you ask?"

"The murderer used your husband's gun to shoot him through the forehead," Nelson said, not even feigning sympathy.

"Oh," she said, stunned, the remaining color draining from her already China-doll face.

Before she could recover, Nelson shot out another question, "And where were you last night, Mrs. Lucas?"

"Last night?" she asked, abruptly looking away from us and staring at her hands, folded on her lap. They trembled slightly as she toyed with an impressive emerald-cut diamond solitaire. "Why should that be important? Edward and Ms. Knowles were murdered this morning."

"We have reasons," Nelson answered, smiling.

This time, I didn't interrupt. I wanted to hear her answer as much as Nelson did. Priscilla Lucas hesitated, obviously considering her response. For my liking, she paused too long, leading me to wonder why, unless she was trying to hide what we'd been told via phone on the drive into Houston. Annmarie's neighbor had ID'ed her photo. Mrs. Lucas was the woman arguing with Knowles the night before. The woman who'd left in a huff.

"Last night I was out until about nine, and then I came home and discussed today's menu for the meeting with the cook. You can verify that with her, if you must," she said, defensively. "Edward was home, going over paperwork from the office when I got here. I didn't feel well. I had an excruciating headache. I went straight to bed."

"Where were you earlier in the evening?" I prodded, needing to pin her down for the period of time the two women were heard arguing. "Say, between seven and eight."

For a moment, the room felt uncomfortably silent. Priscilla Lucas hesitated, once or twice appearing to be ready to talk. Finally, she rose to her feet, her smile as painted on as the hand-stenciled ivy covering the sunroom walls.

"That's something I'm not free to discuss." I wasn't surprised when she said, "This interview is over."

"Mrs. Lucas," I said. "Detective Nelson and I know you were at Annmarie's condo arguing with her last night. You were seen leaving by a neighbor. What you need to tell us is why you were there. What was the quarrel about?"

Beautiful, cultivated Priscilla Lucas, mainstay of Houston society and a woman used to controlling not only her emotions but, by virtue of her vast fortune, the actions of others, frowned, and I noted what might have been her first tears of the day collecting in her eyes. Were they for her dead husband or for herself?

"Lieutenant Armstrong and Detective Nelson," she said, her voice stoic and exuding perfect politeness. "Please leave, and direct all further inquiries to my lawyers. Right now, my children are in the other room. My father and the therapist will be here soon, and I need to tell my children their father is dead."

Five

Detective O. L. Nelson and I left the Lucas house and parted for the night. We'd cover our phones for the weekend, but for now the uniformed officers, the lab techs, and the coroner were in charge, processing the evidence in hopes of finding leads. It was late when I arrived home, and the house was dark and quiet, everyone asleep. In bed, I mentally retraced my steps, back to the beach house and over and over again through the bedroom door to the foot of the canopied bed, where in my half-dreams the two bodies remained frozen in time.

I thought of the Lucas children and the conversation that must have taken place after we left: their mother, grandfather, and a therapist attempting to explain the incomprehensible, that their father was brutally murdered, that they would never see him again.

About three that Saturday morning, I gave up on sleep and went to my workshop over the garage. In college, I had a double major, psychology and art. After graduation, I thought I would use art to work with abused children. Obviously my life took a detour. These days my psychology training is an asset in my profiling. As for my art? Well, that, too, has taken a rather dark turn.

In the workshop, I grabbed a brown cardboard box off the shelf. It was from the Houston M.E.'s office, and inside was a human skull mounted on a sturdy wooden base.

I admit it's an unusual way to relax, but in my off time, especially when I'm mulling over a case, I do facial reconstructions on unidentified remains. Maybe it's not as odd as it sounds. I've always found sculpting in clay soothing, and unlike live models, the dead don't complain that I made them look ten pounds heavier or didn't get their smile right.

A woman scavenging dried weeds to make wreaths had discovered the remains on the bank of a Houston bayou. Insects, heat, and humidity had eaten away the tissue, muscle, and flesh. Animals had scattered most of the bones. Little was found, only the skull, one thigh bone, and the delicate bones of an arm and hand. From the still-forming joint cartilage, the medical examiner estimated that the bones were of a small child, probably not older than five. Even with an entire skeleton, it's difficult to determine sex at such a young age. One worn Superman tennis shoe found near the body initially suggested we were viewing the remains of a boy, an assumption that was later confirmed with DNA.

A week earlier I'd wired together a three-inch fracture, a patch of skull at the hairline nearly crushed by a powerful blow, the presumed cause of death. I'd then cut twenty-one rubber stubs to match the depth of the boy's missing skin and muscle, a thicker stub for the cheeks, thinner on the forehead and the chin. Positioned on the skull, the stubs would serve as guides to the depth of the clay. Along with the boy's DNA, the generous spread of his nasal aperture and the slight elongation of his lower face suggested he was black, leading me to choose clay the color of dry coffee grounds and two plastic eyes with irises so dark they swallowed up the pupils.

Throughout the night, I lost myself in my work, enjoying the quiet and the feel of the clay in my hands as I carefully coated the skull. Well after sunrise, seven hours after I'd started, I was finishing up, using a small trowel to reshape his lips. The boy had a wide mouth, and I fashioned a mischievous grin and a small nose wrinkled in laughter. I sized up my handiwork: full cheeks, thick eyebrows, and a crooked front tooth jutting out from under a frozen smile. He was a good-looking kid.

"I'll call you Ben," I said, wishing the boy could tell me who he was and who had murdered him.

How easily life ends, I thought. If nothing else, the last year had taught me that.

"Mom?"

I didn't respond.

"Mom," she said again, only louder. "Gram says it's time to get ready or it'll be too late to go to the museum." Peering in the workshop door, my eleven-year-old was scowling, a look Maggie reserves for me, I know, when I'm not being quite the perfect mother, which is often.

"Magpie, tell Gram I'll be right there."

"You better hurry," she warned. "Gram's pretty mad."

"Hmmm," I said. I walked over and planted a wet kiss on the top of her head, thinking of the Lucas boy from the night before. Then I held her tight.

"What's wrong?" she asked, squirming.

"Nothing. Nothing at all," I said, as she pushed away. "But I guess if Gram's upset, I'd better be on my best behavior?"

"She's baking," Maggie said, imparting what we both knew was a serious clue to my mother's state of mind.

"Uh, oh, that's not good." I chuckled. "Tell her I promise that I'll be right there."

"She's not going to believe me," Maggie said, shuffling off.

Mom had the right to be miffed. I'd promised I wouldn't let work interfere, that we'd make it to the museum before lunch. I knew I should go. But I hesitated. After all, Mom was already in a slow burn. Why not?

There was no predicting when I'd have time again, so I grabbed my digital camera and snapped four photos of Ben's reconstructed face, and then downloaded the photos onto the computer screen. Within a few minutes, I'd e-mailed the lot, along with a summary I'd already prepared describing where the skull had been found, to Houston P.D.'s missing persons, my office at the Texas Department of Public Safety, and to the National Center for Missing and Exploited Children in Virginia. I had no illusions. It was a long shot. No matter how many post-office walls this kid's face was displayed on, there was little hope anyone would identify the child.

Finished, I put Ben back in the box, then hurried downstairs. I walked through the garage, past Mom's beat-up Ford pickup, feeling vaguely uneasy. Maggie's fearfulness did that to me. For the first ten years of her life as I sculpted faces on skulls, Maggie played at my feet, claiming leftover tidbits of clay to mold into flowers. Back then, sudden, violent death was something that happened only to strangers.

Then Bill died last spring, and now Maggie won't even walk through my workshop door.

Knowing Mom would be on the warpath, I hurried through the garage door and past the corral, where Emma Lou, Maggie's three-year-old, black-and-white pinto, slurped from her water trough. The filly rolled her head, eyeing me. She looked hungry. The half-dozen horses Mom boards were across the yard in the old barn and had already eaten their morning oats and hay. Mom makes sure they have an early breakfast. But Emma Lou is Maggie's job, and there wasn't a feed sack in sight. The horse whinnied.

"Emma Lou," I grumbled. "I'm already running late, girl."

The horse shook its head, its snow-white mane flying, and I thought about shouting for Maggie. Instead, I hurried back into the garage and grabbed a bucket, then dunked it in the yellow oat can. By the time I'd reached the back door, Emma Lou was happily munching.

The truth is that the Rocking Horse Stables has seen better days. The grass and shrubs are overgrown, and there's no way the place will ever make *Rancher's Digest*. It's a hodgepodge of additions tacked onto a dilapidated two-bedroom cabin. The whole thing's covered with rough cedar seasoned battleship-gray. But it's home, and it's convenient, on the outskirts of Tomball, a once Podunk town that's in the process of being swallowed up by the city. Mom and Dad bought the place when I was a kid, and I grew up here, riding horses and raising 4-H hogs. After Bill died, I brought Maggie and moved back in. Pop had passed on years ago, and Mom was alone. The place is only half an hour's drive from my Houston office, and I figured we could all do with having more family around.

"Well, you took your time," Mom chastised when I swung open the screen door. I'd been able to smell the cookies from the porch, sheets of saucer-sized oatmeal-raisin cookies that covered the counter.

"I had something I had to finish," I said, reaching for one. "And I fed Emma Lou."

"I would have done it," Maggie protested.

"Magpie, it's after ten," I said. "You need to—"

"That horse has to be starved by now," Mom scolded, and Maggie groaned.

Mom's bushy white hair was pulled back in a scarf. Dressed in a pink sweatsuit with hand-painted tulips on the front, she looked the consummate grandmother, which she is. Actually, she's a professional. Along with running the ranch, Mom has a second business and a second name, Mother Adams, as in "Mother Adams's Cheesecakes." She sells her baked goods to caterers and the city's fancy restaurants. Her real name is Nora Potts. "Mother Potts's Cheesecakes" just didn't have the same panache.

At five-foot-six, I weigh a hundred and thirty pounds, not bad, but I've got the hips of a woman ten pounds heavier, a deformity I blame on my mother's talent with an oven. Still, since Mom went pro, she usually only bakes professionally. When she takes out the mixer for Maggie and me, it's not good news.

"Sarah Jane Potts," Mom chirped, clicking her teeth, a habit that since childhood has crawled up my spine like spider feet. "You've kept us waiting all morning. You get maybe two weekends off a month. Couldn't you save those days for family?"

"Armstrong," I reminded her, not bothering to again justify my tardiness. Nothing changes. Even if I'm a cop with a gun and a badge out on the street, in Mom's kitchen I'm still a kid. "The name's Sarah Armstrong."

"Gram, you know that," Maggie agreed, dipping a still-warm cookie in a tumbler of milk. "It's Armstrong just like mine and Dad's. Why do you always do that?"

"Well, of course it is, baby," Mom said, wrapping her arms around Maggie's shoulders. "Gram's old. Sometimes she just forgets."

I didn't buy a word of it. Mom loved Bill, but she blamed him for luring me into law enforcement. A daughter who investigates brutal murders doesn't give a sixty-six-year-old woman much peace of mind.

Looking back, Bill Armstrong had been the center of my life for nearly two decades. We met in college, and married the year I graduated. He was a third-generation Texas Ranger, and he coaxed me away from my textbooks with tales he'd heard as a kid, stories about rangers with colorful nicknames like Big Foot, Three-legged Williamson, Lonewolf, and Senior Ranger Captain John "Rip" Ford, who earned his middle name during Texas's bloody war for independence from Mexico. At first, Ford signed condolence letters to the families of fallen soldiers "rest in peace." Weighed down by the sheer volume, he settled on RIP. Those were the bad old days, when rangers ran roughshod over Texas, capturing train and bank robbers, simmering down blood feuds, corralling cattle thieves and rum runners, and holding off lynch mobs.

Personally, I've never been drawn to sepia photos of sour-looking men in handlebar mustaches and cowboy hats. I am, however, fascinated by the human mind. As soon as Bill brought his first case file home, I was hooked.

"So," I asked, grabbing one of Maggie's ponytail ties off the counter and looping it around a fistful of my dark straw-colored hair. "You two ready? I am. Just need to grab my purse and the car keys."

"You bet," Maggie said, her face breaking into an ear-to-ear grin. "And Strings is, too. We can pick him up on the way."

"Ah, that's my girl," I said. "Then, Magpie, we're off."

I planted the second kiss of the morning on her head, thinking how with her shaggy black hair and hazel eyes she looked like Bill. She even had his build, lean, and with adolescence she'd developed that awkward lankiness kids share with puppies, the stage when their arms and legs appear only vaguely connected to their bodies.

At that point, I noticed Mom staring into the oven.

"Well, just a minute," she said, her face flushed red from the heat. "I want to finish the last of this cookie dough. One more batch, and I can take off this apron and we'll go."

I gave her one of my quizzical looks, the kind I use when I've backed a suspect into a corner. "Guess I'm not the one holding up the works then, Mom. It looks like you are!"

Mom frowned and looked flustered. For a moment she was at a loss for words. "Sarah, just get your coat." She sighed, realizing she'd lost. "I'll put the dough in the fridge for later."

"I don't think dinosaurs are really extinct," Strings said, with his usual certainty. "They're alive on some island somewhere, not grown outta that DNA stuff like in *Jurassic Park,* but just alive, 'cause they never all died."

Maggie's best friend, Strings, aka Frederick Allen Jacobs, Jr., was four-feet-ten-inches tall and bespectacled in wire-rimmed glasses. Strings's dad, the Reverend Fred, preaches at Mount Zion African, an old, steepled church tucked into the woods not far from the ranch. The church and the shrinking community surrounding it are all that's left of Libertyville, a once thriving black settlement that dates back to Reconstruction. On Sunday mornings, Alba Jacobs, a tall, elegant woman, wearing bright caftans with matching turbans, leads the choir, and even Mom has admitted that Alba makes the best buttermilk pie in the county. Gifted with his dad's flair and his mother's love of music, Strings plays a mean acoustic guitar, which explains his nickname.

All four of us, Maggie, Strings, Mom, and I, had just spent three hours touring the Natural Science Museum, especially a visiting dinosaur exhibit, and sat resting our feet and eating McDonald's hamburgers in the cafeteria. Half the display detailed the dinosaurs' extinction. It was vintage Strings to now insist he knew better.

"That's really dumb," countered Maggie, ketchup dripping from her bun. "How come no one's seen them?"

" 'Cause they're in a place that nobody's been, that's why. There are places like that, islands, aren't there Mrs. A?" he said, nodding, apparently in hopes that I'd nod along. "I watched a show like that on the Discovery Channel with my dad, about how some fish every-one thought was extinct wasn't. Some guy caught one."

"Now, that's *really* dumb." Maggie frowned, pointing a french fry like a bony finger just inches from her friend's face. "Fish are small. Dinosaurs are huge. How would the whole world miss seeing them?"

"Margaret, it isn't nice to say Frederick is dumb," scolded my mother.

"Actually, someone did catch a fish that was supposed to be ex-tinct," I said, rewarded by a grin so wide it nearly split Strings's face in two.

"Okay, a fish I understand. Like I said. But dinosaurs?" my ever-pragmatic daughter challenged.

"Well," I admitted. "Maybe Strings isn't right about the dinosaurs, but . . ."

"Geez, Mrs. A," Strings protested. "How can anyone know for sure? I mean, really know for sure? In Africa, there are still whole tribes who have never seen a white man."

"Strings does have a point, Maggie," I said, to which my daughter and my mother shook their heads in unison, as if certain they were dealing with the reality challenged.

At home, I checked in with the office. No news on the Lucas case. It was a cool spring late-afternoon, so I moved Maggie's telescope out of the way, the one Bill and I bought her the Christmas before he died, and Mom and I plunked down in the porch rockers to watch Maggie and Strings in the corral with Emma Lou. The air smelled sweet, filled with the heavy scent of the yellow jasmine climbing the porch railing. Maggie wielded a brush on one side of the filly, working on her coat, while on the other side Strings used his fingers to detangle her mane. Tied to a post, Emma Lou shifted back and forth, shuffling left and right, while the kids stepped gingerly to stay out of her way. It looked like a dance of sorts, the horse in the lead.

"I miss your father and Bill," Mom said, suddenly melancholy. "How they would love to see Maggie as she is now, growing up so fast."

Caught up in the moment, the two kids nearby jabbering about Strings's dinosaur theory, the peaceful country evening, I was surrounded by the warmth of family. Yet without Bill, everything felt odd, more remote. Even home.

"Yeah" was all I could muster.

As they had throughout the past year, the tears quickly welled in my eyes. Any thought of Bill's death did that to me. So I did the only thing I could, and I tried not to think of it. Still, on this particular afternoon, it was there, so close I could touch it, and too painful to deny. There was something I'd been wondering. "Mom, do you think there's a heaven?"

"Of course there is," she said, frowning.

"How can you be so sure?" I asked.

She paused for a moment, deep in thought. "How could there not be a hereafter?" she asked. "Think about how strong love is, your love of Bill, the way you love Maggie. How can anything that powerful simply disappear?"

Although I understood any theory on life after death was necessarily unproven, the truth was that I longed for something concrete, something to hold on to. Yet, if nothing else, Mom's words were comforting.

"Do you think Bill and Dad are close enough to watch over us? To know what's going on in our lives?"

Mom sat back and rocked, mulling over her answer.

"Maybe. I hope so. When your father died, at first I felt so alone. But as time passes, I've grown to feel he's with me." She chuckled, and then admitted, "Sometimes I even talk to him, out loud. But don't worry. So far, I haven't heard him talking back."

I nodded at her, but by then I was barely listening, only thinking of Bill and how much I wanted to believe he was close.

If something happened to Bill or Maggie, I'd always figured I'd somehow know, as Priscilla Lucas said she had known with her husband, some kind of premonition. But when Bill died, I didn't have a clue until the captain showed up at our front door. And as much as I wanted to, as much as I prayed to, I haven't felt Bill's presence for even a moment since. As far as I could tell, at the instant he died, Bill left us, and Maggie and I were alone. Part of me did believe in heaven, but the way I felt, it had to be many worlds away.

"I wonder sometimes what it's like, up there," Mom said. She held up her hands. They were thickening at the joints from arthritis. "I wonder about little things like hot water. It feels so good on my hands, takes the pain away. I wonder if they have hot water in heaven, to ease the pain in these old hands."

"But if it's heaven, there's no pain," I said, looking at the grooves in my mother's weathered face. *When had she aged so?* I wondered. Time had passed so quickly, I hadn't noticed.

Wrapped up in our conversation, Mom and I had stopped watching Maggie and Strings. I didn't realize she'd left the corral and walked toward the house.

"Where are they then? Where's heaven?" Maggie shouted. She held Emma Lou's brush in her hand, and her eyes were filled with tears. "I've looked through my telescope at the stars, and I don't see my dad or Grandpa. The astronauts have been to the moon and back and didn't find heaven. We've even sent satellites to Mars. No one's found heaven. Have they?"

"Oh, Magpie," I said, sorry that I'd brought it up. "Please, don't . . ."

"You sound like Strings. The dinosaurs are extinct, Mom. Dad and Grandpa are dead," Maggie said, sounding as sure as she was of the answers to last week's algebra test. "There is no heaven. People die and we never see them again."

I got up and walked over to her. Strings looked like he wasn't sure what to do. He was pulling on Emma Lou's mane so hard the horse was rolling her long, thin head away from him. "My dad says if you believe in God you have to believe in heaven and hell. That a God who loves us would never—" Strings started, but Maggie sent him a chill warning glance and he stopped talking.

"Strings, would you go inside and wait for Maggie? I think we need to talk alone," I said.

He looked at me, again at Maggie, and then did as I'd ordered, but all the while he walked toward the house, the boy kept glancing back over his shoulder at us.

Once Strings was inside, I put my arms around my daughter and held her tight. "Maggie, I don't know where Dad is. I don't know where heaven is. I miss him, too," I said. Then, despite my own doubts, I had to give her hope. I had to give her something to hold on to. "Maybe sometimes we have to believe in what we can't see. Maybe we have to trust that even if we don't know what's best, God does."

It sounded odd for me to be talking about God. Unlike Strings and his family, Mom and I aren't churchy people. But that didn't mean that at my core I didn't believe someone, somewhere was in charge. I'd seen the worst men could do. Yet deep down, where I know the things I can't explain, is a conviction that as chaotic and evil as this world can be, there is a powerful good, something that challenges us to love and care for one another.

"If there was a God, Dad would be here with us," Maggie said, no longer crying. She pulled away from me, looking sad and small and determined. I reached out to her, but she ran toward the house. Before I could follow, Mom grabbed my arm.

"The hardest thing, Sarah, is that children grow away from us," Mom said. "Things happen and we can't fix them. Sometimes, we need to give them room to come to terms without our interference. Give Maggie a little time. She'll come around."

I remembered how I'd felt when my dad died, the pain, the loss. Then Bill. Still, I wasn't a kid. *It must be so much harder for Maggie*, I thought.

I stared up at the house, where Maggie had disappeared inside. I wanted to run to her, but maybe Mom was right. Maybe Maggie needed time to sort through her thoughts on her own. Maybe we both just needed more time.

Half an hour later, I checked on Maggie and found her with Strings on the computer in the family room. Ever levelheaded, she was convinced that with minimal research on the Internet she would persuade her friend and her mother that no evidence existed that pointed to dinosaurs still roaming any part of the earth, not a deserted island, the jungles of Africa, and not, as Strings had suggested in the car on the way home from the museum, caves in the center of the earth. Despite the row it was sure to cause with his science teacher, I silently found myself hoping she'd fail. I wasn't sure I'd like living in a world without the possibility of Strings's dinosaurs any more than I wanted to live in one without believing in God and heaven.

With Mom busy in the kitchen working on a cheesecake order and with no one to complain, I settled down in front of my own computer in the workshop. After reading an e-mail from the National Center for Missing and Exploited Children thanking me for the photos and information on Ben, I tapped into Nexis to do a search on Edward and Priscilla Lucas, followed by another on Annmarie Knowles.

As expected, the morning's papers had bannered the murders. "Lucas family stunned by murders," read the *Houston Chronicle*. "Bizarre murder claims Edward Lucas and lover," read the *Galveston County Daily News*, the only one to have uncovered the lurid details surrounding the deaths, including that the bodies were found nude and posed under a bloody cross.

Although the official autopsy wouldn't be finalized for another week, the M.E.'s office had called me an hour earlier with preliminary findings. Lucas and Knowles had not had intercourse that day, suggesting that they were either escorted to the house by the killer or interrupted shortly after arriving. And, as I'd expected, the puncture marks in their hands and feet were inflicted before death by a long, thin blade. The chest cuts, while gory, only broke the skin deep enough to inflict pain and fear and release a river of blood, blood the killer wiped on the wall in the form of a cross. While Annmarie's bruised throat showed signs of ligature strangulation, that wasn't what killed her.

A not uncommon irony: both victims had been remarkably healthy and probably could have expected to live well into old age, if not for the bullet that sliced through Lucas's brain and the knife that slashed Knowles's throat. In this case, the M.E.'s office had no difficulty assessing causes of death.

A call from the crime lab had proved less helpful. As the captain had suspected, the killer had been exceedingly careful. The fingerprints on the scene had all been tied to Knowles, Lucas, and the family maid. Not a single print from an unknown source—namely the killer. The only forensic evidence found consisted of two long blond hairs, one found on Lucas's shoulder, the other retrieved from the shower drain. Longer than Annmarie's and unbleached, the probability ran high that they had come from the killer. Unfortunately, neither hair had a root, a source of mitochondrial DNA.

How the Galveston newspaper had learned the details of the murders disturbed me. A high-profile case, the word had quickly passed down through the ranks that a media blackout was in force. Revealing too much could jeopardize the investigation and prove disastrous in a future trial, once the murderer was found. Obviously the reporter, Evan Matthews, had worked a good source within GPD. A mention in the second paragraph led me to believe Detective O. L. Nelson might be our leak.

"We're looking closely at Edward Lucas's family situation," Nelson was quoted as saying. "And we have already held our first interview with his wife."

That Nelson could be callous, opinionated, and difficult, I knew. That he could be outright stupid, however, surprised me. With that announcement in the paper, any possible cooperation we might have anticipated from Priscilla Lucas and her lawyer vanished.

Befitting the lofty social status of Mr. and Mrs. Lucas, their Nexus hits riddled the screen. In photo after photo, the couple smiled happily at Houston's finest social events, fund-raisers for the ballet and opera, the symphony, along with a smattering of worthy causes, including breast cancer research and the downtown homeless shelter. In Galveston, Edward Lucas was a member of the exclusive, old-moneyed Mardi Gras krewe the Knights of Momus. A quick reading and it was readily apparent that, as she'd said, Priscilla Lucas had no need for her husband's money. A *Forbes* magazine ranking the nation's wealthiest families estimated the Barker Oil fortune in the $500-million range. The Lucas family's commercial real estate empire edged her out with an impressive $800 million. Together the two families controlled more than a billion dollars.

Annmarie Knowles was another story. Search though I might, I found but one mention of her, in the caption of a photo taken the previous fall. In the black-and-white image she stood behind her boss at a groundbreaking for a Galveston condo project, just the latest of the Lucas family's many real estate ventures. Annmarie, it turned out, was only twenty-seven and nearly two decades younger than Lucas. In the photo, she gazed at him with a proud, proprietary smile. I had to wonder: perhaps Priscilla Lucas had seen the same photo and correctly interpreted the young woman's intentions. There was no doubt that the widow was a woman with secrets.

Six

I'd grown accustomed to the dream, expecting it in those final moments before sunrise. Bill called out to me, surrounded by flames, not from hell but the fire-engulfed car in which he'd died. All the danger our jobs are fraught with, but my husband died in a commonplace car accident on a Houston freeway. In the nightmare, he begged me to save him. Unable to reach him, I screamed that I loved him, as he disappeared in the jagged yellow flames. This morning was no different than the others, and I awoke with tear-streaked cheeks.

The Houston offices of the Texas Department of Public Safety, a nondescript beige brick government building just off the West Loop, appeared a refuge when I arrived at seven Monday morning. I swiped my ID card and made a beeline for my office, next to the captain's, in the section of the building reserved for the rangers, near the rear, overlooking the parking lot and the radio tower used to transmit to the department's Austin headquarters.

After a Sunday spent working with Maggie on her science project, a computer-generated, 3-D, mock-up of the solar system, illustrating the path of a coming lunar eclipse, I was glad to be on familiar ground. Hours of nodding as she discussed her plans, trying not to embarrass myself by asking too many questions, had left me exhausted. My own sixth-grade science fair project has been on a more modest scale, stalks of celery in glasses filled with food-colored water to illustrate how plants draw moisture through roots and stems into leaves. Of course, that was a different era, pre–personal computer.

Although it was all I could think about, I didn't bring up the conversation about death and heaven from the day before. Neither did Maggie. I'd considered it a few times, trying to figure out how best to approach the subject of the hereafter, but decided Mom was right. I had no real answers to share with my daughter. Right after the accident, we'd gone to a counselor a few times, but that hadn't seemed to help, and we'd just stopped going. Maybe there aren't any standardized blueprints for surviving grief.

"Lieutenant Armstrong," the captain called out, as soon as he saw me. "I'd like you to come in here."

That didn't bode well. The captain called me Lieutenant Armstrong only when I was in trouble, the way Mom called me Sarah Jane.

After hanging up my blazer and throwing my black leather purse in a drawer, I walked into the captain's office and found he wasn't alone. One man I recognized, an FBI agent I'd met in the past. The other guy I didn't know. Glancing at the captain, I sensed he wasn't happy with whatever they'd been discussing. He was chewing on the inside of the jowls middle age had settled onto his face, another sign of bad news to come.

"You know Agent Ted Scroggins."

"Sure. Hi, Ted," I said, shaking his hand.

"And this is Agent David Garrity. He's a profiler, like you. Transferred here a few months back from Quantico," the captain continued, motioning toward the other man. The captain's voice was even-toned and resolved, hiding what I knew must have been deep irritation, when he said, "Based on the high-profile of the Lucas family, the governor has asked the FBI to work with us on the Galveston double-murder case."

"We don't need—" I jumped in, ready to defend my turf and point out that the case was well in hand, when the captain motioned for me to stop talking.

"This isn't optional. It's an order from the top."

"But we've only had this for a few days. You know there's absolutely no indication at this stage that this is a case we can't—"

"This isn't a reflection on your investigation, Lieutenant." He cut me off, his deep baritone leaving no room for argument. "These two agents are here to offer help and suggestions. It's still your case."

Then, the order: "Go over what we've got so far with them."

"Of course, Captain," I said, frowning. Despite his assurances, I'd been a ranger long enough to understand that when the feds moved in, they controlled the investigation. It only made matters worse that I knew Detective Nelson undoubtedly felt the same way about my arrival in Galveston.

Still, as I saw it, I had reason not to be happy with interference, especially from Scroggins. He was in Waco in '93, one of those Bill credited with heating things up to the point David Koresh holed in instead of giving up. After the compound burned to the ground, taking everyone inside with it, Scroggins blamed the local police, including the rangers, painting them all as bumblers.

Since then, I've had little use for Agent Ted Scroggins.

On the other hand, Agent Garrity I didn't know. We'd never crossed paths during my months studying profiling at the FBI academy in Quantico. Garrity was tall, not a bad-looking man. I would have remembered. So for him, the jury was still out.

"Let's go in the conference room," I suggested.

I collected my files and met them there.

"This is what we know so far," I said, launching into the con-densed version of the murders of Edward Travis Lucas and Annmarie Knowles, including forensics, the M.E.'s findings, and what Nelson and I had learned from Priscilla Lucas and the murdered woman's neighbors.

"Looks like you don't have much more than we could have got-ten reading the Galveston newspaper," taunted Scroggins, a scrawny man, balding, with small narrow eyes under thick bushy brows. "What about Nelson's theory, that it's a hit ordered by the wife?"

"I'm not saying it's impossible, but my gut tells me it's not her. I just don't buy it," I said, not at all surprised he'd already talked to Nelson.

"Seems to me she had motive and the money to finance it, along with knowing where the guy would be and—"

"This was the work of someone who murders for enjoyment, not money," I cut in. "It doesn't impress me as a murder for hire."

"Maybe Priscilla Lucas didn't want to impress you. Maybe she just wanted to dump the philandering old man to take up with the French teacher," Scroggins said, mocking.

"Ted, back off," snapped Agent Garrity, his voice quietly firm.

Scroggins shot him a hostile glance, and a flush of red crawled up his neck and faded into his monk's fringe of dark brown hair.

I couldn't help it. I laughed.

"What's so funny?" Scroggins asked, furious. Garrity at first looked surprised at my reaction but almost immediately seemed amused. He had a good smile, like a next-door neighbor I wouldn't have hesitated to borrow a lawnmower from. Scroggins shot his col-league a cautioning glance, but Garrity ignored him.

"Nothing really. It just struck me as funny," I said. "Guess this is the way you do it in D.C.? Down here we only play bad cop, good cop with suspects. We assume other officers know the drill."

"Geez, Nelson said you're hard to deal with," Scroggins sputtered. His flush deepened, and he pulled a wrinkled tissue out of his pocket to wipe a sweaty film from his forehead.

Meanwhile, Garrity said nothing but continued to appear pleased with the exchange. With Scroggins's ravings at least temporarily silenced, I took the opportunity to size up the man who'd just come to my defense. Well-formed, Garrity appeared fit enough to spend mornings in the gym. His hair, a sandy brown with just the hint of white at the temples, was combed straight back, but it bushed slightly about his neck and ears, giving him a rugged look. His light gray suit hung haphazardly from his body, creased as if he'd forgotten or just didn't bother to hang it up the last time he'd worn it. The word "rumpled" came to mind, a rather unusual adjective for an agent of the spit-and-polish FBI.

"Ted, the lieutenant's right. We're all on the same side here, and we need to take this a step at a time," Garrity said. "I'm not saying Nelson's theory is without merit, but we've got some problems with it. On the surface, these murders appear too ritualistic to be a hit. Using bindings and a gun from the site, leaving the bodies posed under a bloody cross? What if we're dealing with something else here? Don't we have to consider that possibility, before we reserve Priscilla Lucas a prison cell?"

"Hell, the profilers have spoken." Scroggins shrugged and again faced me, ignoring his fellow agent. "Nelson said you had dismissed his theory about the wife without real consideration, and I can see he's right."

"I'm not writing off Nelson's theory," I protested again, reining in my building frustration. "I'm like Agent Garrity. I haven't ruled out the possibility that Priscilla Lucas is involved. That she didn't come clean about being in the dead woman's apartment the night before the murders is suspicious."

"Well, at least that's something," Scroggins said, with an impatient huff. "It seems to me that when the lady won't admit she argued with one of the victims, that means *something.*"

"Something, but not necessarily that she was involved in killing her husband," said Garrity. "Lieutenant Armstrong is right. This is too early in the investigation to settle into one theory and exclude the other."

"Not excluding theories, there's something we all agree on," said Scroggins, with a forced grin.

I took a deep breath, stifling my irritation and said, as nicely as I could muster, "All I'm suggesting is that we work both angles, until we've got more proof. We're not facing any kind of deadline on this investigation. Priscilla Lucas isn't a flight risk. Why narrow ourselves down to investigate only one scenario when we have time to take a good look at this case?"

With that, the two agents glanced warily at each other, and I thought back to one of Bill's old ranger stories, how in 1934, it took Senior Ranger Captain Frank Hamer 102 days to track Bonnie and Clyde to the Louisiana farm where they riddled them with bullets and ended the careers of the notorious bank robbers. Something about Scroggins's and Garrity's reactions suggested we weren't going to have that kind of time to solve the Galveston double murders.

"There are factors at work here, aspects of this case we all need to be aware of," Garrity said. "There's big influence being parlayed all the way up to the governor's mansion—in fact, all the way to the White House—by both families. Priscilla Lucas's father, Bobby Barker, is calling not only Austin but D.C., trying to use his money and influence to have his daughter ruled out as a suspect. On the other hand, the Lucases have a long history of major political contributions. There's a laundry list of politicians who owe them favors, and they're twisting arms in the opposite direction. They want Priscilla Lucas put under a magnifying glass."

"Why?" I asked. "Because she has a boyfriend? Hell, in this marriage, she didn't have a monopoly on infidelity."

"There are motives for both families," Scroggins said, with a rather mysterious glance at Garrity. "It's easy to see why Barker wants his daughter cleared, but the Lucases have reasons for wanting her charged. Let's just say that it would be advantageous for their entire family if Priscilla Lucas turned out to be involved in the murders."

I had the unmistakable impression that Scroggins was being intentionally vague, so I said, "Ted, I need to know exactly what you're talking about. Lay it on the line. We're working together on this case. Aren't we?" I thought I sounded remarkably calm considering my impulse to pull out my gun and make him start tap dancing.

That fantasy didn't disappear when he blustered, "I understand that, Lieutenant. But you have to understand our position. We're the FBI. We have sources, and we're not at liberty to share everything. We can't just—"

While his fellow agent rambled, Garrity must have realized I was teetering on some kind of precipice, because he interrupted. "Our sources tell us that both families were in on the divorce negotiations, and things got pretty nasty. The late husband and the widow were fighting over the kids. And the fight got so dirty that they were each preparing motions charging the other was unfit to raise the children."

"And?" I prodded.

"Lieutenant Armstrong, these murders have put us in the middle of a power struggle between two of the state's wealthiest families," Garrity continued. "With her husband dead, Priscilla Lucas avoids a scandal and walks away with not only her lover but her children without a court fight. That means the widow had motive. If that's not enough, there's another reason for Priscilla to want her husband dead."

"And that is?" I asked.

"Money. Big money," he said. "Priscilla Lucas didn't lie when she said she didn't need her husband's money. She just didn't tell you everything. The Barker and Lucas fortunes are tied up in irrevocable trusts. Priscilla and Edward's children are the only ones in either family, the only heirs. The family that wins custody of the Lucas children controls more than a billion dollars."

Scroggins glared at him, while Garrity shifted uncomfortably in his chair, perhaps aware of how it sounded, as if power and money could influence the investigation.

"The point is that money talks. Neither of these families will back down until they've got what they want, and they'll use everything they have to get it," Garrity said. "In the meantime, this case is a political landmine for everyone with ties to either family, and here we're talking a who's who of Austin and D.C. One thing Agent Scroggins and I agree on is that we need more than theories; we need answers and we need them fast, before this case spins out of control."

"And even if you and the guru from Quantico here are doubtful, we can't afford not to take a microscopic look at Mrs. Priscilla Lucas," Scroggins concluded.

The discussion wrapped up. Agent Scroggins left for Galveston to work with Detective Nelson. Their job would be to investigate Priscilla Lucas and determine any role she may have played in the double murders. I couldn't help but muse that from my perspective Scroggins and Nelson deserved each other. Meanwhile, Agent Garrity and I began what I call the needle-in-the-haystack phase. Suspecting a serial killer, to bolster our theory, we needed to find other murders, similar enough to have been committed by the same man. We both knew what we were looking for: murders committed with a knife by an UNSUB, an unknown subject, where victims were tortured and posed in unusual positions. The bloody cross, that too was a definite possibility, a high probability of being part of his signature, ritualistically repeated at other murder scenes, an integral element of our killer's fantasy and, therefore, his pattern.

Over the weekend, I'd completed two questionnaires, one for each murder, and reported the Galveston homicides to ViCAP, the FBI's Violent Criminal Apprehension Program, a national database that tracks serial and unsolved homicides. Each characteristic of the killings had to be noted, down to the torture wounds in the victims' hands and feet. Below item 84, elements of unusual or additional assault/trauma/torture to victim, next to carving on victim, I wrote: *superficial cuts to form crosses on victims' chests.* In the proper slot, I'd listed the type of knots used to bind the victims, although it appeared they'd offer little help in revealing the killer's background. Rather than rare Chinese upholstery knots or surgical knots used by docs in operations, the lab described the ligature around Annmarie's neck as anchored with a common slipknot. The bindings on the victims' arms and legs were even less helpful, tied as they were with simple overhand knots. While the knots in other homicides might match, they weren't unusual enough to link these murders to any others on their own or to suggest anything about the killer.

Under the weapons section, I listed the gun as a weapon of opportunity and the knife as the killer's weapon of choice.

Although they'd had to work over a weekend, the research staff at the FBI ranked the case a priority, and Garrity and I already had a screen full of e-mails to follow up on, suggesting cases that shared characteristics with ours.

Computers are an incredible advantage when solving serial crimes, allowing investigators to assess thousands of cases at once. Yet they're also a danger. Become too convinced the answer waits somewhere untapped in a database, and a cop can waste precious hours that should be devoted to pounding the pavement and asking questions instead of sitting in front of an answerless screen. We both knew the risk.

Morning grew into afternoon, and Garrity stood beside me as we worked, pulling up the information on each case, splitting them up into two piles. He would follow up on one; the other would be my responsibility. Before long, I found myself wondering about him. Why had he stood up for me against Scroggins? That hadn't been my experience with FBI agents. They tended to stick together, forming a united front against local police. Distracted as I was, my hands hesitated on the keyboard, and I found Garrity looking quizzically at me, waiting for me to begin again. Embarrassed and annoyed with myself, I refocused on the job at hand. Yet in the quicksand that was fast becoming this case, I wondered if Garrity could be trusted.

By late morning, we'd called departments throughout the state investigating ViCAP's laundry list of unsolved murders. On each, we'd compiled a list of the essentials: names and locations of the victims, any telltale clues that suggested one or another of the cold cases could be tied to the Galveston murders. Slow, tedious work.

There were similarities: a garage mechanic stabbed to death in his backyard and left hunched over an old Buick he was in the process of restoring, an elderly minister discovered murdered in the church sanctuary, the six-year-old murder of a woman who had been found nude in the bathtub with her throat slit. Each time, we quizzed the officers who'd handled the investigations. Each time, we came up dry. None of the MOs were similar enough to our case to suggest a connection.

"What about this one?" I asked, at three that afternoon.

I pointed at a case on Garrity's list, one he'd drawn a star next to. The victim: an elderly woman murdered in Bardwell, an East Texas town cut out of the rich expanse of forests and swamps collectively known as the Big Thicket. Garrity's summary was brief: no apparent means of entry into the woman's house; nothing had been taken. What caught my eye was his notation *two knife wounds on chest.*

"The sheriff wasn't in to answer questions, and no one in the office seemed to know much about the case. I got the info on the chest wounds from the courthouse secretary. But that's the closest I came to a probable match," he said. "You up for a drive east?"

Seven

The drive to Bardwell took about two hours. I parked the Tahoe in front of an aging stone mansion surrounded by oaks trailing heavy, ruffled shreds of Spanish moss. Decades earlier it had been converted into a combination county assessor's office and sheriff's department. Sheriff Tom Broussard had delayed his dinner to meet with us, curious that a Texas Ranger and an FBI agent needed his help.

"Yup, Louise Fontenot was a good old woman. People in this town were mighty upset by her murder," said Broussard, chewing a plug of tobacco that stained the corners of his mouth and made his right cheek bulge. Every so often he paused and spit into a dented Sprite can. "Her family was one of the originals around here. Pioneers. She didn't deserve to go that way."

At the time of her death, Louise had been eighty-six years old. In the photo he showed us, she wore a flowered cotton housedress, her white hair permed into tight curls, her glasses too wide for her narrow face. A tightness about her features gave her a pinched, spinsterish look. She'd been found nude, her throat cut, in her bedroom. There were wounds on the palms of her hands and the soles of her feet that the county coroner, most days the local family practitioner, described as puncture marks. The "two knife wounds on her chest" formed a cross.

With that, Sheriff Broussard drove us out to the old Fontenot place, a deserted frame house that backed up to the woods on the outskirts of town. The yellow paint was faded, and the plastic holly wreath on the front door drooped from sun and weather. Strands of multicolored lights entangled a small bush next to the front door. Louise had been murdered fifteen months earlier, two days before Christmas.

Inside, the house looked as if its owner had just stepped out. Her furniture remained in place, and her cane leaned against a wall. The old woman's Bible waited on a lamp table next to what was undoubtedly her favorite chair, its back covered by a crocheted doily.

"Louise was the last of her family in these parts," explained the sheriff. "For a long time, nobody could agree on what to do with her stuff. The county attorney said no one had a right to touch any of it—until the property taxes were left unpaid and the county seized the place, but there'd been talk about going through and seeing if anything was right for the local history room at the library. The taxes came due about six months ago giving the go-ahead, but the museum ladies haven't gotten around to it yet. I think they're spooked about even walking in this place."

"Is that how the killer got in?" I asked, pointing at a boarded-up window.

"No. We're not sure how he got in. We think maybe through an open window in the back bedroom, although we couldn't find any footprints or fingerprints to confirm that," the sheriff said. "Teenagers broke that, months after the killing. They're the only ones not afraid of ghosts, I guess. They used the house to smoke pot after school, until we ran them off."

"Sarah," David called. "Come take a look."

I found him in the bedroom, standing next to the bed. On the wall above the tarnished metal headboard was a bloody cross, a smaller version of the one wiped onto the wall above the tortured, murdered bodies in Galveston.

"Is this where the body was found?" David asked, pointing at the bed.

"That's it," said the sheriff. "Funny thing, nothing was taken, not even the fifty dollars she had in her billfold."

"How was she positioned?"

"In bed, flat on her back, the covers folded real neat at her feet," he said. "The killer tied her ankles together and her hands. He had her hands propped up, on top her chest. When we walked in the room, it looked like she was praying."

"Anything else strike you as odd?" I asked.

"Well, one thing," he said, smacking the corner of his lips and tapping the straw cowboy hat he held against his thigh.

"And that was?" I nudged.

"The telephone was smack on top of her chest."

"The phone?"

"Yup," said Sheriff Broussard.

"What did you make of that?" David asked.

"Didn't know what to make of it except . . ."

"Except what?" I prodded.

"Folks around here thought it was pretty strange with the way old Ms. Fontenot was, that's all," he said, this time anticipating our next question. "It's not a pleasant thing to talk bad about the dead, but the fact is Louise Fontenot was the town gossip. She was always on that damn phone talking bad about somebody."

David and I glanced at each other.

"And this was well known in town?"

"This was well known in the county," said the sheriff. "Anytime anybody had anything going on that they didn't want their neighbors to know, they did their best to hide it from Miss Fontenot. Anytime I wanted information out, like that if the kids didn't stop smoking in the big oak tree behind the high school, that I was considering raiding the place, I just let it slip while I was talking to Louise. Less than a day and everyone in town had heard about it and no more worries about the school catching fire from a cigarette butt."

"Was Louise talking, gossiping about anyone in particular in the weeks before the murder?" I asked.

"Not that I remember."

"Anybody disappear from town around the time she died?"

"Not that we could tell," he answered. "We thought of that and made a canvass, a deputy and me, but we didn't find anybody noticeable gone. The thing is, around here a lot of people live back in the woods and people don't see them much. That and we have a lot of migrants and the like. It's not the kind of thing where we can really keep track of people."

"Any evidence the killer hung around after the murder?" I asked.

"I considered that possibility," he said. "There were wet towels in the bathroom, and it looked like maybe he cleaned up right here in the house before he took off. He was careful though. We closed the house up and had the forensics people come in from Beaumont P.D. They didn't find a thing."

David glanced over at me and I knew what he was thinking. With the cross, the positioning of the body, and the similarities in the victims' wounds, we hadn't needed more, but here, too, the killer had taken his time on the murder scene, then meticulously cleaned up all evidence. It was another piece of the puzzle that fit perfectly, as well as further evidence of our killer's bravado. This guy wasn't spooked. Dead body in the next room and the killer hung around and made himself presentable.

It was past eight when we finished at the house. The sheriff went home, and David and I found the only non–fast-food place in town, a small dimly lit restaurant with wood tables and a lunch counter. Someone, it seemed, had apparently put a couple rolls of quarters in the jukebox and a George Strait marathon was playing over the tinny speakers.

David ordered a brisket sandwich. When it came, it dripped with a sweet barbecue sauce and shared the plate with mayonnaise-and-mustard potato salad and a pickle. I'd been meaning to start watching my cholesterol but ordered the chicken-fried steak. Together with mashed potatoes and white gravy, it hung over the chipped white plate like a bedspread over a mattress. The gravy had all the finesse of Elmer's glue, which left me nibbling at the peas and carrots. I ordered a Shiner Bock and figured that gave me enough calories for the night.

"We've got two murdered adulterers and a gossip," I said, putting into words what I knew we'd both been thinking. "So we've got a murderer on a mission from God, placed on earth to smite the sinners?"

"Undoubtedly, tells himself he is," said Garrity as he consumed the last fork of potato salad and got ready to start on a bowl of apple cobbler in a puddle of half-melted vanilla ice cream. He'd chosen one of the two wine choices the place offered, the red one, although it actually looked more pink. "Of course, the truth is that he's just a pathetic loser carting around a lifetime of anger, of not fitting in, and a twisted perversion that mixes sexual fantasy with an obsession for power and violence," he said. "What do we know so far?"

"Not much. The guy is blond and most likely white, probably twenty-five or younger," I said, based on the found hairs and national profiling statistics. "My guess is he's from somewhere around here. He had to have known of Louise to know she was a gossip. Lucas and Knowles, on the other hand; he would have known she wasn't his wife just by following either one of them for any period of time. He could even have come to that conclusion from the photo of Priscilla and the kids on the nightstand."

"Anything else?"

"These aren't his only victims," I ventured. "This guy's enjoying it too much to wait more than a year in between."

"Good point," he said. "We've done the ViCAP search, though. It's hard to understand why more victims aren't coming up."

"True," I said. "But I'd be willing to bet a month's pay that they're out there."

David nodded. He concentrated on the cobbler, scraping out the last of the ice cream with his spoon, and then glanced up at me across the table.

"I know I didn't mention this before, but I knew Bill," he said. "Scroggins and I both met him in Waco."

"Garrity," I said. "You know, I remember . . ." Suddenly David Garrity's name surfaced in my memory. Bill ranting and raving about the FBI, complaining that they'd taken over the scene. He was irate with Scroggins, but sometimes he mentioned an agent named Garrity. Bill respected him. Once he paid him what, coming from Bill, was the highest compliment: Bill called Garrity a good cop.

"Those were long days and nights in Waco. Bill and I got to know each other a bit. We talked about you, Sarah," David continued. "He said that there wasn't a string of clues you couldn't crack."

"Bill was one of a kind," I said.

"What's it been now?" Garrity asked. I didn't need to ask what he meant.

"Bill died a year ago last month," I said.

"I'm sorry," he said. "Must be rough."

"Yeah," I said. "It is."

"Write This Down" came on the jukebox, Strait crooning to a heavy country beat, reminding his lover of the place she holds in his heart. It was a favorite of Bill's, and one we danced to often. I used the music as an excuse to close my eyes. Before long I was swaying a little in time with the song, and when I opened my eyes, Garrity was smiling at me. It was beginning to appear that he found me a continuing source of amusement. Embarrassed, I waved at the waitress. In no time, she'd slapped down a second bottle of beer.

"Kind of nice that we're off duty," Garrity said.

"As off duty as two cops on a case ever get," I said.

"That's true, but, well, I was thinking," he said, with a soft, nervous chuckle. "There are things I need to learn if I'm going to live down here. I mean, I hear things are different."

I stifled an urge to laugh. Nearly every Yankee I'd ever met had a preconceived notion about Texas that included cowboys, oil wells, and characters out of that old movie *Deliverance*. The truth is, they were partially right; we have some of all three, especially the oil wells. Still . . . "Well, you have entered a foreign country," I replied in my best Texas drawl, deciding to play along. "We Texans are pretty particular. You don't fit in; we may not let you stay. Some of us aren't too partial to foreigners. We'd rather all of you packed up and went home."

"I've heard that," Garrity said, laughing softly, this time without the uneasiness, and I laughed along with him. The beer was going down smooth, and it felt good to unwind after a long day.

"Well then," he ventured. "Under those circumstances, I'd say it's your responsibility to teach me to fit in. You don't want your partner, even a temporary one, standing out like a dairy cow in a field of longhorn steers."

"What've you got in mind?" I asked. When he didn't answer right away, I suggested, "You know, I could teach you the UT fight song?"

Personally, I thought I was highly entertaining, but this time,

Garrity didn't laugh. Instead he reached across the table and covered my hand with his—thick, solid, and warm.

"Let's dance," he said, standing up and trying to nudge me to my feet beside him.

This was something I hadn't expected. I hadn't danced since Bill died. Drawing my hand away, I said, "You know, there's no dance floor, and I don't think . . ."

"We'll just get a couple of these tables out of the way," he said, doing just that, the table legs making a chalk-on-a-blackboard screech as he pushed them across the wood floor. The place smelled of beer, cooking grease, and decades of cigarette smoke.

"Now I know how to dance, but I hear you do it differently down here," he said, again slipping his hand over mine, gently pulling me toward him. "Come on. Help an old Yank out."

He was watching me, and I felt my face grow warm.

"I don't need any sympathy dances," I said, shaking my head.

"Sympathy dance?" He sighed. "Lieutenant, I'd consider this a personal favor. What if I have to work undercover in a Texas dance hall? How will I fit in if I can't two-step?"

I thought for a minute, listening to Strait's crooning fill the darkened room. "Why not?"

I stood up and put Garrity's right hand on my waist, then wrapped my left arm under and behind him. He took my right palm in his outstretched hand. I waited a minute, and then eased into the strong beat of the music with a quick step forward with my right foot, following it with my left. Then two slides, left, left, with a pause. Garrity bobbled, and we repeated across the dance floor. He had a strong, athletic body, and he moved well, catching on quickly. Before long, he took the lead. Halfway through the song, he pulled me closer. For just a second I tensed, but I didn't pull away. I wanted to remember the heavy sweetness of a man's smell, and the tug of a strong arm gently riding just above my hip.

After our dance, we paid our check and left. David talked on the walk to the motel, but I barely listened. Once there, I hurriedly said good night, agreeing to meet him at my Tahoe at six the next morning. I settled into my room at the Easy Street Motel, with its sagging bed and a nightstand that someone had leveled with the aid of a frayed book of matches, as thoughts of Bill crashed about me. I wished that I could see him, talk to him, one last time. What would I say? That I loved him? Bill knew that, just as I knew without question that he loved me. I pulled on the chain, extinguishing the only light, and crawled into bed wearing the nightshirt from the spare bag I kept in the truck, when it occurred to me that if I had one last chance to be with Bill, I'd say nothing. Instead, I'd hold him in my arms for every second God gave me.

Eight

My hand reached for the telephone before my mind acknowledged the ringing. The sun was just barely up.

"Armstrong here," I said.

"It's Scroggins," the voice said. "I couldn't reach Garrity. Is he there with you?"

Still groggy, I didn't immediately answer. I started to stutter, "No," but it was too late. Scroggins was already laughing.

"I hear those Quantico guys are fast movers, but this has to be a record," he said, still chuckling.

"He's not . . ." Then I realized a denial would only do more damage. "What do you want? It's not even six."

"I thought we'd give you a heads-up," he said. "Nelson and I are bringing in Priscilla Lucas this morning."

"You're what?"

"You heard me," he said, his voice thick with self-satisfaction. "We talked to the Galveston D.A. late last night. He says we've got enough to arrest her. The bitch has lawyered up. With the neighbor's ID of her as the woman Knowles argued with the night before the murders, we've got more than suspicions. Plus, we found another one of Knowles's neighbors who swears he saw the widow Lucas knocking on the dead mistress's door on at least one other occasion."

"That's not enough to—"

"There's more," he said, his voice ringing with excitement. "Get this. We pulled her bank records. Three days before the murders, Lucas withdrew a hundred grand in cash from her personal account. We asked her lawyer for an explanation. Guy practically choked when he had to tell us that his client said it was a personal matter."

I pulled myself up and sat on the edge of the bed. This was serious.

"Ted, I know it looks bad for Mrs. Lucas," I said, straining to shake off sleep and gather my thoughts. "But Garrity and I found another murder using the same MO out here in East Texas. Everything about these murders points to a serial killer. You've got to be careful here. The Lucas family isn't the only one with connections. Priscilla Lucas has not only three kids you'll be putting through unnecessary hell but her own money and influence. Her father, Bobby Barker, and his lawyers will have you for lunch if you're wrong. This could come back to haunt you, big time."

My cell phone was silent.

"Same MO, huh?"

"Nearly identical," I said. "Down to the cross carved on the old woman's chest and the bloody cross on the wall over her head."

Again, Scroggins said nothing.

"That close," he finally said.

I knew I'd hit a nerve when I reminded him of Priscilla Lucas's resources. No matter how much he wanted kudos from the top for closing the case, Agent Ted Scroggins wasn't the type to step too far out on any limb.

"Any fingerprints or DNA on this one?"

"No, same as the last," I said. "The scene was clean."

"Well," he said, restraint edging his voice.

Again only silence, and I knew he was carefully weighing what he'd say next.

"Under the circumstances, I think Nelson and I will have another powwow with the assistant D.A.," he said.

Presuming we'd made some progress, that he fully understood what David and I had discovered in Bardwell, I couldn't believe what happened next. As I listened, Scroggins made a complete one-eighty. I could almost hear the pounding as he hammered on our information, reshaping it to fit his preferred theory.

"But, you know, if you think about it, this really doesn't have to hurt our case against Priscilla Lucas. The way I see it, so you found another murder that might or might not be the work of the same killer. That doesn't necessarily change the situation," he ventured, slowly reclaiming his former confidence. "Think about it. So the same guy offed some old woman in some little town . . . that only confirms our theories."

"How do you figure that?" I asked.

"We're not claiming Lucas murdered her old man herself. Nelson and I have said all along that this was a murder for hire, probably by some asshole who's murdered before. Another body changes nothing."

"It seems unlikely for this type of a killer, with this kind of MO, to be motivated by money."

"Unlikely but not impossible," he said, fully inflated with his old ardor. "When are you and the Quantico guru driving back?"

"We hope tonight—if not, tomorrow afternoon," I said. "We've got work here first. We need to track this guy down or at least find out who we're looking for."

"Well, I'm going to get a pocket warrant," Scroggins mused. "That way when we're ready to pick her up, the red tape will be out of the way."

"That's probably a good idea, if you're convinced you need a warrant," I conceded. Issued and signed by a judge but not recorded at the county clerk's office until an arrest is made, a pocket warrant is kept secret. "At least the press won't be the wiser. But wait until we get back to pick her up. Wait until we know what we've got here. Okay?"

"You got it. We'll hold off," he agreed. "But if Priscilla Lucas doesn't start answering our questions and if you don't find something more concrete, we're gonna haul her pretty ass in and book her. Understand?"

"It would be a mistake," I said again.

"Maybe, maybe not," he said. "But it's the way this case is going down."

Judging by the gully in the center of the mattress and the black cockroach—nearly the size of a small mouse—that crawled out of the drain into the sink, I had little hope for the shower, but it turned out that the Easy Street Motel's water supply was hot and plentiful, even if the towels were wax-paper thin. I pulled my only lipstick out of my purse, a light mauve called rose sunset. In my spare clean white shirt and Wranglers, my boots and blue blazer recycled from the day before, I emerged from my cabin to find David waiting, just as we'd agreed. He'd already had his morning run and shower, but just like his business suit the day before, his jeans and white shirt hung undisciplined on his body. I briefly wondered what he'd look like if he learned how to iron. Over a hot breakfast at the same hole-in-the-wall as the night before, I filled him in on Scroggins's news.

"That lady ought to just tell them what she used the money for, answer the questions," Garrity said, shaking his head in disgust. "If she's not involved, she's wasting their time and this thing could really backfire. She could end up splashed on the front page wearing handcuffs."

"She must have some reason for not talking," I said. "If we can figure out what that is, maybe we'll be able to sort through all of this."

"Sure, she's guilty," he said, using his fingers to comb back an errant fringe of hair falling over his forehead.

"You don't believe that," I said.

He paused, as if considering the possibility.

"No, I don't. My guess is that you've been right from the beginning," he grudgingly admitted. "These murders have nothing to do with money or Priscilla Lucas. We're most likely looking at a serial killer. One who has visions of grandeur, a pathetic loser who tells himself that he's on some kind of twisted mission from God. They just crossed paths with the wrong guy."

"How?"

"What do you mean?"

"How did they cross his path?"

"That's something we need to answer if we're ever going to pull this thing together," he said.

I thought about that for a moment, and then ventured, "But you said, 'If Priscilla Lucas isn't involved.' That means you still believe she might be."

David sighed, as if my insistence tested his patience.

"Sarah, come on, you've got to take those blinders off. Nothing here is certain, and we have to at least consider the possibility. The widow Lucas had motive and means," he said. "We don't really know at this point, do we?"

Stunned, I didn't answer. I couldn't believe David even vaguely agreed with Nelson and Scroggins. My silence hung between us, until David went on.

"One thing I've learned is that you never dismiss a theory until you've got hard evidence that it's wrong. Cases will surprise you. You think you know what kind of guy the killer is and what's motivating him, but you can be wrong," he said. "Remember that case in Virginia, the pretty young teacher everyone thought was killed by her husband? Everything pointed to domestic violence, every bit of evidence at the scene. The local cops easily built that case and nearly prosecuted the poor bastard."

"Yeah," I said. "I do remember it."

"Well, I worked it. Helped the local cops profile the killer. We were right about the murder being an up-close and personal matter—hell, she was bludgeoned to death with a tire iron. The guy smashed her face like a jack-o'-lantern. That's about as personal as anyone can get. We were right about the love-gone-bad motive, but we were wrong about who did it. Of course, we didn't know until later that she was bedding her students, widening the field of suspects who had a romantic motive to kill her. If the lab hadn't found that latent print on the body, we might have convicted the wrong guy of murder. Who would have thought it would turn out to be a shy sixteen-year-old, a member of the high school chess club, no less?"

Silent, I waited for him to continue.

"Right now all we've got is speculation that our guy's a conventional serial killer, as if anyone who kills for kicks can be described as conventional," he said. "Do I think she hired the murderer? No. Am I in favor of charging Priscilla Lucas with solicitation of murder? No. But Ted and Detective Nelson have a lot of years of experience behind them, their own instincts, and an arguable theory with at least some evidence, including the unaccounted-for hundred grand. The biggest strike against Priscilla Lucas's innocence is her own behavior. She's put herself under suspicion."

"You honestly believe there's the possibility that she hired the same person who killed Louise Fontenot to kill her husband and Annmarie Knowles?"

"I can't rule it out," he said. "And neither can you."

Nine

The dense forests that begin in Maine carpet the East Coast and end in Texas, where they spread into the hybrid of woods, streams, marshes, and swamps called the Big Thicket. It's a bucolic setting, but I'd learned early in my career that looks can be deceiving. During Prohibition, moonshiners counted on the Thicket's dense vegetation to hide their stills from revenuers. For decades, escaped prisoners built hideouts in the woods, living off the land and feral hogs they castrated in the fall to fatten for a spring kill. In recent years, the Thicket's spawned more than one sensational killing, including a state congressman shot through the heart by his trophy wife, after he beat her until doctors couldn't repair the damage; and the bizarre case of a small-town doctor, ostensibly happily married for nearly four decades, the father of six, the grandfather of thirteen, who slipped a deadly drug into the soft drink of every suitor his pretty young nurse dated. Since he also served as the county coroner, three young men died before the local sheriff realized that they couldn't all have had weak hearts and that there seemed to be more of a connection than that the doc's nurse was particularly unlucky in love.

On the southern edge of the Thicket, Bardwell rested shouting distance from the Louisiana border and north of I-10, the main highway that connects Houston and New Orleans. The town had a post office, a grocery store, three churches, a Wal-Mart, an old limestone courthouse across from a park, a Sonic, and a Dairy Queen. In the evenings, the locals congregated at a dance hall on the highway outside town to drink and listen to country music. That's where David and I began our search.

A metal building the size of a small house, cooled by fans and open garage doors on all sides, J. P.'s wasn't ready for business yet, but as we drove by, its owner, J. P. Lancett, a stubby yet muscular man with dark olive skin and dyed, thinning black hair greased straight back from his forehead, hauled in stock, a case of Lone Star Beer in longneck bottles hoisted on his right shoulder. I put the Tahoe in reverse and swerved into the parking lot.

Minutes later, we were seated in the clammy shade of the bar. Insects buzzed loudly in the surrounding woods as we inquired about the late Miss Fontenot.

"Bitchy old lady," Lancett said, his bulk uneasily balanced atop a rickety wooden bar stool that wobbled under the strain. "She never had a good word to say about anyone."

"Fifteen months ago, before the murder, was there anyone in particular she was talking about, anything out of the ordinary happening in town?" I asked.

"There's always something going on around here," he said with a frown. A lack of teeth folded his chin into his upper jaw, making it appear that the lower half of his face had collapsed. "Girls turn up pregnant. Maybe some old boy, he's got a lunchtime date with some girl in the Thicket for a little fun. Sometimes wives leave husbands or take up with someone else's. Old Lady Fontenot, she didn't let any of it go without talking it up to the good ladies in town."

"But right before she died," I repeated. "What was she talking about then?"

"She was always talking about someone, but at that particular time, I can't hardly think of who it would've been. If she hadn't been talking, now that would've been news," he said.

"Is there anyone in town you suspected at the time the murder happened, for any reason?"

"Nah, can't say as I did."

"Anyone who disappeared about the time of the murders, maybe a young man with blond hair?"

The barkeep stroked his whisker-stubbled chin and considered my description of the possible killer. "Nobody I can think of," he admitted.

"Did you ever hear rumors that anyone in particular was complaining about Louise Fontenot, for any reason?" David asked.

"Like I said before, I didn't hear anything," he concluded with a shrug. "It seemed to me at the time that people were pretty befuddled by the entire thing, her dying like that and all. Murder ain't particularly something that happens every day in this town. Especially an old lady like that. Just wasn't natural, that's all."

"Well, thanks for your help," I said, taking out a card and scribbling on the back. "This is my cell phone. If anything comes to mind after we leave or if you mention what we've discussed with anyone who believes they might have any information, call."

"Bet I will," Lancett promised.

Despite his avowed enthusiasm, we watched as he tucked the card in among a sheaf of matted, stained papers next to the cash register that looked as if they'd remained untouched for decades.

As we drove away, I asked David, "What do you think the odds are we'll be hearing from Mr. Lancett?"

"About the same as the odds that he's reporting all his liquor taxes," he said with a short laugh. "Sometimes, in towns like this, it's my impression that people make it a point not to notice things."

"Except for Louise Fontenot," I said. "She would have been the one with a theory or two. Too bad she's not here to ask."

With no firmer leads than a list of the names and addresses of the "good ladies" supplied by the sheriff and the barkeep, David and I began circulating through the town to clapboard houses with porch boards that squeaked under our weight. Timid old women answered, their white hair secured with bobby pins. To our insistent questioning, they each maintained they remembered nothing about what their murdered old friend, Louise Fontenot, might have told them in the months preceding her death.

By noon, we were canvassing block to block, house to house, repeating the same questions until they became routine. We always finished with "Do you know of anyone in town who disappeared around the time of Louise's murder?"

"Can't say as I do," said Sally LeBoef, the owner of the Cut and Curl Salon on Oak Street, as she chopped Cyndi Lou Styles's mane of thick, midnight-black hair, at about three that afternoon.

"Think back," Garrity asked. "It could be anyone, but most likely a man with blond hair, maybe in his twenties or thirties?"

LeBoef stared at us, wrinkled up her nose as if deep in thought. Styles shrugged.

"You know, there's lots of people back in them woods. It could be one of them, but I can't say one in particular comes to mind," the hairdresser said. She flicked the switch, and raising her voice she shouted over the hum of a blow dryer. "If you leave your number, though, I'll be more than glad to ask my customers and call if any of them have an idea."

Since no one noticed our guy's absence, David and I decided LeBoef could be right. Perhaps our killer lived away from the townsfolk's prying eyes. So after the Cut and Curl, we gave up on Bardwell proper and focused on the back roads that radiated from town, onto gravel and dirt roads that turned into driveways and ended next to double-wide trailers. When those were exhausted, we followed paths that led to hunting cabins with deer blinds anchored on stilts and camouflaged to blend into the foliage.

No matter how many questions we asked, it seemed we were destined to learn nothing about the three murders.

Early that evening, David Garrity and I agreed on one more day in Bardwell before we admitted defeat and drove home. There were still camps and houses, hidden farther back into the Thicket, we hadn't been able to reach without a guide. Since there was nothing to be done until morning, we checked ourselves back into our rooms at the Easy Street and contemplated dinner at the usual place. I showered, pulled clean clothes out of my stash from the trunk, wishing I'd brought something nicer than T-shirts and jeans, and thinking about my dance with Garrity the night before. As I smoothed a healthy layer of rose sunset on my lips, I wondered what Bill would think of me prettying up for dinner with Garrity.

I looked in the mirror, my shoulder-length dark-blond hair fanned out like I'd been hit with a bolt of static electricity. I wet my comb and tried to tame my hair, but it was no use, so I pulled out a black scrunchy from my purse and yanked my hair into a tight ponytail. In the mirror, my skin seemed paler, more sallow than I remembered, and my face more drawn. I squinted and my forehead furrowed. "Well, Bill," I said to the mirror. "If you're watching, don't worry too much. The way I look, a man would have to be blind."

That reminded me of Mom's admission that she sometimes talked to my dad, and I chuckled. I had time to call home before dinner. The first thing Mom said was that Maggie had been in a blue mood all day. "She needs you here. She seems to be struggling with things but won't talk about it with me. Sarah, I love Maggie like my own child, but she's not. And I can't be a substitute for her mother."

"I know, Mom," I said. "But I can't come home. Not yet. Put her on the telephone. Let me talk to her."

"Sarah Jane . . ."

"Mom, please," I said, not in the mood for an argument. "Just put Maggie on the telephone."

When she picked up, Maggie sounded even less pleased with me than Mom.

"I really wanted you to come home tonight," she said.

"I wanted that, too. But I can't," I said. "What's wrong, Magpie?"

"I don't know," she said, and I thought she probably didn't.

"You know I love you, that I'd be there if I could."

At first quiet. Then, "I changed my science project," she said, her voice still sad. "I'm doing it on singularity."

"Singularity," I said. "And that is?"

"The center of a black hole. The vortex," she said. "Some scientists think it rips apart stars and gobbles them up. But others think the stars get caught in the vortex and it crunches them down to space dust and spits most of it back out. But it's destruction for any star that gets too close."

"Wow," I said. "And it's called . . . ?"

"Singularity," she said, again. "I'm going to call my project the monster void that devours stars. Strings says it's more exciting than a lunar eclipse."

"I think he's right," I said. "And what's he doing? Still the dinosaurs?"

"Yeah, still the dinosaurs," Maggie scoffed. "He's going to prove it's possible that they exist somewhere. I haven't changed my mind. It's dumb. But I'm helping him on the computer. He talks about dinosaurs all the time, how we're going to go dinosaur hunting together when we're grown up and we're both archeologists."

I laughed again. Maggie sounded more like herself, but not over whatever was needling at her. Something was still wrong. "Is that all that's bothering you, that Strings is droning on about his dinosaurs and that I'm not there to help with your science fair project?" I asked.

Maggie was quiet, too quiet.

"I guess," she said, but, of course, that wasn't true. Her voice had that familiar melancholy that always found its mark, the ever-expanding section of brain cells where I stored my anxiety and guilt. If Bill had been there, she wouldn't have missed me so. I knew that, and part of me wanted to get in the Tahoe and drive home. But I couldn't. If we were dealing with a serial killer, it wouldn't be long before he killed again.

"Maggie, I'd rather be home with you. I really would. But I can't come home tonight. It's important that I'm here."

"I know, it's just that, sometimes I wonder . . ." she said.

"Wonder what?"

"Why can't you be like other moms and get a job in an office or something? One where you're home every night?"

I didn't know what to say. All I could do was ask again, "What's wrong, Magpie? Is everything all right in school?"

Again, Maggie was silent.

"Maggie, listen, I love you dearly. You are, barring no one, the most important person in the world to me. If I could, I'd drive home this very minute. There's nothing I'd like more than to be with you. But I can't. For at least one more day, I'm needed here. But I will be home soon, probably tomorrow."

"For how long before you have to go away again?" she asked.

Dodging a question I couldn't answer, I suggested, "Let's do something special this weekend, a whole day together, just the two of us. We'll leave Gram at home and make it a mother-daughter day. All right?"

It was a tempting offer, but Maggie wasn't in the mood to jump at anything that let me off the hook.

"Cross-your-heart promise?" she said, doubtfully.

"Cross-my-heart promise," I repeated. "Now put Gram back on the phone, honey. Sleep tight."

"You, too," she said, her voice sad and distracted. Whatever bothered Maggie when we'd begun talking was still there.

"Sarah Jane, when *are* you coming home?" Mom asked.

"As soon as I can. Probably tomorrow night."

"The truth is that I'm worried about Maggie," she said, her voice low so Maggie wouldn't hear. "It's not just that she seems sad. She's doing odd things."

"What?"

"Oh, nothing dangerous or bad, just odd," Mom said. "Like what she's done to her room. I asked her why she wanted the Christmas lights, but she just said she wanted to look up at night and see stars. She's strung them all over the ceiling."

"Maybe she's telling you the truth," I said. "Maybe she just likes to look at them."

"Could be, dear," she said, sounding unconvinced. "But something's troubling that girl."

"Kiss Maggie good night for me, Mom," I said. "I'll be home tomorrow, and we'll talk."

With fifteen minutes before dinner, I hung up the telephone and turned on the television until it was time to meet David. I tried to focus on a fuzzy sitcom, hoping the inane chatter would occupy my mind. It didn't work. I couldn't stop thinking about Maggie. It didn't help to explain I needed the job to support us. I couldn't lie to her. The absolute truth: if I wanted to, I knew I could find another job, maybe one that didn't pay quite as well, but certainly one that allowed me to be home every night. Yet, despite the fact that I would do almost anything in the world to make my daughter happy, I knew

I wasn't ready to change my life, even for her, not right now. Too much had already changed for both of us.

Minutes later, someone knocked on the door. David was early. I wondered, for just a second, if he'd ironed a shirt for the evening. But when I opened the door, he stood there, rumpled as ever, holding his suitcase.

"We need to head back to Houston, now," he said. "It'll be all over the news in the morning. Scroggins and Nelson are bringing in Priscilla Lucas, charging her with solicitation of murder."

Ten

I don't understand how you can do this," I argued, every muscle in my body tense with anger. "We had an agreement. You said you'd wait. Don't you realize what we've got here?"

We were in Galveston's courthouse, a forty-year-old building with diamond-shaped windows that was slated to be replaced by a new courthouse still under construction. I briefly wondered if the county would relocate both the outdoor monuments to the new courtyard's plaza: a plaque honoring Norris Wright Cuney, a freed slave who in 1867 cared for victims of the island's yellow fever epidemic, and a monument to the Confederacy, a robust soldier carrying a banner over the inscription GLORY TO THE DEFEATED. Inside his chambers Judge Wilford McLamore, a rotund light-skinned black man with one eye that turned slightly in, whittled at his gums with a flat wooden toothpick. We'd interrupted his dinner and he didn't look pleased.

"Seems to me we've been through all this," he insisted, brushing his teeth with his tongue then sucking back to reclaim a loosened tidbit. "What we've got are two viewpoints that don't necessarily disagree. Agent Scroggins and Oliver here, sorry Detective Nelson, have explained that you may have a lead to the actual killer. Well, bravo. But I don't much see that makes a hill of beans difference as far as Mrs. Lucas and this arrest warrant goes. They're not saying she killed her husband and that woman herself. They're saying she hired someone—maybe your man—to do it. They're not charging her with murder. It's solicitation of murder."

"What makes a difference is that we're looking at a serial killer, not a hit man," I said, straining but failing to regain my composure. "Serial killers do not kill for money."

"Hit men are serial killers," argued Nelson, his face tight and red with anger. He was furious. The Lucas case was the biggest collar of his career, the kind that could finally earn him the sergeant's badge he coveted. He acted as if David and I were trying to snatch it away from him. "Hit men kill multiple victims over a span of time. Maybe this time the guy figured he might as well bring in some bucks doing what he enjoys."

As I fumed, David took over.

"Judge, there's a reasonable assumption the man who killed Louise Fontenot may also have committed the Lucas and Knowles murders. For the sake of argument, let's assume that's true," he said, remaining remarkably cool, I thought. "First, we have no evidence anyone paid for the Fontenot murder, which raises the question, is this guy a hit man? I'd argue that it suggests he's probably not. Louise Fontenot had no money. She had no family, no one to profit by her death. Why would anyone pay to have her brutally murdered? Second, we have no evidence linking Priscilla Lucas with the killer. In a courtroom, we're going to need that link or we have no case."

"We all know that, and we know that it'll take time to develop that evidence," interjected Scroggins, his balding head glistening under the fluorescent lights. "But in the meantime, we've already got a perfectly good circumstantial-evidence case against this woman. First, she had motive: they were divorcing and fighting over custody of the children and the control of more than a billion dollars. Second, she refuses to tell us what she argued about with the dead woman the night before the murders, even to admit she was in her apartment. Third, she had the means, withdrew a hundred grand three days before the murder, and won't account for what she did with it. Fourth, and this is something Nelson and I just tracked down late this afternoon, less than a month ago, she was overheard confiding to a close friend that she'd pay anything, give up her entire fortune, to get her husband out of her life, forever."

"Come on," I wailed. "That's your evidence? Have you ever been through a nasty divorce, Ted? Ever wish your ex-wife was out of the picture? You arrest everyone who's ever uttered those words and half the state of Texas will be locked up."

"Lucas was overheard during one of her Junior League volunteer days at the downtown homeless shelter," Scroggins continued. "And this wasn't a whisper. She wanted to be heard. She wanted to get the word out. She was shopping for a killer."

My experience, everything I believed in contradicted their theory, but I had to admit Nelson and Scroggins were painting a damning portrait of Priscilla Lucas.

Perhaps sensing my confusion, David asked, "Judge, how far do we want to reach here? Do we want to jeopardize our case by rushing to make an arrest? There's no need for that."

At that, the judge pulled his round body up onto two thick legs, and I sensed the argument had ended and we had lost.

"Why arrest Mrs. Lucas now?" David argued. "We have no indication she'll flee. To the contrary, she's a respected member of the community with family and business connections both in Houston and on the island. Why not continue investigating and wait until we've got solid evidence before we make an arrest?"

The judge seemed to consider that, searching all four of our faces for the answer. A frown pulled at his mouth.

"Well, Lieutenant Armstrong, Agent Garrity, this is all real interesting, but I left my wife and a slice of pecan pie at home and you've told me nothing I didn't already know," he said, finally. "These two officers have developed what I'd label sufficient probable cause. The district attorney agrees. The warrant stands. When there's something new to report, call me, but not at dinnertime."

It was nearly nine when the meeting ended, and I called home and checked on Maggie. Mom said she was sleeping. The only good news coming from tonight's events was that I'd be home to surprise her at breakfast.

We left Galveston and took the causeway back to the mainland. In the distance, I saw the small towns that border the coastline, where residents live in an uneasy alliance with miles of petrochemical plants, so vast they stretch into the horizon. Jungles of gray-and-silver pipe illuminated by eerie yellow lights, their stacks belch steam into the air, some burning off escaping gases in flames that look like torches against the night sky. More than once in my memory, one or another of these plants exploded in a fury of destruction, leaving a charred skeleton, where search parties combed for the remains of the dead. Lawyers got rich suing for the grieving families, but little ever changed. On the Gulf Coast, livelihoods depend on the well-paid jobs supplied by these plants. Even if it were possible, few residents truly want them to leave.

On the drive into Houston, we silently licked our wounds from the battle we'd so miserably lost. I wondered where Priscilla Lucas's children would be when she turned herself in. Would they see their mother on television, arrested for their father's murder? Of course there was the hope, vague at best, that no one would tip off the television stations. But my guess was that Nelson and Scroggins wanted the circus, the excitement of a big arrest live on the morning news.

Before leaving Galveston, David and I had decided to have dinner in Houston. We'd settled on Campinetti's, a neighborhood Italian place near the house he'd rented in the Heights, one of the city's oldest neighborhoods lying just northwest of downtown. As I drove past Houston's tailored skyscrapers, some still lit for the night with cleaning crews readying offices for the next morning, I realized neither of us had spoken during the entire drive. I felt grateful for the quiet. Too many people were compelled to fill every available minute with useless words. That David was comfortable with silence spoke well of him.

When we arrived at the restaurant, just before ten, Papa Campinetti, a man stooped with age, informed us they'd stopped serving dinner and that the grill was shut down and cleaned, something we might have expected.

"I guess we should have had dinner in Galveston," I said, as we walked back to the Tahoe.

"Why not my place? I'll make pasta and pour you a glass of wine," David offered.

"I should get home. I haven't seen Maggie since yesterday morning."

"She's sleeping," he said. "You have to drop me at my house anyway, and I don't know about you, but I'm famished."

He was right. I couldn't remember being so hungry, and Maggie wouldn't know until morning that I'd come home early. I had no reason to hurry, but my hands felt a bit clammy when I thought about being alone with David.

"You're not planning any dancing, are you?" I asked, with a nervous laugh. "I didn't wear my steel-toed work boots."

"Aw, that hurts," he said, raising his hand to his chest as if blocking a blow. "I may not be John Travolta, but in the kitchen I channel Rachael Ray. Give me a chance to show you."

"That's an interesting prospect," I said. "Do you dress for the part?"

David laughed, one of those deep laughs that sound vaguely dangerous. "You afraid?" he asked. I wondered if I should be.

"I'm not sure," I admitted. "But I'm willing to give it a try."

Like much of Houston, the Heights failed the continuity test. Without zoning, factories, stores, and homes formed a haphazard patchwork. Motorcycle repair shops and muffler manufacturers intermingled with single-family homes on streets shaded by arcs of live oaks or lined with thirty-foot palms. Two-bedroom houses that would be described in a real estate ad as "handyman's specials" sat next to beautifully restored Victorians, with maid's quarters over the garage. David lived in a small frame bungalow a few miles from the restaurant, and I pulled into the driveway and parked in front of the garage. It was one of those houses people in the north with basements really can't understand—no slab, perched on foot-high pilings, leaving just enough room underneath for the neighborhood cats to breed. A porch ran the length of the front, and David had two wood-slat rockers facing the street. Painted a rich tan and trimmed in white, the house had a farmhouse look, which made the view of the sleek downtown skyline surreal.

Once inside, he poured two glasses of a dry cabernet and then banged about in the kitchen, pulling out pots, boiling water, while I circulated through the living room and dining room. Unlike his tousled appearance, the house was well cared for and organized, neatly kept. Books on shelves lined the walls, many of them travel guides, China, Russia, Thailand, and New Zealand. The furniture was dated but comfortable, the brown corduroy couch worn but clean, and the heavily carved oak tables appeared old enough to have been inherited. Black-and-white photos lined the walls, matted and framed, many of a young boy with thick blond hair, freckles, and David's dimple in his chin.

"Did you take these?" I asked when he walked into the room.

Sipping his wine, he nodded.

"They're good."

"Thanks. It's a hobby. The kid's my son, Jack. He's fourteen now and lives with his mother. We divorced about ten years ago."

"I'm sorry."

"Me, too," he said, with a shrug. "Jan's a great gal, an elementary school teacher. We thought we'd stay married forever. She just couldn't deal with the job. Too many hours on the road, too much time for her to sit alone and worry."

"I was lucky that way with Bill. Since we both worked for the department, we both understood," I said. "Do you see Jack often?"

"Every chance I get. But they moved from Houston a few months back, just after my transfer here finally came through. Pretty ironic," he said, with a shrug. "I move in, set up a bedroom for the kid for weekends, and her husband gets an unexpected transfer a month later to Denver. If I didn't know better, I'd wonder if it was plotted. But it wasn't. Just a bad break. Her husband's in computers, software. Nice guy. Jack loves him."

"I can't imagine being separated from Maggie. She's kept me going this last year," I said, instantly regretting my words as I saw sadness wash over David's face.

"Jack and I are okay," he said, with a half-smile and a resolution to his voice that confided this was something he considered often. "The hours I work, I wouldn't be able to spend as much time as I'd like to with him even if he lived in Houston. It's funny. One of the reasons I asked for the transfer from Quantico was that this job came with assurances of more free time."

"Hasn't worked out that way?"

"How'd you guess? But enough of that. Now back to dinner," he said, rubbing his palms together, as if in great anticipation. "The bad news is the only bread in the house is old and hard as a floorboard, but there's pasta and I added mushrooms and artichoke hearts. Sound good?"

"Extraordinary."

"Then, let's eat."

We filled our plates with steaming linguini David tossed with olive oil, basil, and parmesan cheese, and then sprinkled on the artichokes, mushrooms, pine nuts, and capers. At the dining room table, stacks of unread newspapers pushed to the side, we twirled the long strands of pasta on our forks, washing it down with the heavy, dry wine. The food was comforting and the house felt warm and inviting. David laughed easily, and I decided that when he smiled he could easily have been described as handsome. We talked about our kids, Mom, his ex-wife. We didn't talk about the case or our jobs. It felt good for once, pretending to be normal people with normal lives. Afterward, I cleared the dishes and David rinsed them and put them into the dishwasher. He added soap and turned it on, filling the kitchen with the sound of rushing water.

"Let's go sit in the living room," he said, picking up the wine bottle.

The time passed quickly as we listened to music and talking. David told me about the trip he'd taken through Italy, four weeks by car, alone, including a week in a stone house in Tuscany, with a view of a village where every hour the baptistery bells rang and every morning old women draped in black shawls shuffled over cobbled streets to mass. Before long I looked at my watch and it was well after midnight.

"I need to go," I said, not really wanting to.

It had been a long time since I'd been so relaxed with a man, and all evening long, I'd had the urge to simply rest my head on his shoulder. But now when he leaned forward, now that I knew that in moments his lips would be on mine, I didn't know what to do or say, how to react. My body wanted to be touched, and I craved mindlessness, to just not think. I felt David's hands on my shoulders, and I became aware of his body surrounding me, his heavy warm smell, and I yearned just to be free of the past long enough to let myself be with him.

Ever so slowly, his lips met mine, with a long, firm, hungry kiss, the kind I remembered from what seemed like a lifetime ago.

Confused, I pulled away.

"Sorry," he said, with a guarded smile. "I guess you didn't . . ."

"No, I did," I admitted. "I thought, I thought I was ready, but . . ." Suddenly tongue-tied, I searched his face, wondering what he was thinking.

"Sarah, I don't want you to feel uncomfortable," he said. "I'm attracted to you. I have been since our first meeting, but I know it's only been a year. Too soon?"

Again the room fell quiet. I could feel my body reacting to his closeness, the rush of the wine flushing my cheeks, the slight tingle that remained on my lips.

"You know for the longest time, I just waited for Bill to come back," I said, needing David to understand. "Every time I heard the door open at the house, every time the garage door went up. When the phone rang, I thought, 'Oh, it's Bill. He's home now and Maggie and I will be all right again. Life will be normal, good and whole.'"

Lost in my thoughts, I paused, hoping David would interrupt and keep me from saying more. When he didn't, I went on. "All the dead bodies I've seen, you'd think I, if anyone, would understand death. I've touched it. I've smelled it. I've lived with it. But I don't understand. I just don't understand."

My words trailed off, and I no longer trusted my voice.

"I know," he said, softly wiping away a tear that trailed down my cheek.

My body, reminded of all it had lost, ached for more. I didn't know if I felt relief or disappointment when David suddenly sat back, expanding the distance between us. Moments passed and neither of us spoke, unable or unwilling to break the silence, each lost in our own thoughts. Finally, he rose to his feet, grasped my hands, and pulled me up with him. For the briefest instant I wondered if he'd kiss me again. I wanted him to, and I was afraid that he might. Instead, he walked away, leaving me alone, standing beside the couch, waiting, for what, I couldn't say.

When he returned, he held my blazer and purse.

"Tomorrow, we need to reassess these three murders," he said, for the first time bringing up work. "We have a lot of questions to answer."

That night, at home, I stood before the bathroom mirror, just as I had in the motel, staring at my own image. David had said that he'd been attracted to me from our first meeting, that day in the captain's office. I wondered how he could be. What I saw staring back at me was a plain, tired woman. I ran my fingers through my hair and thought about adding highlights and getting a good cut. Something not so harsh around my face, something to camouflage the wrinkles the last year had etched around my eyes. Maybe some new clothes. I couldn't remember the last time I'd gone shopping. A vague sense of guilt gnawed at me, but when I thought about Bill, I reminded myself again that he was gone and that he wouldn't be coming back. I couldn't bring him back, no matter how hard I tried. Still, I couldn't quiet the ball of anxiety in my chest.

In my old blue nightgown, I let myself into Maggie's room. She slept peacefully in her bed. Above her hung a web of hundreds of white lights, Christmas tree lights claimed from the garage and hung in a haphazard pattern that crisscrossed the ceiling. In the dark room, they shone like stars borrowed from the sky. I thought about Mom's words, that Maggie was acting strangely. Yet the lights didn't strike me as odd. I found them comforting.

For nearly an hour, I sat on the floor beside my daughter's bed, watching her sleep, her chest steadily rising and falling. At times, I looked up at her make-believe stars, and I thought about what she'd told me on the telephone earlier that evening, about singularity, the dense vortex of a black hole, where stars are greedily sucked in and crumbled into dust, never to be seen again.

Eleven

"I like your room, Maggie," I said first thing in the morning, as I gave her a quick kiss on the cheek. "Beautiful. Just like being out in the woods and looking up at the stars."

"It's because . . ." Maggie started to say something, and then stopped. In between chomps of Frosted Flakes, she said instead, "Mrs. Hansen wants you to come to school for a parent-teacher conference."

"Is everything all right?" I asked.

I'd expected her to be surprised to see me, but Maggie acted as if I'd never been gone, not even acknowledging our conversation from the night before.

Out of the corner of my eye, I watched Mom inspect a home-made coffee cake, its crust cracked into a cinnamon-and-sugar road map. She'd gotten up early and baked it before sunrise, and I realized she must be even more upset about Maggie than I'd realized. She cut through it, excising a slice that measured a sixth of the cake. I knew it had to be for me, but I didn't protest. I'd learned long ago that with Mom it's always less painful to eat cake and skip lunch. Somewhere, far back in our English/Irish family tree, undoubtedly lurks a Jewish or Italian woman whose food genes waited in hiding until they morphed into Mom. How else can anyone explain a woman who considers an unfinished plate of cake or a refused cookie a personal rebuff?

"I failed my math test," Maggie continued, reclaiming my full attention. She sounded no more concerned than if she'd just announced she'd been tardy to class.

"Your math test?" I stammered, truly stunned. "How could *you* fail a math test? You're a whiz at math and science. It's impossible."

"She hasn't been studying," Mom said as she plopped the cake plate in front of me accompanied by one of those looks that says, *Didn't I warn you about this?* As wonderful as Mom is, as much as I love her, she's never been above a good old-fashioned I-told-you-so.

"Did you do your assignments?" I asked.

"She hasn't brought books home all week," Mom answered for her.

"Gram, I did so. Maybe I just didn't understand it," Maggie answered, her lower lip jutting out, the same way it had when she was a toddler and Bill or I scolded her for not picking up her toys. "Just because I failed one test doesn't mean that I'm not studying. Lots of kids fail sometimes."

"Not you, Magpie," I said, genuinely puzzled. "You've never failed anything."

"Gee, Mom. It's no big deal," she said. "I don't know why Mrs. Hansen even wants to talk to you."

"Because she's concerned about you, just like Gram and I. She knows, we all know you can do better," I said, trying to sort through my thoughts. Of course it was my fault; it was always my fault. I wasn't paying enough attention. I was gone too much. I should be a more suitable mother, the room mother who coordinated the school bake sale and led a Girl Scout troop, taking twelve eleven-year-olds on campouts.

"Well, maybe I can't do better," Maggie said. Clanking her spoon into the empty cereal bowl, she pushed back from the counter and plopped flat-footed onto the rough Mexican tile floor. "Maybe I'm not as smart as everyone thinks."

I paused, considering what to say next, when the telephone rang. Mom answered it.

"Maggie, we've had a rough year," I ventured, deciding to confront it head-on, a pain inching its way up the back of my neck into my skull. "Maybe the two of us need to talk more, spend more time together. Maybe you're not studying because you're upset about Daddy or mad at me?"

"Oh, Mom," she moaned. "Why do parents always think it's something big, just because a kid fails one stupid math test?"

Suddenly the television set on the counter clicked on and Mom flipped to channel two, the local NBC affiliate's morning news.

"Some man named Garrity says there's something on the news you need to see," she explained, pouring herself a second cup of coffee.

"This discussion isn't over," I called to Maggie, who flounced from the kitchen, her backpack hanging like a disfiguring hump from her shoulders. "Get your jacket, and I'll drive you to school."

"I told Strings I'd ride the bus with him," she shouted back.

"We'll pick him up on the way," I said. "Five minutes, you and me, in the car."

I poured myself a mug of black coffee to wash down the two thousand calories of coffee cake, just as Priscilla Lucas, head down, dressed in a pale purple suit fit for a society luncheon, appeared on the television screen, walking into the Galveston County jail for booking, Scroggins and Nelson trailing behind her. My suspicions had been right; one or both had tipped off the press. They wanted the show, the spectacle of arresting one of Houston's most prominent and wealthiest citizens.

Behind Lucas followed a feisty-looking, white-haired man, his face flushed with anger, who looked to be in his seventies, a man I recognized from newspaper photos as Priscilla's father, Bobby Barker. He whispered to another man, fiftyish, in a well-cut suit. Her lawyer, no doubt. Probably from one of downtown Houston's mega firms.

"On Galveston Island, early this morning, Priscilla Lucas was charged with solicitation of murder in the deaths of her multimillionaire husband, Edward Travis Lucas, and a young lawyer, Annmarie Knowles," said the reporter. "Sources within Galveston P.D. allege that, at the time of the murders, Edward Lucas and Knowles were lovers and the Lucases were in the midst of a contentious divorce battle, fighting over custody of their three children. According to the arrest warrant, Mrs. Lucas has refused to answer questions regarding one hundred thousand dollars she withdrew from her personal bank account just days before the murders."

I cringed when the station cut to footage of Scroggins and Nelson in front of the courthouse.

"What we have here is an age-old scenario, jealous wife has unfaithful husband and his lover murdered," said Scroggins, frowning into the camera, as Nelson stood solemnly behind him. "We feel confident that we have enough evidence to ensure that the Galveston district attorney's office will have no difficulty in obtaining a conviction."

"This morning, Mrs. Lucas is free on one-million-dollars' bail. No alleged hit man has yet been charged in connection with the double murder. More news tonight on the arrest that's rocked Houston and the island," said the reporter.

Mom clicked off the television and asked, "Why did Agent Garrity want you to watch? Is that the case you've been working?"

"Yeah, it is."

"Looks like those detectives think they've solved it," she said.

"They were grandstanding. She didn't do it."

Mom walked over and looked at me, intently sizing me up.

"Are you sure? They made it sound pretty cut-and-dried."

"I'm sure," I said, with an edge of resentment I didn't try to hide. "I don't believe for a second Priscilla Lucas had anything to do with either murder. I'd bet my career on it."

Mom was silent, mulling that over.

"Well, can you prove it?" she asked with a frown. "Because if you can't, it appears what you're really betting is the rest of that woman's life."

I turned to Mom, wondering why she seemed so concerned about the outcome of the case.

"I knew Priscilla's mother," she explained, as if she sensed my puzzlement. "We went to school together. Our parents traveled in the same circles."

It wasn't something I thought about often, probably because it predated my birth and had never had anything to do with my life. Mom hadn't always had to scratch for a living. Her dad was a successful wildcatter who'd made millions drilling for oil in West Texas. Someplace in the attic, we have pictures of my grandparents and Mom-the-debutante at her coming-out ball.

Then my grandmother died young, and the grandfather I never met disowned Mom when she married Pop, who Grandpa said would never be able to support her. Financially, the old guy was right. An Englishman who'd come to Texas to make his fortune, Pop used up Mom's trust fund digging dry holes from West Texas to the Louisiana border. Still, my grandfather had been wrong about the most important thing: my father was a good man. When I was a kid, I sometimes wondered how my life would have been different if my grandfather had understood that and hadn't written us off and left his millions to charity.

"I hadn't seen Jessica Barker in years until Priscilla's wedding,"

Mom explained. "But I work with the family caterer, and I made the cake when she married Edward Lucas. Jessica was very gracious, not treating me like an underling. And Priscilla was a beautiful bride, such a waste when everyone in Houston knew Edward Lucas was a spoiled playboy."

"I didn't know that you knew the family."

"There was never any reason to bring it up," she said, frowning. "I knew all those families, years ago, before your father entered my life. Since then, I've been something of a social outcast, not that I've cared. There's more to life than money. Anyway, Priscilla's mother was always kind. I honestly grieved when I read that she died of breast cancer a few years ago."

"You were friends?" I asked, genuinely surprised.

"I guess you could say that. Jessica offered to help us once, a long time ago," Mom continued. "Something that meant a lot to me. I never forgot."

"What's that, Mom?"

"She heard about your father's stroke and offered to move him into the clinic at the medical center, the one the Barker family funded," she explained. "It was too late. Your father was near death. The doctor examined him and said there was nothing they could do. But I never forgot her kindness. When I faced a crisis, Jessica Barker was the only one from my old life who cared."

Mom tilted her head and looked at me closely. "Sarah, are you certain Priscilla Lucas is innocent?"

"I can't be sure. There's the possibility I'm wrong," I admitted. "But my instincts tell me that I'm right."

"Well, then you need to not worry about Maggie and me for a while," she said.

"Mom . . ." I protested.

"No," she said, raising her hand to shush me. "I promise you that I'll handle things here. We'll be all right. Until this case is closed, you just go do your job. Because if Jessica Barker's daughter is truly innocent, you need to prove it."

Maggie and I shared the car but little else on our drive to her middle school. I tried talking; she just didn't answer. Mom was right—something was troubling her and she wasn't yet at the point where she was willing to talk about it. Picking up Strings cut through the silence, and they gabbed about their science projects, his still based on an ever-expanding theory that dinosaurs were not only alive and hiding somewhere on the planet but would someday reclaim the earth after yet another ice age. I couldn't help smiling when Maggie clicked her tongue in disbelief; it was just so Mom. When I pulled up in front of the school, she seemed surprised that I parked the car.

"I'm going to stop in to visit with Mrs. Hansen for a few minutes," I explained.

Maggie frowned, but I sensed she was actually pleased.

As they ran off to talk to friends, I found my way to Emily Hansen's classroom. Mrs. Hansen was Maggie's homeroom teacher, as well as her instructor for math and science. It was Maggie's first year in middle school, but I'd been at the school a few times before, most recently for spring open house. The classroom reminded me of mine in sixth grade: blackboards, books, desks with attached chairs, and a bulletin board full of profiles of ancient scientists and mathematicians, including Galileo and Pythagoras. The class pet, a gerbil named Leo, after Leonardo da Vinci, spun aimlessly inside a wheel, and Mrs. Hansen, a stocky woman in her late fifties with a helmet of highlighted hair, sat behind her desk, making notations in her grade book.

"Mrs. Armstrong," she said, sounding genuinely pleased I had come. "Thank you for dropping in."

"I'm worried about Maggie," I said. "She told me about her math test."

"I think you should be concerned," she said, frowning. "Maggie's having a difficult time, maybe not surprisingly so for a child who's lost a parent, but a hard time."

When I left, Mrs. Hansen's words were still ringing in my ears. "Maggie's having a difficult time." I'd known, but hearing it from her teacher somehow made my daughter's sadness more real. We had only a few minutes before the bell rang and a herd of young bodies invaded the room, but we agreed to talk again by phone in the coming week. She also promised to call if Maggie failed to turn in her homework or wasn't prepared for class. As I was on the way out the door, she handed me a paper brought to her by Maggie's English teacher. The assignment: to write about what makes her happiest.

I read it in the car. It began, "What makes me happiest is being with my mom," Maggie wrote. "But she's gone a lot, because she helps solve crimes, like my dad used to do. My gram takes care of me, but I'm lonely a lot. Since my dad died, everything is different. We don't have fun like we used to when my dad was with us. He'd kid us, and call Mom and me his girls. My dad could make anything fun." Maggie wrote about our trip to the dinosaur exhibit and that Strings and Mom came along. It ended: "We had a good time, but the next day my mom was gone again, working on a case. Her job is important. People die if she doesn't catch the killers, so I guess the truth is that I'm being selfish."

I tucked the paper in my bag and drove to the office, but it was impossible to put it out of my mind.

Twelve

David and Captain Williams were in the conference room when I arrived. They'd already begun compiling the information we'd collected by building a chart on a sheet of poster board. Across the top, they listed the names of the three victims and the dates of each of the murders. Below each name, they noted details of the offense and the murder scene: nature of the wounds, position of the bodies, any forensic evidence. Here they had only the two strands of blond hair to enter. They also wrote in the cross slashed across each victim's chest and the bloody crosses painted on the walls above their bodies. They'd left two empty columns in front of the Fontenot murder and four before those of Edward Lucas and Annmarie Knowles. I knew without asking that they anticipated writing in the names of other, still unknown victims.

Most frightening, they'd left five columns after the Galveston murders, reserved for future victims, a possibility that increased in probability every day the killer remained free.

"This is where you two have a problem, if you're going to prove Priscilla Lucas wasn't involved," said Captain Williams, pointing at the final category, "connection with the killer." That square re-mained empty under Louise Fontenot's name, but under the Galve-ston murders the captain had penciled in *hired by PL* followed by a question mark.

"Seems to me that you two have to find a way to fill that square with hard evidence if you're going to erase Mrs. Lucas's name," he said.

"Maybe when we track down other cases," I said, pointing to the open areas they'd left between the murders. "As we fill in the blanks, we'll be able to determine how our guy made contact with the others, suggesting how and why he chose Lucas and Knowles."

"The captain and I were just talking about the same thing," said David, frowning. "I think it's safe, at least until we uncover other evidence, to assume that there were others before Louise Fontenot. We did a pretty good canvass in Bardwell, and we came up without any clues. We really have no evidence she was his first. After her, of course, we've got a substantial lapse until the Galveston murders. Very uncharacteristic for someone who gets such a kick out of killing."

"So why are we coming up empty on other matches?" I said, posing the question we all knew had to be answered.

"I'm not sure," he said. "Maybe we're wrong and there are no other murders. In my view, as we've already discussed, highly un-likely."

"Or?"

"Our guy is smart. He changes MO, at least enough for the mur-ders not to match on a computer search. That's a possibility," David said. "This guy's sophisticated enough to cover his tracks on the scene. He doesn't leave physical evidence. He's also shown an ability to adapt parts of his MO to fit the situation. He slashed Louise Fontenot's and Annmarie Knowles's throats, but when he found a gun at the scene, he used it to finish off Lucas."

"Any other possibilities?" I asked.

"One. In my opinion, the most likely: for some reason we're missing cases. Some just weren't reported."

"So none of us believe these three are this guy's only victims?" I asked.

David glanced at the captain, and then turned back to me.

"No," he said. "None of us believe that."

"Well, if the only factor here is that the murders aren't being reported, it's going to be nearly impossible to fill in those blanks," I said, unhappy at the prospect that we may have hit a dead end.

"Then we have to ask why these other agencies aren't reporting," said David. "What cases don't make the list?"

"Of course, theoretically, they all do," I said. "But we all know that's not true."

"Right," he agreed. "It could be that the murders are taking place in small towns where police are often too short staffed to take the time to report."

"Also, departments don't report cases if they believe they know who committed the murder and just can't prove it," I added. "They don't consider those cases truly unsolved."

"That happens," agreed the captain. "What else?"

"High-risk victims, vagrants, homeless, prostitutes, drug addicts, or dealers," I said. "More often than not, they're considered nonpersons."

"That wouldn't fit the profile of the murders we've got so far," David said.

"So where do you two start?" asked the captain.

"If we assume it's number three, unreported cases, what's the best way to contact agencies to ask them to look through their unsolved case files?" asked David. "Something that will have a wide distribution."

"We could e-mail a departmental bulletin to rangers and law-enforcement agencies across the state," I suggested. "One asking for information on any murders even remotely similar to the three we're investigating, anything that hasn't been reported to ViCAP."

"That'd work," said David. "But should we extend the search? Go national?"

The captain thought about that. "Since ViCAP is a national database, we should have had hits on similar cases in other states the first time we ran a comparison. I'm reluctant to go too broad with this. Search too wide and we'll be swamped in cases. At least for now, let's keep this in Texas. I'll get Sheila to get the bulletin out," the captain offered, referring to his secretary.

"It'll be a while before we start getting responses. While we're waiting for those to come in, where do we look?" asked David. "How do we fill in those blanks on our own?"

"Why don't we follow through on your second possibility, that the killer may be changing MO?" I suggested. "Maybe the murders are being reported, but, as you said, they're just different enough that we're not tying them to our cases?"

"Okay," he agreed.

"Let's go back over the ViCAP list and reconsider any unsolved murder reported in Texas in the last three years where the murder weapon's a hunting-style knife."

"That's a lot of cases, Sarah," said David.

"Give me another suggestion."

David shrugged. "It's someplace to start."

"Sounds like a plan," said the captain. "I'll talk to Sheila about the bulletin and leave you two to get started."

We began organizing our files to take to the computer, but the captain seemed reluctant to leave.

"I've got a couple other things you should both probably know," he finally said. "Neither one is particularly good news."

When he had our full attention, he went on.

"We received a copy of a letter to Galveston P.D. from the governor this morning, praising Detective Nelson and Agent Scroggins for their speedy action on this case, so there are a lot of important people invested in their belief that Priscilla Lucas is guilty. There's also a newspaper reporter nosing around for interviews, a guy named Evan Matthews. He's been calling here asking for you two all morning. Watch out for him."

"He's the Galveston reporter who had the front-page story the day after the murders, the one that included all the inside information," I said. "But that didn't come from us. You know, we don't talk to anyone about an ongoing investigation. What's your concern?"

"This case is sensational," he said. "Word is that Matthews plans to write a series of exposés on the lives of Texas's ultrarich, including high-dollar divorces and high-society murders. He's anchoring it around a major article on the Priscilla Lucas case. He'll be looking for every bit of information, every innuendo he can find. Be advised, I'll back your investigation one-hundred percent. My gut tells me you two are right and we're dealing with a serial killer, not a hit man."

I was waiting for the "but" and it came quickly.

"Until you have something solid, we need to keep a lid on your investigation. Only those working the Lucas case are to know what you two are working on or that you believe Priscilla Lucas is innocent," he continued. "Even though you might like to share your opinions with others, you can't. If anyone finds out you believe Mrs. Lucas has been wrongly accused, you may find yourselves in the difficult position of being witnesses for the defense during her trial, an uncomfortable situation not only for the two of you but for the rangers and the Bureau."

"We're aware of that," said David.

"Don't forget it," cautioned the captain. "Go ahead and try to prove your case the way you see it. But if you fail and Nelson and Scroggins turn out to be right, you don't want to end up on the stand testifying against the prosecution."

As David had suspected, the expanded list of potentially connected murders proved lengthy, more than a hundred. All had been committed in Texas within the past thirty-six months, all by unknown assailants who used what were believed to be long thin-bladed knives. By telephone, we slowly worked our way through the list. By three that afternoon, we'd found only one probable lead, a woman murdered nearly eighteen months earlier, in the small town of Redbluff, by car seven hours southwest of Houston and just across from the Mexican border in the Rio Grande valley.

"This would have been three months before the Fontenot murder. It's, at best, a long shot. If it's our killer, he was still refining his technique," David said, when he hung up the telephone with the investigating deputy. The woman's naked body had been found propped up in a chair behind her house. Her throat had been cut and her chest was slashed and bleeding. In the autopsy the county coroner had noted no signs of torture.

"It may be long, but it's a shot," I answered. "And at the moment, it's the only one we have."

"Well, I'd like to talk to this officer in person, see the autopsy photos and the crime-scene pictures," David said. "Shall we?"

"Let's go," I answered.

David was on the telephone booking a flight to McAllen and a rental car, when the telephone rang next door in my office.

"Lieutenant Armstrong, we don't know each other, but I'm Bobby Barker," an unfamiliar voice informed me. "Priscilla Lucas is my daughter."

"Yes, Mr. Barker, what can I do for you?"

"Priscilla and I would like to talk with you, if possible this afternoon. We believe it may be beneficial for both of us."

"What's this about, Mr. Barker?"

"We'll discuss that in person," he said.

"All right. I'll be bringing FBI Agent David Garrity with me," I said. "We're working this case together."

"No," he said. "This invitation is extended only to you. My daughter tells me that you seemed more reasonable than the other officer when you came out to the house the day of my son-in-law's murder. She has the impression that, given the right circumstances, you could be trusted."

Thirteen

The trip to the valley on hold, I returned to the River Oaks mansion of Priscilla Lucas. This time I had no need to wait for the maid to answer the door. Priscilla's attorney, Stan Claville, the tall, spindly man with a painfully gaunt face and deep-set brown eyes I'd watched on television that morning, waited outside to greet me. From the cut of his gray pinstripe, I knew the family had spared no expense when considering his hourly retainer. I followed him to the library, where Priscilla Lucas waited in a hunter-green leather chair, drinking an iced tea and watching the smoke from her long, slender cigarette dissipate over her head. Unlike the woman I'd met just four days earlier, she seemed unsure of herself, although she sat with rigid posture and, at what I sensed was great personal expense, looked me straight in the eye.

"May I offer you a glass of tea?" she asked, with a forced smile.

"No thanks," I said, not particularly wanting to make sociable. As I left headquarters, the last thing David did was remind me to be careful, or the captain's concerns could become reality. I could find myself in the untenable position of being used as a courtroom pawn.

"Please, sit down," Priscilla suggested, her impeccable manners still intact, as she motioned toward the sofa.

"I'd prefer to stand," I said. "Why am I here?"

Nervously tapping a top hat of ashes from her cigarette, Priscilla glanced toward the opposite corner of the room at two men who stood together, leaning against a shelf filled with gold-embossed books. One was the man from the morning news broadcast, in his early seventies, a man age hadn't yet diminished, his hands still muscular enough to wrestle a steer or, if need be, an oil well. He had a cap of thick white hair and bushy eyebrows that curled into his hairline, giving him an unsettled look.

The other man appeared his antithesis, in his forties, a fringe of light brown hair falling over his eyes. More than six feet tall, he had fine patrician features and a broad smile, the kind some people are born with and others practice in front of mirrors. He wore a brown cashmere sweater that bagged perfectly over olive-green pants, the collar on his white shirt just peeking above the neckline. The French professor, I assumed. Priscilla's new man.

"This is Scott Warner," the elder of the two said, gesturing to indicate the man beside him. "A friend of Priscilla's."

"It's good to meet you," said Warner, leaning forward to shake my hand, and then quickly retreating to his former stance in the corner.

"And I'm Bobby Barker, Priscilla's father. We talked on the phone. Glad you agreed to come," he said, extending his own hand. "You know my late wife went to school with your mother."

"Yes," I said. "Mom mentioned that."

Barker smiled warmly. "Well, we've been hearing a lot about you."

"Is that right?" I said.

"We've been told by sources within the Galveston Police Department and the county courthouse that you showed some sense about this case. We hear you argued against issuing the warrant for my daughter's arrest," he said, assessing me through rheumy green-gray eyes, the color of a stagnant pond. Again taking the lead, he asked, "Is that true?"

"I just wasn't sure now was the time to make an arrest," I hedged. "Obviously, others disagreed."

"So you're saying it was just a matter of timing then?"

"I think that's probably the best way to characterize it."

"Priscilla was hoping . . . we were all hoping . . ." began Warner.

"I'll handle this," Barker cautioned. It appeared that the old man had the younger one on a short tether. Warner frowned but quickly nodded.

"Lieutenant Armstrong, it's obvious that my daughter is in a rather uncomfortable situation here and, considering what we've been told about your sentiments, we thought you might be able to help by talking some sense into your fellow officers. I'm referring, of course, to Agent Scroggins and Detective Nelson, who seem intent on crucifying her for murders she not only didn't commit but had no involvement in."

"They're just doing their jobs," I said, unhappy at being put in a position in which I felt compelled to defend them.

Exasperated, he audibly groaned.

"You're a businessman, aren't you, Mr. Barker?" I asked.

"Of course," he said, turning his head skeptically, as if to see me better through the corners of his muddy eyes. "I run Barker Oil. My father founded it."

"Well, as a businessman, you know what counts is the bottom line, don't you?"

"You could say that."

"I suggest the most prudent course then is to look at the bottom line in this situation," I said.

"And what is the bottom line here?" he asked peevishly.

"All Mrs. Lucas needs to do is truthfully answer all the questions, and if she's innocent, she can put this matter to rest," I said, slowly turning to focus my attention on Priscilla. Dodging my gaze, she concentrated on stubbing out her cigarette in a crystal ashtray.

"What did you and Annmarie Knowles argue about the night before the murder?" I asked. Priscilla shifted in her chair and shot her father a worried glance, then searched Scott Warner's face as if hoping to find her answer there. The attorney, Claville, who'd been silent up until now, cleared his throat, a tactic I had no doubt he employed often in courtrooms to ensure that he had a jury's attention.

"Lieutenant," he said. "While we understand what you're saying, under the circumstances, since Mrs. Lucas is the prime, perhaps the only identified suspect in these murders, I've advised her not to answer any questions."

"Then I can't help her," I said, looking straight at Priscilla.

"If that's your final word," he said. "I thought as much. From the beginning this exercise was nothing more than a waste of time."

"If that's the case, I'll be on my way," I said.

From the corner of my eye, I saw Priscilla's shoulders heave with disappointment. She shook her head as if my departure were inconceivable, and then glanced about the room at the three men. Claville, apparently unaware of his client's reaction to my imminent departure, blustered on about his opposition to calling me, unconcerned. It was Warner who interrupted him.

"Priscilla, you have to do what you think is right," he advised her. "I'm here with you. We're all here for you."

She stared down at her hands, and I noticed she'd removed the emerald-cut diamond solitaire that had dominated her left hand at our first meeting. She glanced up again at Warner and then smiled.

"Sarah, may I call you Sarah?" she asked, turning back to me.

"Sure."

"I would like to tell you what we argued about," she began.

"Mrs. Lucas, I advise you not to go any further," interrupted Claville, his voice stern as if addressing a child.

"Stan, quiet," Barker chastised. "We know Pris didn't do this. She couldn't. Let her talk if she's ready."

"Maybe if Lieutenant Armstrong understands more about what happened, she can put a stop to this nightmare," Warner said. "What more could happen than already has?"

"Priscilla could be denying these words in front of a jury," Claville sputtered. "That's what could happen. If I'm going to defend her—"

"Let her talk to this woman," Barker ordered, again.

Visibly unhappy, Claville backed down, as Barker turned to his daughter.

"Priscilla, I know you couldn't have done this thing. If you're ready to explain yourself, maybe it's time."

She smiled at her father, and their eyes met. She looked again to Warner who nodded encouragingly. Then she turned to address me.

"Sarah," she said. "I went to see Annmarie to talk sense into her."

"About what?"

"About the children," she said matter-of-factly. "You probably already know that Edward and I were fighting over the children. He wanted them for control of their trust funds. I wanted them with me because I'm their mother, and there are things only a mother can give a child. I want to be there to give those special gifts to my children. I want to be with them, to guide them as they grow. The money means nothing to me. It never has."

"So, why not let him control the trust funds while you raise the children?"

"I offered that. I would willingly have signed over all control of their trust funds, just to have them with me. But Edward was not an easy man to bargain with, and when he wanted something, he wanted it all," she said, nervously pulling another cigarette from an etched silver box on the Chippendale end table beside her. Barker bent toward her to light it, and her hands trembled as she held it to her mouth. She drew in, long and hard, and then exhaled a thin cloud of gray smoke.

"Edward's pride was hurt," she continued. "I was the one who wanted the divorce, and he couldn't forgive that. As much as anything, he wanted to punish me."

"He wanted to punish us," said Warner. "Both of us."

Priscilla smiled fondly at him and agreed. "Yes, Edward wanted to punish both of us."

"If that's the case, what good could it do to talk with Annmarie?" I asked.

"Edward had bragged for days that he planned to marry the girl, just to spite me. He said she'd be the one raising our children, my children," she said, pointing at her chest, her voice restrained but shrill. "He claimed he had enough on me to prove that I was unfit, and that I'd only be given supervised visitation. I knew he couldn't have much to use against me, but there were those times, when we'd fought and I, angry and upset, drank too much in public. You have to understand that much of our life was played out in the public eye, at the country club, one social function or another, after a while they all ran together. It always happened during one of his affairs. At times, you see, it was difficult just to look the other way."

She paused, and I sensed a part of her had returned to that day, to her husband threatening to take her children away.

"With Edward's lawyers, he could have dragged me through the court system until he found a judge willing to give him what he wanted. I couldn't let him have the children. I love my children. They mean more to me than my own life," she said, emotion tearing at the raw edges of her voice. "Are you a mother?"

"Yes, I am."

"Sons? Daughters?"

"A daughter."

"Then I don't have to explain to you how I felt," she said. "I would, any mother would, do anything to keep her children safe and with her. Wouldn't you?"

"Priscilla, please," intruded the attorney, the color drained from his face. "Say nothing more. I'm cautioning you that this could be damning in a courtroom."

"It's the truth, Stan. I'm not going to lie," she said, looking to Warner for support. He smiled back at her and she went on. "I went to her apartment to talk to Annmarie, to explain that I didn't care about Edward or the money, anything she wanted of mine she could have, except my children. She couldn't have my children."

"And her reaction?"

"She refused to help me. She said that the entire matter was up to Edward, that they were his children, too, and that she wouldn't get in the way if he wanted them. Annmarie said that she loved Edward. I couldn't accept that as her answer. How could they take my children? Edward had never had time for them. He never would. She cared nothing for them, hardly even knew their names."

"How did you leave it with her?"

"I told her that she needed to find a way to convince Edward or that we'd both squander our lives in courtrooms and our fortunes on lawyers," she said. "I told her I would never give up my children."

I said nothing.

"Sarah, as a mother, certainly you can understand," she pleaded. "I had to . . . I have to be there for my children. I would not, could never, leave their raising to a stranger."

"Ms. Knowles's neighbors say you were at her apartment on at least one other occasion. I appreciate what you've told me, but there's more going on here. What was your relationship with Annmarie Knowles?" I asked.

For a moment, Priscilla Lucas appeared stunned, surprised at my question. "We had no relationship, beyond that she was my husband's employee and his mistress," she insisted. "Yes, I'd been there before, but it was for the same reason, to talk some sense into her. I couldn't take no for an answer. I kept going back, hoping she'd change her mind."

"And the money, Mrs. Lucas. The hundred thousand dollars? What did you do with it?"

Priscilla Lucas grew suddenly silent, looking toward her father, then Claville, then Warner. I had the impression the men all waited as expectantly as I, not knowing what she might say.

When she hesitated, Warner interceded.

"Priscilla, I know you. Whatever you did with the money, it can't be that bad. I'm sure the lieutenant will understand and that it will be all right," he said. "I want you to tell her what you did with the money. Don't be afraid."

She stared at him, as if she replayed his words over and over in her mind, debating what to do. When she still said nothing, her father broke in, eager to rescue his floundering daughter.

"Lieutenant, there's a misimpression here," he said. "To most people, of course, one hundred thousand dollars is a great deal of money. It would be unusual to deal in such terms, especially in cash. We understand that. But not in our family. Such withdrawals wouldn't be unusual."

"That should make my question easy then. Why should there be a mystery?" I said. "If this isn't a great deal of money, if she used it to buy jewelry, clothes, cover household expenses, anything, all she needs to do is supply us with receipts or tell us whom to talk with to confirm it, and this can all end."

Moments passed and Priscilla said nothing, just stared blankly ahead.

"Priscilla, please tell her," beseeched Warner.

"Mrs. Lucas, I believe you love your children," I said, calmly, watching her every nuance. "Don't you want to clear this up, so that you can be with them, especially now when they need you the most? Why not tell me what I need to know so I can do my job and you can do yours, be their mother? So that you and the professor can begin a new life together."

The room again fell silent and I held my breath, wondering what would happen next.

"I didn't kill my husband and Annmarie. I hired no one to do it," she finally said, in a voice so low it resonated from somewhere deep within her. "But I can't tell you what you want to know."

"Priscilla," Warner pleaded. "Please."

"No," she answered him. "You don't know the Lucas family. You don't know what they're capable of, what would happen to us if they knew. They'd use it against me, to take my children."

The room fell silent. I waited, but I sensed her decision was made.

"Then, we have nothing else to say," I concluded, not really wanting to leave but knowing that nothing more would be accomplished by my staying.

"Sarah, our mothers were friends. Doesn't that count for something? You have to trust me," she argued, her hands, palms up, begging for sympathy. "The money had nothing to do with the murders. But telling you could jeopardize all our futures, everyone I love."

"I can't just trust you," I said, my voice harder than I felt toward her. "I'm investigating two brutal murders."

"I realize that," she said, fighting to keep her voice steady. But her eyes betrayed her by filling with a thick, glossy coat.

"Then you understand why I'm not able to just take your word. I need to know what the money was used for. I need more than your assurances."

After a few silent moments, she said, "I do understand. But I'd hoped if I told you the rest, you'd understand that I'm not the type of woman who'd do such a thing and that you can believe me."

"Lieutenant, isn't it obvious Priscilla is telling the truth, that she's attempting to cooperate?" Warner pleaded, sitting beside her and protectively wrapping his arm across her shoulders.

"Please understand, summoning you here, this was not an easy decision." her father interjected, his own voice heavy with emotion. "Are these the actions of a guilty woman, inviting the hunter into her den?"

Perhaps they were right. I believed Priscilla Lucas was innocent, but with the evidence against her mounting, in the end what I believed might not matter.

"Mr. Barker, as your attorney feared, all I've heard only gives more reason to suspect your daughter might be involved, not less," I said, turning to Priscilla. "I need to know what she did with the money. Nothing else has the power to make all this disappear. I'm sorry, Mrs. Lucas. I truly am."

From somewhere in her dwindling reserves of strength, Priscilla Lucas pulled together a weak smile and nodded.

"Unless there's something else then," I said.

"Nothing?" she said, her voice weary and resolved. "There's nothing you can do to help me, then?"

"Nothing," I said.

With that, I turned to go. I didn't realize until I'd nearly reached the door that her father had followed.

"Lieutenant, perhaps you can clear up one point for me," he said, his face crimson with emotion but his voice soft and pleading.

I turned back.

"What's that, Mr. Barker?"

"You argued with Judge McLamore against issuing the warrant. I've been told it's because you and Agent Garrity believe that the man who killed Edward and Miss Knowles is actually a serial killer and that their deaths have nothing to do with my daughter."

He waited, but I said nothing.

"Is that true?"

His eyes appealed for hope, any shred of reassurance I could give.

"I can't tell you what we're investigating, Mr. Barker," I said, quietly. "I can assure you that Agent Garrity and I are following every lead that presents itself in this case. And that we're doing our very best to find all the answers."

"You do believe she's innocent, don't you?" he said, a hint of hope in his voice. "You are looking for someone else, someone not connected with Priscilla?"

Barker searched my face, and I sensed he found his answer without my uttering a word. Nothing more was said. I quickly turned and left, the mansion's massive double doors thudding to a close behind me.

Fourteen

What awakened me in the early hours of the morning, just before two? Down the hall, in their own rooms, Maggie and Mom were peacefully lost to their dreams, but I jolted upright, searched the shadows and listened. Through the slats of my shuttered bedroom windows, the back porch light funneled through the darkness, and rain padded softly onto already sodden brown earth, flowing into muddy ribbons that flooded my mother's favorite azalea bed, where wet boughs bent under the weight of just-opening fuchsia blooms.

I was certain of only these things: that my eyes opened before the telephone rang, that I knew before I picked it up that I would hear David's voice, and that before he'd uttered the first word, I knew what he would say.

"Another murder. I'll pick you up in half an hour. The helicopter is waiting."

Two hours later the sun had just come up, and I stood in the bedroom of a ramshackle white wooden frame bungalow in a San Antonio neighborhood of small houses, with cars in various stages of disrepair parked under spindly oak trees on burned-out lawns, staring at the nude body of Mary Gonzales, a twenty-eight-year-old waitress and the mother of four young children. Mary had been a beautiful woman, with long, flowing black hair and a complexion the color of tea with honey.

The detective in charge with the San Antonio P.D. had already reconstructed her last hours. Mary worked an early dinner shift at a Riverwalk restaurant, serving margaritas, quesadillas, tortillas, and tacos al carbon to tourists and conventioneers. At seven-thirty she'd punched out. Instead of picking up her children, she'd left them at their babysitter's house. Coworkers said Mary had been excited about that night's date with her boyfriend, Santos Maida, a construction worker. They said Mary loved to dance to hot salsa music. Mary and Santos never made it to the club that night, where the music played and the dancing went on for hours after she died, awash in blood, her throat slashed, her fists clenched in rage.

From the evidence he left behind, it appeared the killer found Mary much as we did, sitting on a wooden bedroom chair, looking into the cracked mirror atop her battered dresser. Her work uniform, a white peasant blouse with her name tag still pinned in place over the left breast and a brightly colored serape-style skirt, lay discarded on the floor. Her hairbrush was found on the floor beside her, leading us to believe she may have been brushing her hair into soft waves and pulling it back in the ribbon that still held it at the nape of her neck, when he made his presence known.

What horror she must have felt. A stranger. An intruder in her house, her room.

How long had he been there? Did he tell her how he'd watched her, as he tied her ankles to the chair, bound her body to the chair frame, cinched her hands together in her lap, wedging between them the long, flat handle of a pink plastic mirror, a child's toy that belonged to her toddler daughter? How long did he remain? Minutes? Hours? Touching her, torturing her, mocking her? Cutting off her bra and panties and throwing them on the floor.

I imagined Mary's pain as the blade cut into her hands, into the soles of her feet, caught on tendons and muscle, wrenching them into tight knots. When did she understand? I wondered. When did she know without question that he would kill her?

One thing I knew: Mary Gonzales had waged a valiant fight.

In amongst the precise torture wounds from the knife tip into her hands, a signature that along with a bloody cross on the wall behind her and the two intersecting gashes that mutilated her chest, there was something new. Mary's cold, still palms bore jagged defensive wounds, indicating that she'd not given in easily and had attempted to shield herself from his blade. One cut nearly severed her right forefinger; another, on the left hand, gaped to the bone and looked as if she'd seized the knife by the blade in a failed attempt to wrench it away from the demon who'd invaded her home and her life.

As he had with the other victims, the killer took his time with her. Before or after her death, he adorned her with dusty crepe paper flowers, the kind sold at Mexican markets, torn from a straw basket beside the bed. He'd posed three white-paper calla lilies between her bare thighs, where they reminded me of a macabre Georgia O'Keeffe painting. The rest, he'd woven into her hair, mimicking a flowered headdress of the type worn by brides. And he'd employed her makeup, casually discarded on her battered dresser, painting her eyelids a frothy green and her mouth a deep red that spilled over her lips until it formed a grotesque clown's smile.

"Vanity," David whispered. "This time the sin is vanity."

The knots on the rope that bound her hands and her legs matched those in the restraints cut from Lucas and Knowles and the specimen Sheriff Broussard kept in an envelope marked *Fontenot Murder* in his evidence room.

"Any possibility this isn't your killer?" asked Detective Mike Morales of San Antonio P.D.

"This is our guy," said David.

"No question?"

"No question."

"What have you got for us?" I asked, trying not to think about the children whose toys lay scattered about the house: an infant's swing, a teddy bear, a teething ring and rattle, a Barbie convertible, a broken plastic *Star Wars* laser, and a colored wheel with primary-colored tabs. Maggie had one like it as a baby. When she pressed the buttons, a cow, lamb, dog, horse, and goat popped up emitting mechanical cries.

"Not much. We think he gained entry through an open back window. It was still open when we got here. We found a few threads of black fabric caught on a nail protruding from the ledge. We've sent them to the lab. No footprints. The place is littered with finger-prints, most of them small, probably from the children. Others may belong to Ms. Gonzales. Of course, we'll check them all," he said. "We found one partial fingerprint, on the nightstand, smeared with blood. It could be the killer's. It's possible that in the fight she ripped a hole in one of his gloves."

"That's something," I said.

"Let's hope," David said. "At least it's a chance."

"Drops of blood, believed to be from the victim, lead to the bath-room and what appears to be a ring of diluted blood around the sink drain. Looks like our guy cleaned up. No murder weapon has been found," Detective Morales added. "As far as the boyfriend can tell, nothing's been stolen. She had nearly thirty dollars in tips, untouched, on the kitchen counter."

"Is the boyfriend the one who found the body?"

"Yeah. He called it in from the neighbor's house. Ms. Gonzales didn't have a phone. Probably couldn't afford one."

"You've questioned him?" I asked.

"Sure. We thought at first he might be involved," Morales admitted. "But his alibi checks out. Based on body cooling, the medical examiner figures she died sometime before ten o'clock last night. Maida's currently working with a crew on a ranch outside town, putting up a new barn. The foreman said he left the site sometime after ten-thirty. He couldn't have gotten here much before eleven, just three minutes before his call came in to the nine-one-one dispatcher. Then, one of the guys in the office remembered your e-mail, and we figured maybe we had another case for you."

"We're grateful you called and that you kept the scene intact for us," said David.

"Where's the boyfriend?" I asked.

Detectives ringed a diminutive man seated in a chair when David and I walked into the bare, white kitchen, with an old gas stove and a chipped porcelain counter, the kind that's shaped in one piece to form a sink. Santos Maida couldn't have stood more than five foot three, slightly built but strong, with the well-defined muscles that come from working construction. Dressed in what I assumed must have been his best clothes, ones fitting for a date with Mary, he wore a carefully pressed blue-plaid shirt and blue jeans with heavily starched creases. His face was buried in his hands, and until I spoke, he didn't seem to either sense or care that we'd entered the room.

"Mr. Maida, I am very sorry for your loss."

He looked up, his eyes searching my face.

"*Gracias,*" he said. "Mary was a good woman. Why would anyone do such a terrible thing to her?"

David and I said nothing.

"Did she suffer?" he asked. "Did this devil make her suffer?"

"That's a question we can't answer until the autopsy," I said, secretly hoping by then he'd forget to ask. Of course, if we caught the deviant responsible, I knew this man would probably sit in a court-room someday, where expert after expert would recount how the woman he'd loved had been tortured.

"What will happen to her children?" he asked. "Who will care for them?"

"Do they have a grandmother, an aunt, any other relatives?"

"In Mexico."

"After we're finished talking, why don't you tell the detective what you know about them, so they can be notified," I said, hoping that gave him some, even if little, peace. When he nodded, I asked, "But first, tell me about Mary. Had she complained at all that anyone bothered her, frightened her, in any way?"

"No," he said, pushing hard against his knees, his brown-black eyes smoldering. "If she would have said those things, I would have found the man and made him afraid to do this. I would not have let this happen."

"Did she tell you about anything unusual, anyone unusual or threatening, anything out of the ordinary?" David asked.

"Nothing," he said. "She was happy. We were going to get married. We were going to have more children and live here, in this little house, together."

"Can you tell us anything at all that might help us find the person who did this?" I asked.

Santos pondered our questions. Before long, his head bowed and he again succumbed to tears. He shook his head and whispered, "No."

It appeared we'd again leave with little physical evidence, so far only a few black threads and the possibility of a partial fingerprint, a clue Mary had fought valiantly to provide. But just then, Detective Morales called us outside. There stood Lily Salas, waiting in the street, in front of the house, an elderly woman wrapped in a loose flowered cotton robe, Mary's next-door neighbor.

"Santos said she's dead. Is Mary dead?" she asked, her shoulders stooped, her hands spotted from decades of exposure to the sun, trembling with age.

"Yes," I said. "Mary's dead."

"*No, Dios mio*," she cried. "How could someone kill Mary? How could he do this? She was such a good woman, a wonderful mother."

Lily sobbed for a few moments, Detective Morales helping to support her as she appeared ready to collapse from the weight of the tragedy.

"Señora Salas," Morales said, softly. "*Digalos.* Tell the officers what you saw."

Slowly she fought back the tears, collecting her thoughts.

"Señora Salas," I prodded, holding her frail hand in mine. "Please help us find the person who did this to Mary."

She nodded and took a long steady breath.

"Last night," she said. "I saw a man, outside, on the street. Dressed all in black. I nearly hit him with my car, when I drove home from the market. I didn't see him until he was before me, and I could hardly stop."

"What did he look like?" David asked.

"Young, about the age of my grandson, Ramon. Maybe nineteen, as old as twenty-four or twenty-five, no older, I think. He had blond hair, long and straight. And he had terrible eyes, blue eyes, like ice, cold and dead. I rolled down my window and apologized. I said, 'I am sorry. I did not see you in the dark all dressed in black.' I think, nothing is really hurt. I didn't touch him. At the most he is maybe frightened. But he is not frightened. I can tell by the way he says nothing, just looks at me with those eyes, *peligroso, muy peligroso.*"

"Dangerous," Detective Morales interpreted. "Señora Salas is saying that the man looked dangerous."

Lily fell silent, lost in her thoughts.

"Tell us what happened then," I asked.

She nodded and continued. "I was frightened, very frightened. How I knew this man was bad, I can't explain. It's like I know other things in life," she said, her hand fluttering to her heart and then her head. "It is here, inside me, that something told me to say nothing more. I roll my window quickly up and I drive home. Just here, it happened, a few houses from my home. He stood there," she said, pointing perhaps a hundred feet away. "And he watched me, even until I walked inside and locked my doors."

"What time was this?"

"Maybe eight, a little earlier."

"What happened next?"

"A little while later, I am watching television, and Perroito begins racket that is so loud, I know something is not right."

"Perroito?"

"My dog. He is in my backyard, fenced up. I name him Little Dog, but he is big and very mean."

"And then?"

"I look out the windows but see nothing. I listen but hear nothing, until I hear Mary drive up, just like every night after work at the restaurant," she said, her eyes filling with fresh tears. "And then nothing more happens, nothing until Santos runs to my house screaming that Mary is dead, that someone has slaughtered her like a beef or a hen."

Two hours, I thought. The dog barked, and if he planned to make Lily Salas his next victim, he knew he'd lost any hope of surprise. Instead, it was Mary. She drove up, parked her car, walked inside. He saw her. Climbed through the rear window. Perhaps he confronted her then. Maybe he waited, watching her undress, watching her prepare for a night with Santos. And then . . . two hours later she died. Perhaps she begged for death when it finally, mercifully, came.

"Thank you, Señora Salas. This is very helpful," I said. "Would you do something for me?" I asked.

"Anything."

"Would you sit down and talk to me, tell me what this man looked like, while I draw what you remember?"

Lily Salas nodded.

We sat in her living room together, alone, Lily Salas and I, while she described the details that made up the man's face. I carefully monitored every word I said, not wanting to implant any images in Lily's mind, to in any way distort her memory. I wanted her clear, un-polluted recollection of the killer's face. In college I'd sketched portraits of my friends; now I drew a brutal serial killer.

"Around here, the chin, it was round but not too round. The cheeks were very high, thin. He carried little weight in his face, in his body. A slight young man, all bone," she said.

With a charcoal pencil on a sketch pad the detective had sent to the scene for me, I outlined a lean, thin face with a slightly rounded chin.

"No," Lily said. "That's not right. Make his chin longer and he was thinner in the cheeks. Very thin and long, but at the base of the chin round."

I erased and began again. "Ah, that's right," she said. "And let me tell you about the mouth . . ."

Ninety minutes later, Lily looked down at the face we'd drawn together and nodded.

"That's him," she said. She'd remembered incredible detail, so much more than most witnesses. Her memory was fresh, and it helped that she'd had time to look at the man before she became frightened of him, before her mind switched from curiosity of the stranger to alarm.

Back at Mary Gonzales's house, where David waited for me, I gave the sketch to Morales.

"Fax us a copy as soon as you get to the office," I said. "Then start using it to canvass the neighborhood and in the local newspaper."

"It'll be waiting for you in your office when you land in Houston," Morales said, as I shook his hand.

"Well, we'll be going then," David said to Morales. "We'll be in touch with you later this afternoon, when we're back in Houston, to find out what else you've uncovered. Fax us a copy of the fingerprint fragment as soon as you can, too?"

"Certainly," said Morales. "Along with anything else we're able to pull together from the scene."

"Thank you," I said. Then, turning to Lily, I added, "Señora Salas, I thank you. What you've done tonight may help us stop this animal."

"I will do everything I can to stop this beast," she said. "Anything."

"I am truly sorry for your loss," I said. "I can tell that you adored Mary and her children."

"She was a good woman, a good mother," she said. "Why would anyone do such a thing?"

"For some questions, there are never good answers," David said, taking the old woman's hand in his. "Perhaps you can help Detective Morales and Señor Maida help find the children's grandparents in Mexico?"

"I can," she said, her face brightening at the prospect. "I know the village where they live in Oaxaca. Mary told me once. And I know her mother's name."

"Good," I said. "That will make it easier to reunite them with family."

We'd been there for nearly five hours, and I hadn't noticed the press milling on the street in front of the house until David and I walked toward his car, but they'd obviously noticed us, and one of them, a photographer, fired off frames before we'd even reached them. A man I judged to be his counterpart, the reporter he traveled with, ran toward me.

"Lieutenant Armstrong," he shouted. A wiry man in his thirties with a bristly manner, he followed along beside us as we hurried past. "Is this murder in any way connected to the killings of Edward Lucas and Annmarie Knowles?"

Startled, I turned to confront him.

"What?"

"Evan Matthews of the *Galveston County Daily News*," he said, extending his hand.

I didn't take it.

"I'm working on an article on the Lucas murders, and I've been told by someone close to the investigation that you and Agent Garrity have an alternate theory, that you believe those deaths can be linked to others, and that they're all the work of a serial killer."

I said nothing, as David nudged my shoulder and urged me away.

"Shouldn't people be warned if this is the work of a serial killer?" Matthews shouted. "Shouldn't they be told to take precautions?"

How could he have known? I wondered. *Who told him about the Gonzales murder so quickly that he made his way to San Antonio to confront us here?*

David and I rushed to the rented green Saturn Ion. He hit the keypad and the locks popped open. I swung open the door and got in, just as Matthews inserted his knee between the car and the open door.

"Lieutenant, do you deny that you and Agent Garrity are investigating a serial killer and that you believe this killer is actually the one responsible for the Galveston double murder?" he prodded.

"You're off base here, Matthews," David shouted.

"Am I, Agent Garrity?" he asked. "Is that true, Lieutenant Armstrong?"

I said nothing.

"Didn't you, in fact, argue strenuously against charging Priscilla Lucas with solicitation of murder?"

"This is an ongoing investigation," shouted David. "We'll make no comments at this time."

"Is that true, Lieutenant?"

Finally regaining my composure, I pulled on the door. "I have no comment on this case, the Galveston murders, or any other case currently under investigation," I said, vainly attempting to push Matthews out of the way. He didn't move.

"Don't you have a theory that this murder is linked to the Galveston killings? Isn't that why you're both here," he shouted, as I pulled harder, this time succeeding in pushing him back and slamming the door hard on the tip of his knee.

"Damn," he cursed, as he pulled his leg out in obvious pain. "Damn it, Lieutenant, just answer the question."

I yanked the door shut and David threw a U-turn, gunned the engine and we were gone. As we drove toward the airport where the chopper waited to take us home, he shot me an exasperated glance.

"How did he know all of that?" he charged. I could see the anger in his hands as he gripped the steering wheel. "Did you tell anyone, anyone at all what we were working on?"

"No," I answered. "Don't you know me better than that?"

David was angry, furious at the confrontation with Matthews. "So how did he find out?"

"I don't know."

"Take a guess."

"Someone in Galveston is talking. Nelson, Scoggins, maybe Judge McLamore?" I said. Then I mentioned something I'd kept to myself about my meeting the day before. "All I know is that when I got to Priscilla Lucas's house, her father knew we'd argued against charging his daughter with solicitation of murder and that we were chasing a suspected serial killer."

"You didn't confirm that?"

"No," I said. "I didn't deny it, but I told them nothing about the investigation."

"Come on, Sarah," he chastised. "Think about it. You didn't have to confirm it. That you wouldn't voice some kind of a denial, even a vague one, was enough for him to call Matthews and clue him in. What better for his daughter's defense than for the newspapers to contaminate the Galveston jury pool with speculation about a serial killer?"

"David, this isn't coming from me and it isn't coming from Bobby Barker, at least not without a police source, a well-placed informant. Barker had no way of knowing about Mary Gonzales's murder so quickly. It's got to be, as Matthews said, someone close to the investigation. He must have gotten the call and left for San Antonio not long after we did."

David thought about that for a minute. "So who's responsible?"

"My guess is Nelson."

"Why?"

"I don't think Nelson needs a reason, that he dislikes me is enough," I snapped. "But the truth is that we've got history between us, not a good situation, and sticking me in the hot seat wouldn't give him a moment's hesitation."

David chewed on that for a few minutes, and when he spoke again, his voice was calm but strained. "Let's not jump to conclusions," he said. "Why would Nelson jeopardize his own investigation?"

"Maybe he doesn't see it that way," I speculated. "Or maybe he wants me in a position to take the blame if his case against Priscilla Lucas falls apart. We both know that the evidence he and Scroggins pulled together is full of holes. A good defense attorney will make fools of them."

"Well. Maybe," he said, considering the possibility. "Nelson *could* be setting you up as a scapegoat."

"So, where does that leave us?"

David considered the possibilities.

"However it happened, you're now in the frying pan with flames licking the sides," he said, with an angry frown. "We'd better find this killer before you end up in the fire."

Fifteen

Sarah," Mom called out the following morning, a Friday. "You've got a phone call."

"The phone?"

"The captain," she said.

I stepped out of the shower, toweled off and threw on a robe.

After leaving San Antonio, the rest of the previous day had been long and unproductive. David and I went over the Mary Gonzales homicide in detail with the captain, and then followed with a briefing session for Nelson and Scroggins. We'd been ordered to bring them up to date, but they were less than grateful. In fact, they showed up at the office loaded for bear, ready to shoot down any and all theories that didn't implicate Priscilla Lucas. I finally gave up and kept my mouth shut while David contended with them. Still, I couldn't keep from watching Nelson, wondering if he was the one who'd tipped off the reporter. I purposely didn't mention the confrontation with Evan Matthews to the captain. David and I decided I hadn't really given him anything to run with. Why cause a problem when none existed? At least, that's the way we saw it at the time.

"Armstrong here."

"Lieutenant, have you seen this morning's *Galveston County Daily News?*" Captain Williams growled. "How about the *Houston Chronicle?*"

"No, I haven't. Why?"

"Well, I suggest you take a look. And I also suggest you get yourself into this office, pronto."

"Hell," I said. "Matthews?"

"Yes. Matthews. Agent Garrity is on his way. We've got a situation. The Galveston D.A.'s office is furious. Even the governor called. Get in here. ASAP."

With some difficulty I sidestepped Mom's pancakes, kissed Maggie, and arrived at the office an hour later. Friday morning, one full week after the Lucas murders, and the whole place bristled with unexpended energy. Sheila, the captain's secretary, gave me one of those withering stares she reserves for those who've made her boss's blood pressure climb. I, of course, was the cause of all the anguish, my photo from the day before under the headline "Texas Ranger tracks serial killer." The subhead read: "Suspect in Lucas double murder."

A week on this case and I'd made the front page of both newspapers, the *Chronicle* picking up the *Daily News* piece off the wire. The photographer caught me with a glint of surprise in my eyes, just as Evan Matthews popped the question, "Is this murder related to the Galveston double murders?" My non-answer, as David feared, was lost near the bottom of the article and hadn't put the matter to rest. Instead, it only made me appear to be hiding information, which, of course, I was. *Matthews must be having a good day,* I thought. Scooping the big-city rival newspaper twice on a case was a major coup.

"Sarah," David said, as I entered the conference room.

"Good morning," I said, warily glancing toward the captain who pulsed with anger. Behind him hung the chart he and David constructed a few days earlier to compare the murders. David and I had already written in the Mary Gonzales information, what little we had to work with.

"Didn't I tell you this could happen?" my boss said, slapping both newspapers down onto the table before me.

"Captain, let me explain."

"Explain? How can you explain?" he scoffed. "Isn't this precisely what I warned you and Agent Garrity about?"

"Yes, but—"

"But? There's a but? I don't think so, Sarah. In fact, I know better."

I'd never seen the captain so angry, not even the day a novice ranger crashed his squad car on the interstate, injuring himself and two civilians, during a high-speed pursuit of a guy who turned out to be just evading a traffic ticket.

"The governor's already called headquarters, and they want answers. What am I supposed to tell them? That one of my best rangers couldn't keep her mouth shut?"

"That's not fair."

"Not fair?" he echoed.

"No, it's not fair," I said, my voice rising. "I told Matthews nothing. This is coming from someplace else. David can tell you. He was there."

"Is that the truth?"

David nodded.

"I wasn't at the Lucas estate when Sarah talked with Bobby Barker," he admitted. "But I can tell you that she told Matthews nothing. He arrived knowing everything that's in that article. At most, Sarah never denied his assertions."

"How could I do that?" I asked, my voice rising in indignation. "It's the truth. We've got another murder, same MO in San Antonio. We've got a serial killer. Evan Matthews is right."

"Right?" shouted the captain. "What's he right about?"

"Instead of hiding information, we should be warning people," I said, standing up and walking toward the chart. "This morning, our chart has another murder. Number four. How many more before we own up to the fact that we've got an active serial killer on the loose?"

"I'm not going to jeopardize the case against Priscilla Lucas, not yet," said the captain. "Not until we're sure."

"We've got a sketch, the San Antonio composite," I said, feeling my own anger rise. "Shouldn't it be on newscasts across the state tonight? Isn't that the best way to warn the public and bring this guy in?"

"No," said the captain, pounding his meaty fist on the table with a heavy thud. "Circulate a flyer on the Gonzales murder across the state. Identify the guy only as a possible witness in the San Antonio homicide. But in no way tie him to the other murders. It's too soon, Sarah. Think about it. We need more time."

"More time for what?" I said, seething. "So this guy can supply us with more tortured bodies?"

Captain Williams flinched as if I'd slapped him.

"That's not fair," said David.

With that, the captain and I looked at each other, and I felt my anger subsiding. I'd just attacked a man I truly respected, one I'd trust with my life.

"Sarah." He sighed. "What's going on here?"

"I'm being unfairly reprimanded. That's what's happening here. I said nothing to Matthews. I told Bobby Barker absolutely nothing about any of our suspicions or the investigation. They both knew everything before I met them. Someone else is talking."

The captain sat down in a chair and pushed back, staring at the ceiling.

"Sarah, the least you could have done was warn me, so I wasn't blindsided," he said.

"You're right. I'm sorry."

"So, what do we do now?"

"We do nothing differently than we do every other day. We find the murderer, solve the case, just like we always do," I said, hoping the uncertainty welling in my chest didn't give me away. "We prove once and for all who killed Edward Lucas and Annmarie Knowles, and we put this matter to rest. We save lives by stopping this SOB."

"And how does that happen?" the captain asked. "What next?"

I'd anticipated that question but hadn't been able to come up with a ready answer. Grateful, I heard David speak up.

"We heard from San Antonio this morning. The partial print doesn't match anyone known to have been in the house. There's a good chance it's the killer's," he said, my hopes rising. "We can run it through the computer and look for a match on the national database."

"While the lab guys do that, David and I will head to the valley," I said. "We've got an eighteen-month-old murder there that could help tie these cases together."

"All right," said the captain. "But do what you need to do and make it quick because, as I see it, this thing's only getting worse."

The Southwest Airlines flight home from McAllen, Texas, that night took only seventy-five minutes but felt like one of the longest of my life. It had been a day filled with disappointment and bad news. First, shortly after we'd arrived in the Rio Grande valley, the captain called to say the fingerprint Mary Gonzales had fought so valiantly to provide us proved too small a sample to compare with the database.

"There's just not enough there to work with. If we get a full fingerprint, there's not enough to say if we have an exact match, but we will be able to determine if it conforms to what we have," he explained.

Then, our afternoon in the small town of Redbluff, fifty miles north of the Mexican border, fell far short of what we'd hoped.

Driving from the airport, I was struck by how much the valley had changed, even in the five short years since I'd been in the most southern reaches of the state. Among the citrus orchards growing Ruby Red grapefruit and oranges were subdivisions of trailer homes populated by snowbirds, seniors from the North who in winter flooded area grocery stores.

Still, this wedge of Texas has historically been a hotspot for crime, and that hadn't changed. Nearly a hundred years ago, during Prohibition, rangers stationed on the border intercepted burro trains of bootlegged liquor crossing into the States. Today the cargo's different: illegals and drugs.

In his office, where a poster on the window announced an upcoming golf tournament, Sheriff Tim Hagen, wearing tennis shoes, khaki shorts, and a blue polo shirt, pulled out his file on the murder of Sheryl Wilcox, a forty-eight-year-old health-care aide. Before us we had an incomplete autopsy report with photos, conducted by the local mortician, photos of the crime scene, lab results, and witness statements. A former detective from Corpus Christi, Hagen ran down the case as he knew it. Wilcox had been found on the deck outside her mobile home, in a rural section outside of town. In the crime-scene photos, she was nude, her throat cut, her arms and legs tied to a battered aluminum-frame lawn chair. Her chest was bloody with gashes. On the copies that came over the fax to our office, the gashes could have been interpreted as forming the pattern of a cross. Yet within minutes of arriving, David and I knew our trip had been a waste of time and resources.

We'd known before we arrived that the knots in the rope were wrong, square, not slip and overhand knots as in our four murders. And there was no bloody cross over the body. Still the murder had sounded enough alike to pique our interest. But when we looked at the crime-scene photos and talked to the sheriff, it became clear: this wasn't our guy.

The deciding factors were the gashes in her chest. Looking at the actual autopsy photos, it was easy to see that they bore no resemblance to our victims' crosses. Instead, they appeared to be the result of a heated battle between the woman and her killer. Finally, the cause of death, not a clean incision as in our cases, the wound to her throat was a jagged, sloppy laceration that left the skin torn and bruised.

While disappointed, to keep the trip from being a total loss, we reviewed the evidence with Sheriff Hagen.

"This woman knew her killer," I said, looking at the photos of the woman left with her legs spread wide. "The murderer posed her to humiliate her. There was incredible anger."

"Sheryl had been working for an elderly couple," he explained. "She cared for the wife, who was dying from liver cancer. We thought at first that the husband might have done it. For an old guy, he's in good shape. There were rumors that they'd had an affair. Figured it had gone bad and he hadn't been able to take the rejection. But he had an alibi. He was on the golf course with three friends at the time of the murder. We sent him to Corpus for a polygraph and the guy admitted he'd had the affair, but he said he knew nothing about the murder. The examiner said he was telling the truth. The test came out clean."

"What about the wife?" asked David, inspecting a close-up of wounds on Wilcox's chest.

"We never seriously considered her," the sheriff admitted. "We questioned her about her husband's connection, but she claimed she knew nothing. She seemed heartbroken about the killing. Why do you ask?"

"Because my guess is that your killer's a woman," David said. He picked up the sheriff's wire-rimmed reading glasses off the desk and used them like a magnifying glass to examine a photo of the dead woman's face, then another of her upper body.

"See these marks?" he asked the sheriff, pointing to the woman's chest.

"Yeah, what about them?"

"Send these photos to the M.E. in Houston, tell them we requested they take a look. They may disagree, but my guess is that they weren't made by a knife," he said. "Looks like she's been gouged, maybe by long fingernails."

"You think that sick old woman could have done this?" the sheriff scoffed. "That's possible?"

"I'd question her."

The sheriff frowned.

"Missed our chance. She died about three months after the murder," he said. "The husband still lives here, but from the results of that lie detector, I doubt that, if she did it, he knows anything about it."

There were a variety of fingerprints found at the scene, and to ensure we weren't prematurely dismissing the possibility that the case could be linked to ours, we took the precaution of e-mailing them to the captain. We both felt confident, however, even before the lab confirmed it while we waited for our return flight at the airport, that they didn't match the San Antonio fragment.

That evening, we skimmed above a shelf of gray-white clouds, on our way to Houston.

"Now what?" David asked.

"The composite should be in the San Antonio papers on Sunday morning," I said, grabbing at the last remaining straw. "That always starts the phones ringing."

"Sunday," he said, pressing the gray button in the armrest and pushing his seat back. His eyes closed, and we flew the rest of the trip in silence.

Sixteen

S ee if you can catch me," Maggie taunted, gliding backward.

"Maggie, you know I can't ice skate."

"Come on, Mom. You can do it. Just follow me," she ordered, sprinting away with a giggle.

Ice skating was something kids in Houston didn't do much of years ago, when I was growing up. We get an inch of snow here about every five years, and hardly ever ice. But I was willing to try.

Determined, I pushed forward. Breathing deeply, I concentrated on putting one foot in front of the other, keeping myself upright on the blades. I built speed, thinking it wasn't all that different from roller-skating, and I began to gain confidence, skating past a young mother coaching her toddler son and a pack of teenage boys with camouflage clothes and earrings who conferred in the center of the rink. I grinned with sincere satisfaction as I skated toward my daughter. Nearly close enough to touch Maggie, I held out my hand to her, then glanced to the right and realized that I was still moving and my skates were aimed directly at the padded barrier bordering the rink.

I swiveled, hoping to stop, the way I remembered those Olympic figure skaters doing at the ends of their performances.

It didn't work.

Instead, my right ankle shot out from under me. On one foot, unable to regain traction, I slid forward, fluttering like a sparrow in water. Then my skate caught on a groove in the ice and I jarred to a stop, in control, both legs firmly on the ice.

"Good work, Mom," Maggie said, grinning. "Way to go."

Triumph.

Just then, my blades wobbled, and my skates shot out from under me. I fell, knocking my tailbone, hard. Flat on my back on the ice, I surveyed the amused faces of spectators peering down at me from balconies circling the ice rink in the center of the Galleria, the sprawling shopping mall that housed layer upon layer of Houston's ritziest stores. I was trying to remember why I'd suggested ice skating instead of shopping, when Maggie, peering down at me as if I were the child, asked, "Mom, are you okay?"

"Fine," I said, holding up a hand. "Now pull me up."

We turned in our rented ice skates and headed to a second-floor restaurant to watch the other skaters try to outdo my performance. After baked potato skins and Cokes, we were in the process of inhaling hot fudge sundaes when I noticed David across the mall.

"Well, imagine this," he said, holding up a bag. "We both get the same idea on our Saturday off."

"Not really," I said. "We were here for the ice rink. You didn't happen to be watching, did you?"

"No, should I have?"

"You missed a good one," Maggie said, grinning. "Mom plopped right down on the ice."

"Maggie, please," I said, feigning embarrassment. "David, this is my daughter, Maggie. Maggie, this is Mr. Garrity."

"You're the FBI agent working on that case with my mom, aren't you?"

"What case is that?" I asked, surprised.

"The one in the paper where those two people got killed in Galveston," she said, licking a scoop of sundae off her spoon. "You know, where that lady got arrested, but you think it's really a serial killer?"

"I didn't know you'd heard about that," I said, motioning for her to wipe a fudge trail drizzling down her chin.

"Gram hid our newspaper, but Strings had one at his house," she said, with a shrug. "I don't know what the big deal is. You chase killers all the time."

"Well put, Maggie." David laughed.

"I didn't like your picture though," she said, scrunching up her nose.

"No?" I said. "Didn't do me justice?"

"It made you look really old," she said.

Deciding it was undoubtedly better not to comment, I asked David, "Would you join us?"

"Mom, this is mother-daughter day," Maggie whined, a scowl replacing her grin. "You promised."

"Maggie," I said. "Just for a few minutes . . ."

"I can't anyway," David protested. "I'm hunting for just the right sweater to go with the shirt I bought for my son. It's Jack's birthday next week. I need to get his present in the mail. Nice to meet you, Maggie."

Maggie just stared at him.

"Maggie!" I admonished.

"Nice to meet you, too," she said, lips pursed.

After David left, she turned to me. I had the feeling she was studying my face.

"Do you like him?" she asked.

"What do you mean? We just work together."

"You look like you like him. Are you going to date?"

"Maggie," I scolded, wondering just how transparent I'd become.

At home that night, Maggie appeared to forget our meeting with David. Mom created her special leg of lamb with a thick mustard-and-parmesan-cheese crust. Afterward, we cleaned up the dishes, while Maggie went outside to bed down Emma Lou. It was just getting dark, the days getting longer, leading toward summer.

"Any progress on the Priscilla Lucas case?" Mom asked.

"A few more pieces have fallen into place," I said, deciding to emphasize the positive. It wasn't a lie. We did have the composite and the fingerprint fragment.

"Then, it'll all be over soon?"

"I can't say that, Mom," I admitted. "I don't know when or how this will end."

As I was bending down to put the washed roasting pan away underneath the stove, I heard Mom say, "Well, look at that. What's that girl up to now?"

I joined her at the kitchen window and stared out at the corral. Emma Lou stood off to the side warily watching Maggie, who'd hauled a cardboard box out from the garage. Under the elm tree in the center of the corral, she was digging through, pulling out what looked like string. She had a ladder propped up on the thick tree trunk.

"What's she—"

"Christmas lights," Mom said. "More Christmas lights."

Mom threw off her apron, and I followed her outside.

"Maggie, what are you doing?" Mom shouted, as she stalked toward the corral. "Now if that isn't the most ridiculous . . . you'll get hurt up there, you know."

Climbing up on the ladder into the tree, Maggie shouted back. "It's okay. I can do it."

Mom was right. Maggie's behavior seemed odd. It wasn't like her. "Why?" I asked. "Why are you stringing lights in the tree?"

"Because it . . ." She started to answer, then stopped. She looked down at me from near the top of the ladder and said, "Just because I want to look out at them from my bedroom window."

Mom and I walked through the creaky corral gate, the one I'd been meaning to oil. All the while, the filly paced back and forth at the fence, uneasy.

"You're going to give Emma Lou a scare, lighting up her corral like that," Mom said. "Look, you've got her nervous already. And it's spring, Maggie, not Christmastime. You shouldn't—"

I put my hand on Mom's arm, and she stopped talking.

"Why, Maggie?" I interrupted. "Why the lights?"

I stood at the base of the ladder, holding it still while Maggie climbed higher, toward the top of the tree, the crinkled cord of the white Christmas lights trailing behind her.

"Because I want them, Mom," she said. "I want to be able to see them."

Perched on a limb just leafing out with its Spring foliage, she turned around and stared down at me.

"Because, maybe it's like what you and Gram talked about. Maybe Dad's up in heaven," Maggie said.

"Well . . . what does . . . ?" Mom stuttered.

"Explain it to us, Maggie," I said. "Gram and I need to understand."

Maggie inched out a ways on a limb, where the tree was barely thick enough to hold her. She stopped when it swayed.

"You and Gram talked about Dad being in heaven and wondered if he could see us," she explained, her eyes narrow and serious. "I thought about what you said, about believing in what you can't see."

"And the lights?" I asked. "Why the lights, Maggie?"

Again she paused. I sensed that this was something vastly

important to her, and she wasn't sure she could trust us to understand. When she did speak, her voice was edged in sadness.

"The lights kind of look like stars," she said. "I figure that if Dad's in heaven, then he's up there with the stars. I thought maybe if I brought the stars closer to us, Dad would be closer, too. The lights were the only thing I could think of. They make me feel like maybe he's not so far away."

My daughter's eyes were glistening with tears in the last light from a bright gold sunset.

Mom glanced at me, and I nodded at her.

"Come on," I said. "Let's help."

I threw down the dish towel I was holding into the dirt under the tree and grabbed another strand of lights.

"Sure," Mom said. "You two get started. I'll go for the bigger ladder. We can get them up higher. Might as well do this job right."

Two hours later, we'd strung all twenty strands of outdoor Christmas lights in the corral tree, and Maggie held the end of the cord with the plug. Emma Lou was in the stable. She'd have to spend the foreseeable future in the rear pasture with the other horses, to keep her from tripping on the extension cord I'd run out from the front porch outlet.

"You ready?" I asked.

"Yeah," Maggie said. "But I want to say something first."

"Okay, say away," I said.

Maggie took my hand in hers and then took her grandmother by the other hand.

We were three generations of women holding hands under the still-dark elm tree.

"God," Maggie said. "If you've got my dad up there, I've got a favor to ask. I know I can't get him back. But I'd like him to be able to visit here sometimes, to be with us. If you can work it out, it would be really good if he got to see me grow up."

Maggie looked up and smiled at me, and I leaned down and kissed her cheek, not bothering to wipe away the tears that were rolling down my own. Mom pulled a tissue out of her back jean pocket and dabbed at her eyes.

"So this is kind of an invitation," Maggie said, looking up at the dark sky and the true stars shining far above us. "We're going to light this tree up and maybe, if you don't mind, you can let my dad visit sometimes. Just to see that Mom and Gram and I are okay. And that we miss him."

"Your grandpa, too," Mom said. "Ask God to let your grandpa come visit?"

"Oh, yeah, God, Grandpa, too."

With that, Maggie let go of our hands and turned her full attention to inserting the plug into the extension cord. Moments later, the lights flicked on and lit up the corral bright as daybreak.

"Amen," Maggie said.

"Amen," Mom and I repeated.

Seventeen

The drive into the office on Monday morning was a dismal one. A heavy rain clogged the 610 loop with cars jammed like logs bottlenecked in a stream. I didn't care. I'd called in off and on all day Sunday hoping to have to rush into the office to follow up on a lead. I knew nothing waited for me at the office except another confrontation with the captain. We'd come up dry. Typically after broadcasting a composite of a suspect, we'd be flooded with calls, but not this time, not a single lead, although not only newspapers but TV newscasts across the state had displayed the sketch along with our 800 number. It was as if this guy, whoever he was, didn't exist. We didn't even have reports of any strange cars in the neighborhoods at the times of the killings. Why didn't someone at least see the guy's car? With the exception of his run-in with Lily Salas, this psycho was invisible.

Making my morning even more perfect, I'd have to face the captain alone. David had called the day before from the airport. By now he was in Quantico, at FBI headquarters, consulting on another case.

"Morning, Sheila," I called out as I walked past her desk, grabbing a stack of phone messages and mail from my cubbyhole. "Captain in yet?"

A round, motherly woman with curly gray hair and a penchant for polyester slacks and brightly flowered rayon blouses, she frowned at me as if I were an errant child in need of discipline. From the beginning, she'd treated me better than the other rangers, all men, who often caught her pointed barbs. I'd always assumed she was proud that a woman had finally broken through the ranks. Today, she didn't seem sure.

"He's been asking for you," she answered, her voice echoing my disappointment. "He wanted to know first thing this morning if any leads came in over the weekend. I gave him the bad news."

In my office, I flipped through a one-inch stack of pink message slips, hoping Sheila had missed something. I found a message from Friday, Maggie's teacher, Mrs. Hansen. "Last few days, homework on time," it read. I couldn't help but smile.

The next was from Laurie Thomas, assistant to the director at the Center for Missing and Exploited Children.

"Ben," I whispered, picking up the telephone and pushing the button for an outside line.

"We have a hit on the reconstruction photos you e-mailed in," said Laurie. "A kid named Darryl Robbins, age four. Disappeared about six months ago in Centerville, Texas. The mom and her boyfriend reported him missing."

"Dental records?" I asked.

"Kid doesn't have any," she said. "We've called the medical examiner's office, and they're going to compare the DNA they've got on file from the little guy's skeleton to a sample from the mom. Put a rush on it."

"Thanks for filling me in."

"No problem," she said. "I'll let you know as soon as we have more news."

"If it's him, who's our suspect?"

"Centerville P.D. is working on that, too, of course. We'll call when they have something."

"Good."

Between Mrs. Hansen's good news and Ben's—maybe I'd soon be able to call him Darryl—I felt vaguely reassured about my place in the world, as I hung up the phone and shuffled through the handful of mail that had accumulated in the week I'd been too busy to bother with such mundane matters. Captain Williams, I knew, would be waiting. I was procrastinating, no doubt about it. Instead of admitting I had no idea where to go with the investigation, I paged through the departmental newsletter, skimming an article on a Dallas case solved by carpet-fiber analysis. Then, on the bottom of a stack of memos from headquarters, I found a slim, white, business-size envelope, my name printed in a small, precise, even hand.

Minutes later, I stood at Captain Williams's office door.

"I think you'd better look at this," I said.

I handed the captain a sheet of unlined, white paper—the kind used in a copy machine or a laser printer—one I'd encased in a protective plastic evidence sleeve. In the same careful hand as on the envelope, someone had written:

Why do you pursue me?
Don't you know that I do the work of another?

"Our guy?" he asked.

"It came addressed to me, here at the office. This was in the envelope," I said, handing the captain a similarly preserved newspaper clipping—my photo cut from the front page of Friday morning's

Houston Chronicle, the one taken as David and I left the scene of the Mary Gonzales homicide. The envelope was postmarked the same day the article ran, from a downtown Houston zip code, and must have arrived in Saturday's mail. It had been sitting on my desk all weekend.

"What's he trying to tell us, that Lucas hired him?" asked the captain.

"Or that he's on a mission from God, which fits the profile Garrity and I have of him."

"Sign them into evidence and take them to the lab," the captain said. "Let's hope he's finally made a mistake and unknowingly sent you something we can use."

"Let's just take a look," said Frank Nguyen, a slight man with high cheekbones and an uneven trim of charcoal-black hair. Nguyen, whose parents had immigrated to Houston from Vietnam, was one of our best techs. I'd never run into him outside the DPS lab, a cluttered collection of equipment in a fluorescent-lit room down the hall from our offices. At times, I wondered if he existed outside the lab walls. I'd entertained a recurring fantasy that when we turned the office lights off at night, Nguyen unrolled a cot and slept next to his DNA separating apparatus.

Wearing latex gloves, Nguyen examined all three items, looking for fingerprints. He came up empty on the note and newspaper clipping but isolated two on the envelope. A quick comparison confirmed that neither matched the fragment from San Antonio. He then fed the prints into the computer and keyed in a command to compare each with AFIS, the Automated Fingerprint Identification System, a library of prints from past offenders across the nation. The computer clicked through until NO AVAILABLE MATCH printed across the screen.

"My guess is when we run them through the civil service files on post office employees we'll come up with matches. They most likely belong to whoever handled the letter in transit at the post office," he said. "They could even be someone's in our office, like Sheila's, since she sorts the mail. We'll do a broader search, but since the letter itself and the newspaper clip are clean, I don't think we'll get lucky."

"What next?"

"Let's see if any evidence piggybacked on the paper," he suggested.

Under the stereomicroscope, Frank examined the letter, starting at a magnification of six and working his way up to twenty-five. With each increase, the field of view diminished, and the white, smooth paper gradually transformed from a slick sheet to a substance that resembled tufts of layered cotton. It was a painstaking procedure.

"Here's something. It looks like electrostatic dust," he finally said.

"What's it made up of?"

"Give me a minute," he answered, sounding excited. There was nothing better than this, I suspected, for Nguyen, using his equipment to zero in on hidden evidence.

He motioned, and I peered through the eyepiece and had no trouble identifying what had drawn his interest, jagged-edged, translucent flecks adhering near the lower edge of the letter. After examining the newspaper clip and the envelope, he again turned the microscope over to me. On both, easily identifiable, was what appeared to be an identical residue.

Saying nothing, Nguyen, who had the manner of an irritated Pomeranian when he was hot on the trail of a bone, collected a microscopic sample of the substance from the lower right-hand corner of the sheet of paper, followed by examples from the news clip and envelope.

"Let's test its IR," he said, with a broad grin. Nguyen held a palpable esteem for his infrared microscope. Although it resembles any other microscope, the IR has one big difference: instead of lenses, it relies on mirrors that reflect a specimen's infrared energy, so it can be charted and identified.

Readying the sample, he focused in on the material through clear glass optical windows. Nguyen then swung the windows out of the way and lined up a series of curved mirrors. During the process, infrared energy passed through the microscope into the sample, where the mirrors redirected the energy to sensitive detectors, resulting in a chart of peaks and valleys, resembling an electrocardiogram of a heartbeat.

"What is it?" I asked when he'd finished, prompting him to look at me as if I were the specimen under his microscope.

"Haven't the foggiest," he said, plainly irritated. "Give me a minute."

With that, Nguyen keyed in a command and the IR microscope transmitted its results to a computer designed to compare the readout to a library of known patterns. The results came quickly.

"It's a polycarbonate," he said.

"You mean a plastic?" I asked. "What kind? Plastics leave dust?"

"Plastic resins do," he explained. "In a raw stage, like the plastic pellets used in manufacturing."

"So, what does this tell me?" I asked, eager for anything that could break the case out of its current slump. "Tell me how we can capitalize on this to find this guy before he tortures and kills someone else."

"I'm not sure," Nguyen admitted, looking uneasy. I suspected that, isolated in the lab, he rarely thought of the bigger picture, the ramifications of his work. To him, that dust was merely a specimen to analyze. To me, it was a clue to the identity of a killer who had already butchered four people, including the mother of four young children.

"If this is a generic plastic resin, it may not help at all," he admitted reluctantly. "But if it's a more specialized compound . . ."

"How do we find that out?"

"I'll work on the samples and run a few more tests. We'll also send the envelope in to start having it checked for DNA, in case our guy was dumb enough to lick it shut," he said. "I'll let you know as soon as I have any answers."

Two hours later—after Nguyen tapped the FBI lab for assistance—I was on my way to the Harkins Plastics Company in southeast Houston, an unimpressive compound of three vast metal buildings on a dead-end street in a neighborhood populated by blue-collar families with roof-top satellite dishes and chain-link fences. Nguyen and his counterparts at the FBI had discovered not only a UV stabilizer in the plastic resin, added to keep the clear material from discoloring when exposed to light, but an antibacterial additive so new it was still under patent to a Massachusetts chemical corporation. One call to the main office in Boston and I discovered that Harkins was the only company in Texas using resin containing the additive.

As I waited in the lobby for the owner, Theodore Harkins, I examined a dusty display case. Next to trophies won by the company softball team sat heavy, bright yellow-and-red plastic pipe fittings, probably built to specification for one of Houston's many oil companies. I bent down to get a better look. My eye was drawn to a spiral of clear plastic tubing on the bottom shelf.

"That's our medical line," said Harkins, who'd walked up behind me. "That's what we discussed on the telephone, the product we're building with the new additive."

I followed Harkins, a slope-shouldered, thick-necked man with curly hair and a wide mustache, to the main conference room. One complete wall held shelves of product guides from plastic resin manufacturers. The sign outside boasted that Harkins had been family-owned for sixty-five years. From the look of this room, they'd done little to update. Dusty and worn, the thin green carpet buckled in places under our feet. The Formica-topped conference table bore the scars of decades of use.

"I'm not really sure how we can help you," Harkins said, with a wary smile. "Yes, we use that type of plastic in manufacturing, but all our employees have been here for years. We're a family business, and I trust all of them."

"Can you show me where the tubing is made?" I asked.

Harkins nodded and turned, and I followed. Through the door at the rear of the room we entered a storage area. We were surrounded by large bins of pea-size plastic pellets—white, black, some bright red, yellow, and blue.

"That's the resin, the way it comes in to be used in manufacturing," he said. "All different types of polymers specialized for individual jobs."

"Which one has the additive?" I asked. He indicated containers near the back of the room, and I walked over and picked up a milky-white pellet, rubbed my thumb over it, and a powdery residue came off.

"It's an exciting new product," Harkins said. "Perfect for medical usage."

The clanking of heavy metal machinery reverberated off the walls as we walked through a second set of doors and snaked through the factory, past two rows of massive steel machines attached to computers, each monitored by a silent worker. Through a window in one of the machines, I watched as liquid plastic was drawn into a mold and expelled into dies which cast it into tube-like branches, of the sort that hold together the pieces of a model airplane. This time, however, each branch ended in a one-inch cube. A stooped, gray-haired woman sat, patiently cutting the boxes from their plastic stems, trimming off the excess with a tool similar to a wire cutter and then methodically assembling two cubes to form small white plastic boxes.

"Postage stamp containers," Harkins explained. "We have a regular contract. But come this way. What you want to see is back here."

After passing workers piecing together a specialized toothbrush
for dentures, Harkins and I left the building for a smaller structure
bordering the parking lot. Inside, a dozen sparkling new machines
churned. In contrast to the rest of the plant, this building was meticulously clean and well lighted. Focusing so intently on their work
that they failed to acknowledge our presence were six white-smocked
workers, one middle-aged black woman, three Hispanic men, and
two Anglos, one man and one woman. The first four didn't fit the
San Antonio description. Of the two Caucasians, the woman appeared in her fifties with salt-and-pepper gray hair. The man caught
my full attention. He was young, slender, with chin-length blond
hair. From the side, I examined his profile. Could he? Could he be
the killer? I felt for my pistol under my jacket and slipped my hand
around the grip.

"These machines extrude the resin into the tubing using three
hundred and sixty metric tons of hydraulic force," Harkins said, picking up a yard-long spiral of the clear plastic tubing. "We got the contract about two years ago. It's a component for a new dialysis machine.
The antibacterial qualities of the plastic . . ."

In the background, I heard Harkins drone on about the plastic
and the additive's promise for the future, principally in medical
applications. I couldn't take my eyes off the young man with the
blond hair, who bent over a carton filled with more yard-long
sections of the finished tubing, expertly maneuvering a long thin-
bladed knife to trim any imperfections on the cut ends. He was the
right height, the right coloring. The curve of his face resembled
the outline of the composite, and I began to ease my gun out from
under my jacket.

He must have felt my eyes boring into him, for he suddenly
looked up and returned my gaze. Full-face, his bone structure was

wrong, as were his eyes, a dark, dark brown. But something else convinced me this wasn't our killer; the man had a half-dollar-size birthmark the color of red wine across his right cheek. Lily Salas would not have missed that in her ID.

The man smiled at me and I smiled back, gingerly taking my hand off my pistol in the holster.

"Who else has access to this room?"

"Just the cleaning staff," Harkins said.

"I'd like to see your employee records."

In the privacy of his office, I took out a copy of the San Antonio composite.

"No one I know," said Harkins.

"You're sure?" I asked, and Harkins nodded. "If you don't mind, I'd still like to take a look at your files."

Since the company had a small contract for a component for NASA, plastic hinges used in the shuttle galleys, all of Harkins's employees had a base-level security clearance, including file photos and fingerprinting. After a quick look-see, I left the plant carrying copies of the files on all the company's employees—including the cleaning staff—for the past two years, the length of time they'd used resin containing the antibacterial additive. None resembled our guy, but I couldn't take chances; I had to be sure. If the letter hadn't been exposed to the resin there, then where?

At the office, later that afternoon, I'd just handed the files to Sheila to give to Nguyen to start on the fingerprints, when the captain cornered me.

"You got another one. Today's mail," he said. "It's in the lab."

Nguyen already had the letter under the microscope when the captain and I walked in.

"Anything?" Captain Williams asked.

"Nothing," he said. "Same as before, a few prints on the envelope and nothing on the letter. Nothing remarkable about the paper itself.

It's standard copier paper, just like the last letter. No debris except what appears to be traces of common dirt."

"Let me see it," I said.

Wearing latex gloves, Nguyen inserted the letter and envelope—postmarked Saturday from a Dallas zip code—in evidence sleeves then gave them to me.

Some are chosen to live, others to die.
This is destiny.

The hand that wrote it was the same as the first, and I had no doubt he was our killer. He was warning me, but at the same time taunting me with his power. His murders gave him control over the lives and deaths of his victims. Now, the killer believed he could control the police, the investigation. He believed he could control me.

"Sarah, we need to talk," the captain said, and from the tone of his voice I knew he wasn't about to compliment my investigative techniques. This was bad news. "We just can't have this. This has gone too far. This guy's fixating on you. I'm sure, when you look back on this, you'll agree. I really have no choice other than to remove you from this case."

The captain's words hit me full force. One thing I was sure of—I would not be replaced. If for no other reason than me with the letters, the killer had made this personal. For my own safety, so I could sleep at night, I had to make sure he was found and put away, forever.

"I'm making progress, I can find this guy. I know I can," I protested. "I'm your best hope and, until this creep is stopped, he's going to keep killing."

"I don't doubt that. None of us do. But it's too dangerous; there's just too much risk for you, personally, to continue on," he said.

Maybe the captain was right. But in my heart, I felt certain I was the best person to stop this nightmare. "Bringing someone new on now, it'll take days for them to get up to speed. In the meantime, this guy's out killing people," I argued.

"I know that," the captain shot back. "But this guy's focusing on you. We can't take any chances that may put you in jeopardy. If you're not worried about yourself, think of Maggie and your mother. If he can't get to you and he figures out how to get to them . . .'"

My stomach tightened into a ball at the thought that the killer could go after Maggie and Mom. But I knew that couldn't happen. "How would he find them? They're safe on the ranch. The place has nothing to do with me. None of the property records, the utilities, not the phone, nothing out there is in my name. It's all in Mom's name. On paper, I haven't existed since Bill died. My car's titled to the department, and even my cell phone is state-issue. My mail comes to the office and a post office box. This guy can run a complete computer search on me and not find an address or a telephone number that links me to the ranch, Maggie, or Mom."

"You're sure?"

"I'm sure," I said.

"No, I still don't . . ." the captain began.

"Three days, seventy-two hours," I countered. "Give me three days, and if I haven't made an arrest, I won't argue. If you still want to, you can take me off the case. I won't fight it."

"It's not your performance. It's for your own good, your safety."

"Mom and Maggie are safe at the ranch, and I can take care of myself," I said, meaning it. "Three days, Captain Williams. That's all I'm asking for, just three more days."

The captain didn't appear to know exactly what to do. "You'll be careful?"

"Yes. I'll be careful."

"All right," he conceded. "But keep a low profile. A very low profile."

"Agreed," I said, relieved but wondering if I could live up to my part of the bargain. My latest clue had just proven yet another dead end. The evidence was mounting, but it led precisely nowhere.

"Three days," I repeated. "Then, if I haven't made an arrest, I won't argue."

At ten that evening, I was in the office conference room reviewing evidence, rereading the two letters, searching for any overlooked clues, feeling overwhelmed and exhausted when David walked in.

"Thought I'd find you here," he said. "I heard about the letters."

"I know the answer to all this is here somewhere right in front of me. It has to be. Why can't I see it?"

"You're tired, Sarah. It's been a long day," he said, in a tender voice I felt certain he reserved for those he deemed to be precariously balanced. "Let's get a drink and then both go home."

In David's car, we drove to a nearby Tex-Mex restaurant and claimed two stools at the bar. I chewed on chips with queso and green sauce. My first margarita went down quickly and I ordered another. Silent, David lingered over his scotch and soda. I knew he was doing the same thing I was, rethinking each piece of evidence, wondering what we were missing, why we didn't have the answers we needed. Halfway through my second drink, I just wanted to go home.

"I'm sorry, I'm not very good company tonight," I admitted.

"This was a bad idea," he agreed. "We're both too wrung out for this to help."

He stood up.

"Come on, I'll take you back to the office for your car."

The drive took only minutes. In the parking lot, he pulled into the slot next to my Tahoe and waited. I hesitated. I suddenly didn't want to leave. The truth was, at that precise moment, I wanted more than anything not to be alone. If I'd been honest, I would have admitted I was both frightened and lonely. If Bill had been waiting for me, I'd have had him to talk to. He would have found a way to make it all go away, at least for tonight.

David made no move to suggest he thought I should leave. Before I even realized what I was doing, I'd turned toward him and lightly skimmed his cheek with the back of my hand.

"Five o'clock shadow," I said, smiling. "Long day."

"Very long," he agreed, taking my hand in his.

This time I made no move to pull it away as he gently turned my hand over and kissed my open palm.

"Am I overstepping?"

"No, you're not," I said, edging forward, feeling a bit like a bashful adolescent with a new boyfriend. I ran my other hand through his tousled hair. "There, I've been wanting to do that," I said, smoothing it back.

"You didn't need to ask," he said, bending toward me. "You could have done that the first day we met."

Our lips met full and hard, and I felt his hands beneath my blazer, pulling me toward him.

We said nothing as he drove out of the parking lot toward his house. There, in his bed, surrounded by his photographs, his books, we made love. We came in a rush of pent-up anxiety. For those brief moments, I felt the ache of the past year dissolving. In the morning, I knew, the world would be as I had left it, full of loss and frustration, but for just a little while, nothing existed outside that room and the feel of his firm naked body pressed against mine.

"I told you this before, the first time you came to this house with me, and I meant it. I have wanted you ever since I first saw you," he said, nuzzling the side of my neck, his breath warm and moist.

"I think I knew that," I said, lifting his face toward me and running my mouth over his. He tasted of scotch and me. "I think maybe I felt the same way."

David gently skimmed his hands over my bare breasts and fondled my nipples. My body quivered, and I pulled him closer, until he rolled on top and pressed hard against me. Wanting him even closer, I wrapped my bare legs around the small of his back and pulled him tight. This I had missed, the feel of a man's body, hard and firm.

His tongue caressed my neck and ear, searching for my lips. David arched his back, and my body relaxed and tensed. For a moment, the past was the past and nothing existed outside the walls of David's bedroom, not grief or anxiety or guilt. Nothing but the feel of his body and the sparks it ignited within mine. My legs tight around him, I rolled onto my side, taking him with me and pushed him down onto the bed.

"My turn," I said, and David chuckled.

"Have your way with me," he whispered.

"Ah, just the way I like a man," I said.

I ran my hands over his solid muscles, his thick arms. I climbed on top of him, and he bent his knees and brought up his legs behind me, and once again I felt my body respond.

"Oh," I whispered. "David, I . . ."

"We can talk later," he said, grabbing my neck and pulling me toward him. The kiss was long and slow, and I hoped it might never end.

At that precise moment, on the nightstand his cell phone rang.

David caught it before the second ring. I didn't feel rejected. I would have done the same. Ten minutes later, we were dressed and on our way to the airport, where the captain had arranged to have a DPS helicopter waiting.

Eighteen

Nothing in my years as a Texas Ranger prepared me for what awaited us on a quiet street in Fort Worth. The house was a massive redbrick colonial in the city's premier old-money neighborhood. Cynthia Neal sobbed silently in the kitchen, attended to by her personal physician and her adult daughter. The impeccably dressed woman in her sixties had discovered the body upon her return from a performance of the Fort Worth Symphony. Her husband had complained of a cold coming on and decided not to attend, so at the last moment she invited a friend.

We arrived just after 4 A.M. The two-story living room, arching into a cavernous cathedral ceiling, radiated heat, as yellow-blue flames licked the gas logs in the green Italian marble fireplace on the far wall. That's where he'd posed it, above the mantel, nailed to the burled walnut paneling. Arms extended, legs straight, feet overlapping, head drooping to his chest, there hung the cold naked corpse of Dr. James Neal III.

It was a crucifixion.

"Do you think our guy did this?" I whispered, as we stood below the body.

After a pause, David nodded. "Yeah, it could be."

For the most part, serial killers don't drastically vary their killings. They know what turns them on, what pushes the right buttons to escalate their excitement, how to get the biggest thrill out of each and every gruesome kill. They are creatures of habit. As their hunters, we count on that. Their patterns help us not only link their killings but offer windows into their minds. These recurring details define the killers and eventually help us find and stop them. But sometimes, and apparently this time, their fantasies escalate. The wounds in the hands and the feet of the previous victims, it appeared now, hadn't been torture. He'd been experimenting and toying with the bodies, working up to Dr. Neal, who bore the stigmata of Christ.

"I know this doesn't match your other cases exactly. Hell, what could match this?" asked Detective Les Maddock, an avuncular man with a thick head of graying hair and washed-out blue eyes. When we failed to answer, he went on. "I still figured I'd call. It reminds me enough of your cases with the bloody crosses to make it worthwhile to take a look-see. Doesn't it?"

After the briefest pause, he again jumped in. "That cross cut on his chest, for one thing, that's similar," said Maddock. "Another's the wounds in the doc's hands and feet."

"Our victims had small knife wounds not nails driven through their hands and feet," I said, slowly. "This isn't the same, but . . ."

"Hell, maybe it's not one of yours," said the detective, pushing back the sides of his faded navy-blue sport coat. He thrust his hands in the pockets of baggy tan slacks. "Sorry I called you two in the middle of the night. Guess all I accomplished was depriving you of some well deserved sleep. You might as well be on your way and leave this mess to us."

Neither David nor I moved. Both of us stared, transfixed. Dr. Neal reminded me of crucifixes I'd seen in Mexican churches over the years, before Maggie was born, when Bill and I took the occasional winter vacation. Not sanitized like those in churches in the States, these were liberally painted with streams of blood, and the expression on Christ's face was always of inconsolable suf-fering.

"It's in the fifties outside tonight. Not exactly fireplace weather. Who lit it?" I asked.

"We think the killer," said the detective. "The doc's wife says he had allergies and never liked having the fireplace on, so it's doubtful that he would have."

David said nothing, but I knew what we were both thinking. Dr. Neal had been crucified over flames, like the flames of hell. It wasn't a reach. Protruding from the slash in the dead man's side was a thick-handled, wide-bladed kitchen knife, more precisely a butcher knife.

"Was Dr. Neal a gynecologist?" I asked.

"Yeah, how'd you know?"

"He performed abortions?"

The detective shrugged and said, "Beats me."

When we'd arrived, I'd noticed a sixteen-foot stepladder, used by the crime-scene photographer, against the wall. Wanting a better look, I walked over to get it. David helped and we set it up a few feet from the corpse. I kicked off my shoes and climbed up to the third rung from the top as David held the ladder steady on the thick carpeting.

"His throat's been slashed," I called down to David. "There's so little bleeding from the wound in his side, I'd bet that came post-mortem."

"Staging," David said. "It's all for effect."

"You did the right thing calling us. There's a good chance this is our guy," I told the detective, once I was standing firmly on the floor. "It looks similar enough, at least, to make that a possibility. What has your forensics team found so far?"

"Looks like the butcher knife came from a set in the kitchen," he said. "The medical examiner's office hasn't gone over the body yet, but that'll happen later today, sometime before noon. We left it there on purpose so you could see this firsthand."

"We appreciate that," David said.

"The hair-and-fiber guys took one swipe through with trace lifts and collected bags of stuff, but we don't know if any of it means anything. We'll transport the body wrapped in a trace-evidence sheet as well, of course. We've collected fingerprints. We've got quite a few, but we don't know if any belong to the killer," the detective continued. "We do have one on an outside bedroom window, a nice one off the glass. We think that may be the point of entry, like maybe the guy screwed up and hadn't put his gloves on yet. The window was unlocked. The wife says Dr. Neal liked to sleep with an open window."

"Anything in the bathroom?" I asked.

"Blood around the sink drain, like the guy cleaned up some before he left."

"Seems more likely all the time, doesn't it?" I said. This time it was David's turn to nod.

"We have a partial fingerprint from a San Antonio murder, Detective," David said. "The rangers will e-mail it to you as soon as we contact them. Please compare it to everything you have from the crime scene, especially that print from the window, ASAP."

"And I've brought additional copies of our composite," I added, pulling a stack from my bag. "Give them to all your officers canvassing the neighborhood. Someone has to have seen something. Any strangers, any unusual cars, anything."

"Will do," said Detective Maddock. "We'll call in with a report as soon as we have something."

I'd half-expected Evan Matthews, the *Galveston County Daily News* reporter, to be waiting in ambush as David and I exited the Neal home. He wasn't—just a group of unfamiliar TV and newspaper reporters and photographers, held back by an army of Fort Worth P.D. officers. Instead of heading back to Houston, I suggested we visit the doctor's office. "Our guy picked Neal out. He knew about him, what he did for a living. Somehow, he found out where Neal lived," I said. "This one isn't like Maria Gonzales. This wasn't a chance meeting."

After breakfast, bagels and cream cheese, we arrived at the clinic, on the second story of a low-rise office building near downtown Fort Worth, minutes after it opened for the morning. The plaque on the door read, JAMES NEAL III, M.D. GYNECOLOGY, INFERTILITY.

Inside, resting on chairs, reading magazines, the morning's patients had already queued up. I rang a bell next to a sliding frosted-glass window and a thin, tightly wound woman in a white uniform, with a pencil perched behind her right ear, stared out at me.

"You and your husband will have to sign in," she ordered. "If you're new patients, there are a few forms to fill out. And, I might as well warn you, Dr. Neal hasn't come in yet. He's running late."

"We're not—"

"Then just sign in and sit down. What time's your appointment?" she demanded. "I thought everyone was already here for the doctor's first of the morning."

I gave up explaining and pulled out my badge. The receptionist blinked, then said, "Come in."

A buzzer sounded, and I felt the curious eyes of the couples in the room follow us as we opened the door and walked into the office's inner chambers, a maze of exam rooms, counters, clerks, and nurses.

"No explanations, just tell your patients the doctor won't be in today," I instructed the receptionist. "Then bring the staff together."

Moments later, nurses and techs in white uniforms and surgical scrubs gathered in the doctor's private office. Plastic models of ovaries, fallopian tubes, and uteruses lined shelves, interspersed among books on gynecology and silver-framed photos of Dr. Neal, his wife, and their children and grandchildren.

"I have a sketch here. I'd like all of you to look at it," I said, pulling out the San Antonio composite. "Have you seen this man? He's in his early twenties, blond hair, and he has a slight build."

"Has something happened to Dr. Neal?" one nurse demanded.

"We'll explain in just a minute. First, look at the sketch."

Murmurs ran through the room as they passed the sketch from hand to hand, until it reached a small, ponytailed woman who looked to be in her early thirties. The white plastic name tag on her pink surgical scrubs read: NANCY KRAMER R.N.

"You know who that is," she said to the others. "That guy who hung around out front with the protestors. He was there yesterday."

"Tell us about him," I said.

"Not much to tell, really." She shrugged. "We have a steady stream of anti-abortion protestors out front. They're here maybe four times a week. Yesterday, there was this new guy with them, dressed all in black. We saw him from this window, right here," she said, pointing to a window that looked out on the parking lot. "He wasn't holding a picket sign like the others. He just stared at the building, up at our offices. Dr. Neal and I watched him through the office window. We thought it was really strange."

"Why so strange?"

"First, because the guy was just weird, scary weird, the kind who makes your skin crawl," she said. "Second, because none of the protestors ever pay much attention to us. We're not the reason they're here picketing. They're here because of the family-planning clinic on the first floor. Dr. Neal only worked with infertile couples."

"He didn't perform abortions," David repeated.

"No, never," she insisted. "If he ever did, I don't know about it, and I've been with him for eight years. Dr. Neal says a doctor can't treat infertile patients who want children so much they'd do nearly anything to have one and still do abortions."

"How do we find this anti-abortion group?"

"They should be gathering any minute now. Right outside. Wait near the street entrance to the parking lot and they'll find you. It won't take long," she said. "But first, tell us why you're here and why you referred to Dr. Neal in the past tense. What's happened?"

We walked out the office building front door to find a handful of protestors, three elderly men and two twenty-something women with small children, unloading a handful of picket signs from the trunk of a white Isuzu SUV. They read ABORTION IS MURDER and IT'S NOT A FETUS, IT'S A BABY.

I passed around the composite, and they immediately recognized the young man as someone who'd stood on the sidelines of their group the day before.

"What can you tell us about him?" I asked one man.

"He was here off and on all day," he said. "Just walked up and stood nearby while we picketed. Nothing much to tell."

"Did he say anything to you?"

"No," he said. "A couple of us tried to talk to him, but he wouldn't even acknowledge us. He kept staring up at the building, and then went inside for a minute. When he came out, he left."

"Did you see his car? Can you give us a description, a license-plate number?"

"No," said the man. "Like I said, he just kind of appeared. He must have parked on one of the side streets."

David and I asked more questions, trying to uncover any clue to the man's identity. They offered no answers.

"He just came out of nowhere," said one of the women, quieting a crying toddler she bounced on her hip. "He sat on the curb for a while and watched and then left. He didn't have anything to do with us."

In the rental car on the way back to the airport where the helicopter waited, David sighed. "So he went after the wrong guy. Saw Dr. Neal's name on the building directory and assumed he was an abortionist."

"Looks that way."

The reaction of the murdered doctor's staff only made the killing seem more tragic. They described Neal as a good man, who volunteered his services to those who couldn't afford hefty fees. One wall of his office was nearly wallpapered with photos of babies he'd helped bring into the world. Two evenings a week, he worked without pay at a clinic for indigent women.

"We've got to catch this guy, sooner rather than later," I said. "Thursday at five P.M., two days from now, without a damn good lead, I'm off this case. I can't just walk away until we've got this guy in custody. The killing has to end."

Nineteen

When we reached Houston at just after eleven that Tuesday morning, the DPS office was in chaos. Outside, reporters milled and rushed forward as David and I walked toward the entrance. Front and center, Evan Matthews was not to be denied.

"What about these letters the killer is sending you, Lieutenant Armstrong?" he asked. "Why is he writing to you? What do they mean?"

"How do you know about the letters?" I demanded.

"Sarah, ignore him. Come inside," David said, tugging on my elbow.

"Are you attempting to prove that Priscilla Lucas is innocent? Is that what all this is about?"

"The letters don't prove Priscilla Lucas's guilt or innocence," I said.

"Well, this says they do," Matthews said, holding up a copy of that morning's *Galveston County Daily News.*

"Serial killer behind island murders: He claims a mission from God."

In a box, in bold print, ran the text of the first letter: *Why do you pursue me? Don't you know that I do the work of another?*

"Don't you ask for comment before running stories like this?" I shouted.

"That's why I'm here, Lieutenant. Tell me the truth. If there's a serial killer murdering people in Texas, the public has the right to know. You have an obligation to warn potential victims."

When I hesitated, he went on. "Are you or are you not tracking a serial killer? Isn't that why you've just returned from Fort Worth? Wasn't there another murder there just last night? A doctor?"

"How did you . . . ?"

"Sarah," David said, pulling me by my arm.

If the captain's brusque manner when I walked into the office wasn't enough evidence that I was in trouble, the sight of Jack Smith, the department's only senior ranger captain, who reported directly to the director, settled the issue. As my pop was so fond of saying, I knew my goose was not only cooked but covered with gravy and on the dinner platter.

"Captain Smith," I said, holding out my hand. "Good to see you. It's been a long time."

"Cut the crap, Lieutenant," he ordered. "What's going on here?"

"I don't know," I said, lowering my unclaimed hand. "As far as I know, I'm just doing my job. You're going to have to tell me what's wrong."

"Well, for starters, where's this reporter, Evan Matthews, getting his information?" he demanded. "And how did he get a copy of that letter?"

"I don't know," I said. "I wish I did."

"Lieutenant, the governor's furious about all this. The rangers are looking like buffoons, running off at the mouth, unable to control a high-profile investigation."

"I'm sorry, sir," I said. "All I can say is that I'm not the leak."

"The lieutenant and I have had this conversation, sir," interjected the captain. "I believe she's telling the truth. She's not the source of the newspaper stories."

"Well, the rest of us aren't so sure," he said, shooting Captain Williams a warning glance. "Lieutenant Armstrong, you are to report to Judge McLamore's courtroom in Galveston in two hours for a pretrial hearing in the matter of *Texas versus Priscilla Lucas*. My guess is that the good judge is deservedly more than a little angry. If I were you, I'd keep my mouth shut and let him get it off his chest."

"I'll tell him the truth, that I'm not the source."

"Then be prepared for an avalanche," said Smith. "This morning the judge slapped a gag order on this case. He's furious about the pretrial publicity, and there's no doubt that you're the one he's after."

"Well then, Lieutenant Armstrong, how *do* you defend yourself?"

Glaring down at me from the bench, Judge McLamore cut an imposing figure.

"I'm telling you the truth, Judge, I'm not the leak. I did not release that letter."

The courtroom was packed. David watched from what during a real trial would be the prosecutors' table, as newspaper and television reporters hovered in the gallery taking notes and shooting footage for the nightly news. In his vast and unquestioned wisdom, the judge allowed cameras into the courtroom. It was obvious that he intended to make an example of me.

"Then who is responsible?" asked the prosecutor in charge of the case, a pale, nervous man, openly peeved.

"Judge McLamore," interceded Stan Claville, Priscilla Lucas's attorney. "We contend there is no real problem here. This is an over-reaction to a few harmless newspaper stories."

"We also have an objection to the placement of a gag order on this trial," shouted another voice in the courtroom. The speaker, a painfully thin man with a narrow mustache tracing a barely present upper lip, stood to get the judge's attention. *Who is he?* I wondered. Just then I noticed Evan Matthews perched beside him.

"Sir?" said the judge. "I don't believe we've had the pleasure."

"Your honor, I've been retained by the *Galveston County Daily News* to represent the newspaper in this matter," he said. "We believe it is in the public interest for citizens to be kept informed about the lieutenant's investigation. If there is a serial killer on the loose, the people of Texas have a right to know. Our readers deserve to be kept abreast of the lieutenant's investigation, not barred from information that could save their lives."

The judge, who relied on those same citizens to reelect him to office every four years, looked perturbed by this glitch in what he undoubtedly thought would be the simple task of dressing down one errant Texas Ranger. Meanwhile, I listened anxiously, uncomfortable that a media hired gun and the accused's attorney were speaking on my behalf. Then again, besides David, they seemed to be the only ones in the courtroom on my side.

"Mr. Claville," said the judge. "And, you sir, what is your name?"

"Jack Ballard, your honor," the attorney said. "With the Houston firm of Quincy and Ballard."

"Well, as I was saying," the judge said, clearing his throat. "Mr. Claville and Mr. Ballard, of the Houston firm of Quincy and Ballard, I understand why you're not particularly concerned about the leaks and why it's in both of your best interests for me to allow people involved in this investigation to be able to run off at the mouth about any old thing they're investigating, whether it's a real lead or the result of someone's overactive imagination. But the prosecution

has as much right as the defense to a jury pool that hasn't been con-
taminated over their eggs and orange juice by innuendo and baseless
theories, proliferated by inflammatory headlines. I suggest you both
sit down while I talk to Lieutenant Armstrong and get to the bottom
of all this commotion."

Looking disappointed but resigned, Claville followed orders.
Ballard, however, planted his feet and looked sternly at the judge,
obviously ready to wage war.

"Judge, to be of assistance to you and this court, my office has
compiled briefs offering an indication of how other Texas courts
have ruled in such matters," he said, his voice, raspy and raw, laced
with a hint of condescension. "My clients and I believe that after reviewing these cases, you'll agree with our conclusion, namely that
many less restrictive avenues open to you offer more reasonable al-
ternatives. The gag order you issued earlier today, with all due respect,
your honor, is the most extreme of measures, overly drastic in circumstances such as these."

"Mr. Ballard . . ." the judge growled.

"Along with our belief that this is too drastic a measure, your
honor, is our growing concern for the public safety. Our readers, in
fact all Texans, have a right to be forewarned when a danger exists.
The citizens of Texas desire and have a right to be alerted, to be given
notice to take precautions, if it is true that a dangerous murderer
roams unimpeded through our fair state, killing innocent citizens
like Ms. Knowles and Mr. Lucas."

If the circumstances had been different, and I hadn't been standing before him awaiting judgment, I might have enjoyed watching as
the judge's anger seeped into the courtroom, a crimson flush crawling
up his fleshy neck from the cusp of his unbuttoned white shirt collar
where it peeked out from under his black robe. But the judge let his
irritation smolder and calmly addressed Mr. Jack Ballard, of the
Houston firm of Quincy and Ballard, in an unemotional and precise

voice, his teeth gritted in a determined smile. "Sir, I'm sure that you're a good attorney and that the *Galveston County Daily News* is acting in good faith by bringing you before me today. I'm certain that my friends at the newspaper, who have endorsed me every time I've run for office since first winning this seat in 1984, would not waste this court's precious time simply in an effort to gain access to a cock-eyed theory about a serial killer that's only of use as material for tomorrow's sensational headline, now would they?"

"Of course they wouldn't, Judge," said Ballard, studiously scoffing. "The *Daily News* asked me to come here today to speak to you only out of concern for the safety of our citizens, the voters who elected you."

"I'm sure you are here for only the reasons you've stated," said the judge, his smile edging downward. "And I can assure you that I am going to take your concerns under consideration as I monitor this case."

"Thank you, your honor," the attorney said. "I appreciate that, but—"

"Mr. Ballard, I promise you personally, and I promise all my fellow citizens, that should anything, and I mean anything, come across my desk that I believe is information necessary to ensure the safety of the good people of Texas, I will not only rescind this order but I will call the editor myself to get out the word on this phantom serial killer you keep alluding to. Is that sufficient for you, Mr. Ballard?" With that, Judge McLamore stared down at the attorney from his bench, his expression that of a school principal with a repeated truant before him.

Not to be denied, the attorney objected, "But, Judge, we believe time is of the—"

"I know what you believe, Mr. Ballard. You've already told me," the judge interrupted. "Now, may I proceed with this hearing?"

"Yes, Judge," the attorney said, resigned. "But I'd like our objection to your gag order formally recorded in the record, so we may appeal your decision to a higher court."

Judge McLamore turned to the stenographer recording the hearing, a long-necked woman with dyed red hair, who wore a tight leopard-print dress and black high heels. Her name was Molly Sanchez and courthouse scuttlebutt had centered for years around her alleged affair with his honor the judge.

"Mrs. Sanchez, have you entered each and every one of Mr. Ballard's objections and every single one of his golden words spoken in the courtroom today carefully into the official record of this hearing?"

"Yes, Judge."

"Well, then, Mr. Ballard," Judge McLamore said, his smile carefully anchored as he stared down at the man before him. "I ask you again, may I now proceed with this hearing?"

"Certainly, Judge," said Ballard, who reluctantly reclaimed his seat beside Matthews.

That matter now disposed of, the judge returned his gaze to me, and I knew that I would be the recipient of all the added animosity Mr. Ballard had generated in a man I'd already heard from the bailiff had promised he'd have "that damn woman ranger" for lunch.

"I ask you, Lieutenant," he said, seething. "Tell me, if you're not the leak in this case, who is?"

"Judge, I've been too busy chasing a killer and working toward solving this case to worry about finding the leak."

I'd never imagined that statement would put the matter to rest, but the judge leaned forward and frowned dolefully at me, waiting for something more from this troublemaker whose very presence had brought bedlam into his courtroom.

Just then, I heard a cell phone ring. The judge craned his neck about the room, looking for the offending party, but said nothing as David hurried from the courtroom. Maybe I wouldn't have said next what I did if I hadn't noticed Scroggins and Nelson in the gallery's back row. Both, but Nelson in particular, looked delighted with the spectacle the case had become, especially with my awkward position before the judge. In a calmer moment, I would have realized that this tack would win me no favors.

"I suggest the leak might as easily be here on the island," I said, turning back to McLamore. "All the information I've gathered with Agent Garrity has been shared with Galveston P.D. That agency and all their officers working the Lucas case were shown copies of the letter and all other evidence uncovered during this investigation. Perhaps GPD should initiate an investigation to determine who on their force might have released the information."

"Are you insinuating, Lieutenant, that a Galveston officer investigating this case is leaking information to the press?" the judge asked, his voice thick with sarcasm. "Why would any officer working for GPD, the agency that initiated the warrant against Mrs. Lucas, leak information that could bring into question their case against her?"

I now faced a choice. I could explain my theory: that I was being positioned as a scapegoat to take the fall when the case against Priscilla Lucas disintegrated. I had no doubt that my suspicions were true and that Nelson and Scroggins knew they had a weak case. Neither was man enough to accept the blame when their indictment proved no more than a groundless accusation. But to do so, I'd have to publicly question—in an open courtroom—the validity of the evidence against Priscilla Lucas.

"I don't know," I said.

"You don't know?" he said incredulously. "Did I hear you say that you don't know?"

"Yes, Judge," I repeated. "I don't know."

"When I was a young boy growing up here in Galveston, and I told my daddy stories he thought might not exactly be fact, he used to say to me, 'Son, that bird ain't gonna fly.' Lieutenant, that's what I'm saying to you now, in front of all the people in this courtroom," the judge concluded.

Peering down at me, McLamore cinched his round face into a steely frown. "From this moment on, I want it known," he said, ready to do what he'd intended to before I'd even walked into his courtroom. "Anyone on either side of this case, from the police, the prosecution, or the defense, who talks to the press regarding the murders of Edward Travis Lucas and Annmarie Knowles will be held in contempt of court and jailed. I promise you that I will tolerate no further leaks."

Pounding his gavel, Judge McLamore frowned directly down at me. There was no doubt in my mind, and I knew in the minds of everyone in the room, exactly whom he was talking to.

"Judge," I said, planning to protest my innocence one last time. But when I saw David gesture toward me from the back of the courtroom, I changed my mind. He had something. I knew it. "Judge, thank you. I assure you, I will respect your order."

"I hope you do, and that you fully understand the punishment if you don't. Putting it bluntly, not only your career but your freedom is on the block here, Lieutenant," he said, then standing up, "This court is adjourned."

Outside in the car, David explained what he'd just learned, that we had a possible break. In the lab, they'd discovered the dirt on the outside of the second envelope wasn't garden-variety soil as initially assumed.

"It's slag dust," he said. "Residue from a type of rock-like substance formed as a byproduct of smelting copper."

"So we've gone from plastics to copper smelting?" I said. "What does this mean?"

"That's the $64,000 question," said David. "The guys at the FBI lab are making phone calls. They should have some answers for us by the time we hit the office."

He'd overestimated the wait. Moments later, while we were still in the car, my cell phone rang. It was Nguyen.

"I've got some information for you. First, the Fort Worth lab just called. The fingerprint from the Neals' back window matches the partial print from San Antonio. The bad news is that we ran the full fingerprint through the system and we still don't have a match on AFIS, so we still don't have a name," he said.

"At least we've now got a complete print," I said. "That's something."

"There's more. I've done some investigating. Turns out, this type of slag has a couple of specialized uses that may help you."

"They are?"

"This is going to bring back some bad memories, Lieutenant Armstrong," Nguyen said with a worried sigh. "It seems that the prime user of this compound is the railroad. It's routinely used in a couple of ways, under track beds and as ballast in empty cars."

"The railroad," I repeated.

It was one of those moments every investigator dreads. How could I not have known?

Twenty

"I don't know why you're so certain this involves the railroad. It's not like last time, is it? It couldn't happen twice?" Roger James said, scratching his head over a visit from a Texas Ranger and an FBI agent, unannounced and late on a Tuesday afternoon.

"It could be," I said, still fighting the nagging doubt that it was possible, that there was any chance such horror could be repeated.

We were at the South Central Railways main office, a three-story brick building skinned with smoky mirrored windows, hidden behind a row of trees in far north Houston. I'd worked with Chief Special Agent James, in charge of South Central Railway's police, years back, on one of the most terrifying serial murder cases in the state's history, that of Angel Maturino Resendiz, dubbed by the press "The Railroad Killer." For two years, Resendiz rode the rails, haphazardly choosing victims. An illegal immigrant who'd begun his career in crime as a burglar, he developed an insatiable taste for killing. In all, he admitted to at least nine murders in three states—Illinois, Kentucky, and Texas—including the brutal killing of a Houston doctor, the case which earned him a cocktail of lethal drugs as Texas's thirteenth execution of 2006.

How could we not have realized? I wondered. Why didn't it occur to any of us that we might have a copycat?

Even as I second-guessed our investigation, I knew why: because these murders were so different from those of Resendiz, who raped then bludgeoned his victims to death. Because copycats were incredibly rare. And if we were right, he mimicked Resendiz in only two ways. First: if he was riding the rails, he most likely learned the tactic from watching Resendiz evade authorities for months as he circulated on thousands of miles of track that crossed not only city, county, and state lines but in and out of his native Mexico.

The second similarity: motive. Like our sadist, Resendiz claimed to be on a mission from God.

Should that have been enough? Should we have known?

No. If we connected every crime where the killer believed he or she was on a mission from God, we'd have enough gruesome cases to fill an anthology of murder. Every city has one, every year, men and women who kill their spouses, their neighbors, even their children, all claiming divine instruction, some delusional, others just plain evil.

In most ways, our killer was on the opposite side of the serial killer scale from the so-called Railroad Killer. Resendiz had been disorganized, left behind scads of fingerprints, clues, DNA. He'd attacked his defenseless victims while they slept. There'd been no bondage, no torture, just torrents of unleashed anger as he battered his victims to death. The bodies were discarded as they lay, sometimes covered with a sheet or a blanket, not posed as they were in the recent murders. And while our guy took no souvenirs, Resendiz pilfered small pieces of jewelry, little mementoes, gifts to bring his wife on his trips back home across the border.

I'd worked the Resendiz case only in a minor capacity, as a profiler, and I ran into James for the first time when we collaborated on a statewide two-day roadblock of all trains in Texas. A blond, blue-eyed man with the build of a football player, he coached his young son's soccer team and collected fly-fishing lures. During the Resendiz investigation, James proved resourceful, worked hard and long hours, and never backed down, not even when the case erupted into a public-relations catastrophe for the railroads. In the final weeks, as the frenzy built, Texans became so spooked that train whistles no longer evoked dreams of romance and faraway places but brought home the realization that Resendiz could be anywhere, at any time. Folks across not just the state but the nation, even those in small towns, locked their doors and windows. Families who lived near tracks kept their children inside.

"Let's not talk about all this just yet," I said. "Right now, we need to see if our suspicions are even probable."

"We do use slag for ballast, but all the railroads do. So, how does that help you?" he asked. "This guy could have run across it anywhere. You know, it's used to line track beds for every railroad in the country. He could have walked across a railroad track and picked it up."

"We called Harkins Plastics on the way here," I explained. "They ship their specialized resin, the dust that was on the first letter, ex-clusively on South Central trains. We could be looking at a guy who rides all the trains, but we're also wondering if our guy is a South Central employee."

James's face turned a pale shade of yellow, and he looked sud-denly ill. "Yeah, sure that's possible. But he could have gotten that plastics debris other places, too, right?"

"Sure, anything's possible," I said, understanding why James didn't like my line of reasoning. "Maybe I'm wrong, but just play along with me for a few minutes. We need to go over your map of the railway lines through Texas. All of them."

"Hell, you know where that is from last time," he said, a certain resolution in his voice. "Come on. Let's get this over with."

Moments later, we'd left his office and walked into the dispatching center, where the railroad's traffic controllers watched computer monitors tracking the progress of trains throughout Texas and Louisiana. On the screen, red lines indicated track down for repairs. Yellow signaled occupied track. Green represented open track, available for passage.

"They communicate with the engineers through a radio system and signal lights on the tracks," James explained to David, a first-timer in the inner-workings of the railroads.

Just then a red light flashed on a pole above one of the cubicles. The corridor manager ran from his office and peered over the shoulder of that booth's controller, deep in thought with sweat coating his square forehead.

"Got a problem," James said, nervously. "Just a minute."

We all watched as the manager, portly and fifty-something, shouted orders to the controller: "Tell the southbound to slow down and pull the northbound into the siding, two miles ahead," he barked. "Get that train outta there."

For five tense minutes, no one spoke. Finally, just as the southbound train hurled toward it, the northbound, indicated by a second arrow on the screen, swerved onto a siding. Relieved, the manager demanded, "Damn, George, why didn't you tell me sooner you had a situation developing here? How'd that happen?"

George, a wiry man with a thick white pompadour, shrugged. "I didn't realize they were that close. Shouldn't have happened, but the northbound was delayed. Someone mudded a signal outside Corpus again. Cut the time between the trains too close."

"We've got more problems these days." The corridor manager sighed. "Swear I've got to get out of this business. Like to give me a heart attack, I keep this up for another ten years."

"That happens often?" David asked James.

"Lately, yeah," he whispered. "The lieutenant here knows most of this from the last go-around. The illegals will do about anything to stop a train and get on board. They cross the Rio Grande and hop the nearest train, not particularly caring where they end up. They fan out across the country that way. To get a train to stop, they cover up a signal lens—packing it with mud or old clothes. Without a signal indicating the track ahead is clear, the engineer is forced to stop. While the crew's investigating, the illegals cut the seal on a box-car and get inside or hide at the ends of hopper cars."

"Is that how you transport plastic resin? In hopper cars?" I asked.

"Yeah. And the slag is dumped in open gondola cars. The illegals climb on top of the rock and sit on it."

"You know, James, this could be just like the Resendiz situation—our guy's a rider. There's no reason, at least not at this point, for any-one to assume he's an employee," said David.

"Maybe that makes the most sense," I admitted. "As active as this guy has been, as unbalanced as he is, he'd have a tough time holding down a job."

"That's a good thought. Let's hope you're right," said James, lead-ing us to a large, highly detailed map of Texas, framed and hung against a back wall. Black lines hatched with slashes represented train track.

"Okay, here we go," I said, dialing my cell phone. I'd already alerted the captain, and he'd pulled out our map pinpointing the murder locations. One by one I relayed the addresses to James. On the map, the first, Louise Fontenot's home in Bardwell, fell within half a mile of a train track. Mary Gonzales's San Antonio rental house, another match, with a track just behind her dead-end street.

Next I read off Dr. Neal's Fort Worth address. The nearest track was miles away.

"Looks like you've struck out." James shrugged, looking relieved.

"Find the address of Neal's office," I asked the captain.

A match: the office was situated within a five-minute walk from one of Fort Worth's busiest railroad lines. Finally, I repeated the address of Edward Lucas's extravagant beach house, but even before James plotted the exact location, we knew we'd hit a snag.

"Doesn't work," said David, pointing at the map. "Not a single track extending that far down the island."

Pausing for a moment, I recalled the afternoon I'd been called to the scene. It seemed like a lifetime ago, not less than two weeks. Something nagged at me, something I'd noticed that first day. Where was it?

"Give me the address for Knowles's apartment," I told the captain.

"Bingo," said James, when he'd located it on the map. "Can't be half-a-dozen blocks from the main Galveston freight yard."

"So, he originally targeted her, not Lucas," David said.

"This answers a lot of questions," I said. "Especially, why no one at any of the scenes has reported a strange car."

Yet suspecting that the killer circulated via the railroad brought up as many questions as it answered. Who was he? And there were still those fifteen months between the murders in Bardwell and Galveston. Where was he then?

"What kind of records have you got on your employees?" David asked. "We need to at least explore that possibility."

"Regular employment histories including fingerprints," said James. "But we've got more than six thousand employees, and none of the prints are on computer."

"What if we just checked your employees in South Texas?"

"That's doable," he said. "That cuts it down to twenty-six hundred. We bring in enough help, we could have something for you by 'day after tomorrow."

"No," I snapped. Both men looked at me, perplexed. "That's too late. By then we'll have another body. This guy's pace is building, and we don't have long before he kills again."

For all we knew, while we stood speculating with Roger James, our guy was targeting his next victim. "Let's assume that our earlier ideas are right and that our guy would have a hard time holding down a job," I reasoned. "What if we concentrate on former employees, anyone who worked for South Central and left in the last two years?"

"You bring in some extra help for me, and with my people we can scan them into the computer," said James. "We're talking a few hundred at most. We can have that by morning."

"Okay, and at the same time we need to investigate our other possibility, that this guy's not an employee at all, that he's jumping trains, like Resendiz."

"Our guy's not Hispanic," said David. "He'd stand out like a sore thumb."

"We've got an agent who specializes in keeping track of what's going on in that population," said James. "In fact, he's infiltrated a white gang we've been tracking."

"A white gang?" I asked.

"Yeah," he said. "People have the wrong idea about who's riding the trains. We don't have hobos anymore. There are really only two populations. The illegals you got an education in last time around, Lieutenant. They've got their bad apples. Hell, Resendiz is proof of that. But for the most part they're folks looking for work, migrant workers, sometimes whole families looking to start a new life. The other group, they're white and dangerous. The core is made up of a gang, maybe five-hundred members, who call themselves the Freedom Fighters," said James. "Like the illegals, they circulate throughout the country riding the trains. But they're not riding to get anywhere. They see the rails as their territory."

"What do they do?" David asked.

"Steal mostly, shipments of anything they can sell, especially electronics," he said. "You know, this could be something. We've never been able to prove it, but we've speculated for the past five years that they're behind many of the dead bodies found along the tracks. The victims are usually poor illegals, mostly men, but even some women and children, murdered, their bodies thrown off a train. At least, that's what we've always assumed."

"How many bodies are we talking about?" David asked.

James shrugged. "Riding the trains is a risky business these days. Seems like there are more all the time, maybe twenty last year. But we don't know if we're hearing about all of them. Since the trains cross city, county, and state lines, there's no way to tell if the local agencies are tying the deaths to the trains and contacting our office."

"How are they killed?"

"All different ways. Some shot, some beaten to death. We've had a rash in the past couple of years, bodies thrown off trains with their throats slashed."

I felt David's eyes on me.

"How soon can you get your guy here?" I asked.

James looked at his watch. "I'll have to track him down. Give me a few hours. Say nine P.M., here in my office. I'll tell him to bring along his file. He's put together a notebook. It's sketchy, but it has all the information they've collected on the individual gang members."

"We'll be back here at eight-thirty. In the meantime, I'll get my office to fax you the Fort Worth fingerprint," I said. "I'll also ask the captain and Houston P.D. for staff to help compare our print with those in your former employees' files."

"Yeah," said James. "Send me help, and I'll get it done."

"Come on," I said to David. "There's someplace I need to be."

Twenty-one

Science Fair always brought out the masses, and this night the gym at Maggie's middle school bustled with murmuring parents and teachers. I searched until I spotted Mom's bright white mane in the crowd, near the center of the gym, standing next to Strings's mom and dad. Alba had her youngest, Teesha, in her arms, and six-year-old Keneesha held on to the billowing sleeves of her mother's flowing turquoise dress. Strings once told me that his mother planned to name him Kantigi, which means a faithful person. Fred Sr. objected, wanting his son to share his name. Of course, now no one ever calls the kid anything but Strings.

To get to Mom, David and I inched our way through a particularly dense circle of parents, kids, and teachers. As I nudged in beside her, I saw Maggie and Strings standing side-by-side in front of their science projects. Preoccupied, Maggie didn't notice my arrival. An older student was asking her questions, while another was taking photos for *The Armadillo*, the middle school's student newspaper. I figured Maggie had probably placed again, no great surprise since she always did well in math and science contests. Still, I couldn't understand why there was so much excitement, until I saw there were two ribbons. Maggie had a second-place ribbon, but Strings had won first place.

"Both of them?"

"Uh, huh," Mom said.

I'd been gone so much, I hadn't seen Maggie's completed project. Now it glittered behind her. A computer-generated mock-up of a black hole, with a whirling vortex at the center: marked SINGULARITY in bright red. Every few seconds a wayward star got within sucking distance, and it exploded and vanished. On the compulsory three-panel display behind the computer, Maggie had dissected such complex issues as worm holes, tunnels through space that led to, well, no one knew, but maybe a parallel universe. Real celestial mysteries.

Eager to see Strings's project, I slipped in behind Maggie to get a better look. Usually not as inclined toward academics as guitar practice, he'd done an outstanding job. On his laptop computer screen, an animated dinosaur trudged through a tropical setting. No T-Rex, as he'd originally described, the dinosaur in question was smaller, its presence more easily concealed. A birdlike raptor with jagged awful-looking teeth, it stalked through a tropical rain forest, at the right of the computer screen, stopping to rear back on its haunches and emit a screeching howl. For some reason, the dinosaur's surroundings reminded me of the honeymoon trip Bill and I had taken to Hawaii.

"Is that . . . ?"

"Yup, your old video. I don't know how they did it, but Maggie and Strings fed it into the computer and then inserted that dinosaur," Mom whispered. "Remarkable, isn't it?"

"Remarkable," I agreed. "Bill would have loved this."

"Yes. He really would have," Mom said. Then she whispered, "Look at the examples Strings found to make his argument."

On the poster board behind his computerized dinosaur, Strings had drawn a map of the earth, with unexplored territories, mainly tropical islands and dense rain forests, colored a bright red. *Where could they be hiding?* he'd written above it.

The two side panels backed up his theory that somewhere on the earth dinosaurs might still roam without necessarily being encountered by man. REDISCOVERED: PYGMY MADTOM AND PHASMID DRYOCOCELUS AUSTRALIS, read the panel to the left. According to Strings's research, the Pygmy Madtom, a diminutive catfish, was thought to have disappeared from Tennessee's Clinch and Duck Rivers in the mid-nineties, a victim of erosion and fertilizer pollution. The other reference was to a type of prehistoric walking stick with long hooked legs that hadn't been seen on its native Lord Howe Island, off Australia's east coast, in nearly a hundred years. The insects were preyed on by rats that arrived on the island after a shipwreck. Strings illustrated the walking stick's apparent demise in a comic book drawing, the hungry rats, saliva dripping from their mouths, devouring the fleeing insects. Yet despite the presumption that both species were extinct, specimens of each had recently been found alive. *If they can be mistakenly declared extinct, why not the dinosaurs?* his project asked.

Just then, Strings, grinning wider than I'd have imagined possible, stared up at me.

"Pretty cool, Mrs. A?"

"Very cool."

"Mom, we both won," Maggie, who'd finally noticed me standing next to her, called out above the noise in the gym.

"I know, Magpie," I said, leaning down to give her a hug. "Congratulations. You and Strings should be very proud."

I felt someone tap me on the shoulder and turned to find Mrs. Hansen at my side.

"Did you get my message?" she asked.

"Yes, I did. Thank you," I said.

"I think Maggie just needs reassurance that you're there for her," she whispered. "I feel better about her these last few days, but I'll keep you posted."

"Thank you," I said. "More than I can say."

The Science Fair so satisfactorily completed, Maggie didn't seem displeased to find David waiting in the crowd as we collected her things.

"Are you two still looking for that serial killer together?" she asked him.

"Yes, we are, Maggie," he said.

"I wish you'd get him soon," she said, wrinkling her nose in a ball. "Mom promised we'd go ice skating again when she has a day off."

"It'll happen soon," David said.

"Unfortunately, Agent Garrity and I have to go back to work tonight. We're following a lead." Maggie looked instantly disappointed, until I added, "But we have time for a celebration first. Where would you and Strings like to go?"

Strings looked at Maggie, and Maggie looked at Strings.

"Saigon," they said in unison.

Minutes later, we sat in a booth along the back wall of our favorite Vietnamese restaurant. In between sips of his Sprite, Strings enthusiastically recounted the moment the blue ribbon became his.

"I could'a fainted, Mrs. A," he said. "I figured Maggie had it. She always wins."

"I wasn't surprised at all," said Maggie. "I knew you were going to win."

"For real?" he challenged. Maggie nodded.

"How'd you know?" Strings asked, looking more than a little doubtful.

"Because the judges kept smiling while they looked at your project," said Maggie. "And I heard that man judge tell the two women judges that you had real imagination."

Intermingled with conversation, we dunked thin-skinned spring rolls packed with rice noodles, mint, and shrimp into thick, sweet peanut sauce. Usually, I insist Maggie and Strings eat lemon chicken or cashew shrimp along with their favorite delicacy. Tonight, there was no such rule. In fact, when the first platter disappeared, I ordered a second.

Finally satisfied, the doings of the night fully recounted and celebrated, Strings turned to David.

"Are you a real FBI guy?" he asked, looking somewhat skeptical.

"Yes, I am."

"I watch a lot of those shows on TV, where cops are looking for bad guys," Strings said, one brow arched, his dark eyes curious, as if concerned about what he planned to say next. "You know, on TV, sometimes the bad guys are smarter than the cops."

"Frederick, that isn't nice," Mom chastised.

"Well, my mom's smarter than *any* bad guy," Maggie said, defiantly. "Aren't you, Mom?"

"We hope we are," I said. "Sometimes we even pray we are."

Twenty-two

I've been riding the rails on this job for the past six years," said Mick Keitel, an unlit cigarette dangling from his thin lips. On the table before him, next to his black leather jacket, lay a loose-leaf binder, dictionary-thick with sheets of battered white paper. "A white guy would stick out like a prostitute in a convent if he rode with the illegals. Plus, the illegals don't turn on their own, never let us in on Resendiz and what he was up to, although I'd bet some of them knew, but they'd turn in your guy in a heartbeat. Guaranteed."

"We agree," I said. David and I had discussed the possibilities on the way back to the South Central offices. We knew our blond, blue-eyed killer would stand out among the sea of illegals jumping trains. He'd be likely to try to blend in, to become an anonymous member of the white gang subculture.

"So in your opinion our most likely scenario pegs our guy as traveling as part of this gang," confirmed David.

"Yeah. He'd feel right at home. They're all real thugs," Keitel said. "Let me show you."

Although Roger James sat nearby, he let Keitel, clearly the authority when it came to this band of criminals, control the meeting. Just down the hall, Scroggins and Nelson had arrived to lead more than a dozen hastily gathered agents and technicians from Houston P.D., the rangers, Galveston P.D., and South Central as they compared former employee photos with the composite drawing. They'd been ordered to scan the fingerprints of anyone who looked even vaguely similar into a computer and e-mail it to ranger headquarters in Austin, where the department's top fingerprint expert waited to compare it to the Fort Worth fingerprint.

As we watched, Keitel, his dark hair rubber-banded in a ponytail, brandishing a tattoo of a grinning skull on his muscular left arm and a marijuana leaf on his right, swung his binder open to the first page, a copy of a grainy driver's license photo of a forty-something man, long dirty blond hair, a beard, wild eyes, and a missing front tooth. Underneath the photo, Keitel had detailed all he knew about this guy, a hoodlum who operated under the nickname Pilgrim.

"Pilgrim is unusual, simply because we know a lot about him," said Keitel. "When he was arrested last year on a rape charge, we got access to his record. Guy has a twenty-page rap sheet, going all the way back to elementary school."

"How long's he been riding trains?" I asked.

Here James took the lead. "Near as we can figure, about fifteen years," he said. "Many of the Fighters go back a long way. I've been hearing about them since I started in this job eighteen years ago. This is a way of life for them, traveling around the country. They want a change of scenery, they just hop the next train. Most don't care much where they end up."

Keitel had compiled a long list of suspected offenses under Pilgrim's name, which culminated the previous year when he entered a Louisiana penitentiary.

"Most of the Fighters we don't know much about," explained

Keitel. "Like Pilgrim, they all go by handles or nicknames. Without a real name, it's tough to know where they come from."

"How well organized is this gang?" I asked.

"Not well," he admitted. "Pilgrim, for instance, is a relatively minor player. No real power. There's a loose hierarchy, but it's meaningless. About all that sets this gang apart is that they have a uniform of sorts. They always wear all black. And they have a symbol."

With that, Keitel pulled a small flag out of his pocket, a replica of the original U.S. flag, thirteen stars in a circle. "They allege that they're patriots, living the freedom the founding fathers guaranteed," he explained. "They say that government has corrupted American ideals and invaded personal freedoms."

"We've found railroad cars painted inside with the thirteen stars," added James. "And we've found bodies—illegals—murdered, the women raped first, with the stars cut into their chests."

David and I exchanged a glance. What we were hearing was different but eerily similar to our guy's victims.

"Of course, it's a thinly veiled argument few if any of them really care about," continued Keitel. "Beneath all the rhetoric, it's simply an excuse to do whatever they want. Over the years, we've arrested and successfully prosecuted a few for stealing, drugs, got one guy for murder, but for the most part, we've got a disappointing record. The truth is that even with post nine-eleven homeland security, we can't police the majority of the trains that ride our tracks. There's just not enough money or manpower. These guys know how to hop on unnoticed. They fall asleep and the next morning they're in a new state, a new city. They stay until they're either bored or the police pay too much attention. On the trains, the illegals pouring in from over the Mexican border are their most common prey. They steal from, rape, and sometimes murder them. First because they hate anyone who's not born here. Second, that population is available and easy."

"And when they disappear . . ." I began.

"No one misses them, except their families in Mexico, and what can they do? Nothing," Keitel continued. "Someone throws an illegal's body off a train while it barrels through some little town, and to the people there, it's a stranger. There's rarely any identification, and it's someone no one in town cares about. Their deaths rarely warrant any public notice."

"There's no pressure to find their killers, and no one reports the murders to ViCAP," said David, looking at me, as we both began to realize how all the pieces were locking into place. "They were invisible from the beginning, and now they've just disappeared."

We sat silently for a moment, thinking over all Keitel had told us.

"Did you tell Mick about our murders?" I asked James.

"No," he said. "Thought you and Agent Garrity should be the ones to explain what you're looking for."

"Of course," David said. "What we've got here are a series of at least five killings. . . ."

Keitel listened intently as David continued. He nodded at times as if he anticipated what he might hear next. When David finished, concluding with the account of the most recent murder, that of Dr. Neal in Fort Worth, he pulled out the composite drawing.

"This is our guy," he said. "Now, does he look familiar, or does any of what I've told you fit anything you've seen or heard?"

"Yeah," Keitel said. "It sure does."

With that, he shuffled through his notebook until he came to a nearly blank page. The name across the top read *Gabriel*. No picture, it offered only a description, slim build, blue eyes, and blond hair. Age: early twenties. Under favorite weapon, someone had noted: hunting knife.

"If this is your guy, he's going to be tough to catch," said Keitel. "I've never had the pleasure or the misfortune to meet him in person, but he's legendary in the Fighters. The other members rarely talk about him. It's almost like a superstition: if they don't mention his name, he doesn't exist. And he's someone none of them want to cross paths with."

"What do you know about him?" I asked.

"We know he's ruthless, that he kills simply for the love of killing," said James. "We know he's probably the one responsible for at least a half-dozen murders on the railroad during the past two years, most of them illegals with their throats slashed."

"And we know he's a religious fanatic," added Keitel. "On the train, he holds court, preaching to the others on the will of God."

"That sure sounds like our guy," I said. "Anything else that can help us?"

"He's been trying to recruit, pull together an army from the Fighters," said Keitel. "So far, no one we know of has enlisted. These guys are bad news, but to a man everyone I've met is afraid of this guy. No one wants to get too close."

"The name, of course, is from the Bible. Gabriel was one of God's angels," James noted.

"Yeah," said David. "Gabriel the archangel was God's messenger. He's the one who broke the news to Mary that she was carrying Christ."

"This guy hardly seems the bearer of good tidings," said Keitel.

"But it fits," I said. "This is the way our guy sees himself, his delusional self-image."

It was then that the door opened and Scroggins walked in, just as David asked, "How do we find this guy?"

Twenty-three

Five o'clock the next morning, just as the sun came up, I stood in the waiting room of the white clapboard train station in the center of Killdeer, Texas, a Hill Country burg north of Austin. The biggest thing in this little town? The Dewberry Festival.

For one weekend every June, the local police chief blocks off Main Street, and booths spring up where housewives sell their wares, handmade dolls, everything from paper-towel holders to tennis shoes decorated with bluebonnets, and homemade dewberry jam, tarts, and wine. Next to the largest structure in town, the high school football stadium, a traveling carnival raises a temporary camp, providing the townsfolk with the opportunity to ride a Ferris wheel or win a stuffed animal. When hungry, they line up at trailers, where grills fashioned of thick black oil-field pipe belch smoke. Their proprietors sell chopped or sliced beef brisket, smoked long and slow over smoldering mesquite, served on buns, topped with onions and pickles, and smothered in a rich, thick barbeque sauce. When they cut the meat, fat runs like juice from an overripe tomato.

The thought of it made my mouth water. There'd been no time

for anything, especially eating or sleeping, since the previous evening's spring rolls. The night had evaporated in a flurry of activity.
By midnight, Captain Williams, David, and I had pulled together a
task force at South Central's main office consisting of the higher-ups
at DPS, HPD, and sheriffs' departments from all the surrounding
counties. It felt like déjà vu. We'd done the same thing to try to
catch Resendiz. It didn't work then. I had my doubts that it would
work now.

Be that as it may, to pull off our plan, we needed cooperation and
officers from nearly every police outfit in Texas. Our intention was to
stop and search as many trains as possible in the next forty-eight
hours, for the purpose of apprehending our bad guy. The fingerprint
comparison of past South Central employees had drawn a blank, and
we were now even more certain that the man we looked for was the
one who called himself Gabriel.

With hundreds of trains barreling through the state each day,
Roger James helped us map out our strategy. As we'd done during the
Resendiz go-around, we would focus on railroad hubs, locations that
boasted a concentration of activity. In addition to dewberries, little
Killdeer had another peculiarity: nearly forty trains crossed through
this town daily.

They came because of the train yard. Bordering the town, adjacent to the terminal, it covered more than fifty acres. Filled with
hundreds of idle railroad cars, the yard was contained within a rusty
chain-link fence. On miles of track, laid on top of the slag that first
connected our killer with the railroad, the cars lay idle for days,
months, and sometimes years, waiting to be needed, at which time
they'd be scheduled for transport, made up into a train, and hauled
away.

Altogether we had twenty such search sites and nearly three
hundred officers, barring none, the largest single task force in Texas
history. While I supervised twenty deputies in Killdeer, six hours

away, north of Dallas, David headed a similar operation in another small town. Scroggins was in charge of the activity in a town thirty minutes east of Houston, while Nelson spearheaded a large contingent of GPD officers monitoring the Galveston train yard. Captain Williams oversaw the activities in Houston's busy railroad terminal, bordering downtown. Meanwhile, watching over all of us, James surveyed the action on the computer terminals in South Central headquarters, hovering over the controllers' stations on the lookout for anything suspicious. We communicated on a private radio band, set up just for the task force.

"Damn," I muttered when the snack machine in the terminal ate my fifty cents and failed to deliver peanut-butter crackers.

Just then the radio crackled.

"Lieutenant, it's Roger James."

"Go ahead."

"We're ready to go, and you've got the first one, an eastbounder. It should arrive within five minutes. It's approximately three-quarters-of-a-mile long, mainly hoppers of resin, gondolas filled with rock, and boxcars and chemical tankers headed to the ship channel. The engineer has already been notified that he'll be stopping at the Killdeer yard for a search."

"Got it," I answered. Clicking off the radio, I called out to the dozen men milling inside the station. "We're moving. Train number one will be here in five minutes."

Then, on the radio, I hailed eight other deputies stationed along the track. "Get ready, any minute now," I ordered. "Watch for anyone jumping off that train."

We took our places. My post was outside the yard office, next to the main track. It was there we planned to stop each train for inspection. Once we searched them, we'd send the trains on their way and set up for the next.

The roar of that first train storming toward us reached us well before we could see it. I felt my pulse quicken as it drew closer, felt the rumble of the earth beneath my feet even before it rounded the final bend, becoming visible down the track. I'd forgotten how imposing a train is close up until it stopped within a few feet of me. The engine loomed twenty feet high, its cars stretching far into the distance, disappearing behind a grove of oak trees. My crew went into immediate action. Two officers at the head of the train walked toward the rear, covering both sides. Simultaneously, four split off from the center of the train, two walking forward while their counterparts proceeded toward the rear. At the same time, two officers stationed at the rear ran toward the center. As the men passed each hopper car, they checked the platforms that bordered the fronts and backs, where the cars angled inward, leaving enough room for a man to ride. At each container car, they inspected the numbered tin seals that secured the doors, to see if any had been cut, an indication someone might be inside.

All went without incident until, a thousand feet away, I heard someone shout "Stop." A man dressed in dark clothing could be seen running from the train, with a deputy in pursuit. "Police, stop now or I'll shoot," the officer ordered again. Still, the man raced ahead until the officer pointed his gun toward the clouds and pulled the trigger. As the warning blast echoed through the train yard and surrounding woods, the man fell to his knees, where he was handcuffed and brought to his feet. As the others continued the search, an officer escorted his prisoner to the terminal.

"Not our guy," he shouted out as he approached me.

Instead, the man the officer urged toward me had dark hair and eyes, a complexion the color of a deep golden tan. "Illegal," he said. "Can't understand a word. Keeps saying something like qui-dad-dough?"

"*Cuidado*," I explained. "He's asking you to be careful with him."

"Ah."

I was just about to order the officer to run the man's prints, to make sure he wasn't wanted for anything, and then release him, when the captain's voice blared over the radio: "All stations. We've had a change in plans. We're already accumulating a number of illegals. This situation will certainly worsen throughout the day. Under the Homeland Security laws, INS will be dispatching agents to each outpost. They've asked to have all illegals detained."

"I thought we'd decided not to do that this time. We had swarms after the last go-around, and they had nothing to do with our guy. If we detain them, I have to assign men to guard them. I need every body I've got to conduct the searches," I radioed back. "Our priority is to find Gabriel, and we just haven't got that much manpower."

"As I pointed out to the captain, we can't do that," Scroggins cut in. "Under federal law, we're required to detain them for INS, Lieutenant."

"Agent Scroggins is right. Can't be helped," the captain agreed.

The radio clicked off and I turned to the man, whose entire body trembled with fear.

"*Lo siento, señor. Necesitas esperar el INS,*" I said, explaining he had to wait until an INS officer arrived.

"Take him inside," I ordered the officer. "Find out where he can be locked up, and then get back out here. We need your help."

As we would do with each train that afternoon, we took our places to inspect the hatches on the tops of the hopper cars' bins as the train departed the terminal. We knew from the first operation that riders often unlock the lids and then lower themselves inside, lying horizontally on top of the cargo, like the plastic resin. "In the south, in spring, fall, and especially summer, the boxcars and container cars get too hot to ride inside," James had explained to the newcomers at a hastily called task force meeting in the wee hours of the morning. "So they ride on top of the cargo in the hoppers, where they can leave the tops open, get fresh air, and stay cool with the breeze."

On twenty-six-foot ladders, at four different positions, I placed men to inspect the tops of the hopper cars as the train moved slowly out of the terminal. Halfway through the long chain of cars, a deputy suddenly yelled, "Found something."

I radioed James who communicated with the engineer, ordering him to stop the train again. We ran up the track after the train, the deputy who'd said he'd seen "something human" leading the way. In the sixth car we searched, we found what had attracted his attention. Protruding from a bin of plastic pellets, we found a motionless, cold arm.

"We need to pull this train into the yard," I ordered the engineer. "Notify your dispatcher and make it happen."

I knew what we'd find—a body. If they didn't ease themselves carefully on top of the plastic pellets or the gondolas of rock, maybe bring along a flattened cardboard box to lie on, a certain number of the riders were drawn into the cargo. Unable to pull out, the plastic pellets slowly sucked them in, like quicksand, suffocating them.

Ten minutes later, we had the train safely tied down on a yard track. As my crew searched another train that had just pulled into the terminal, two switchmen cut the car with the body out of the train. Then they coupled the remaining cars to the train and signaled the engineer. Nearly half an hour after its scheduled time, the first train was on its way.

The local police chief monitored the operation as his men unloaded the small, bright yellow balls of resin that covered the body. Although no one suspected the man might be alive, the town doctor stood vigil nearby. Uncovered, the arm belonged to a young Hispanic man, maybe even a teenager. The officers laid the body out on the ground and the doctor slowly removed the clothes and examined it. "No surprises. My guess is he suffocated," he told me a while later. "You can order an autopsy, but this doesn't look like murder to me."

By noon, with another day and a half ahead of us, we had one body on its way to the Houston medical examiner's office and thirty-five illegals—men, women, even two children found with their parents inside an otherwise empty boxcar—detained in the yard office lobby, guarded by five officers I couldn't afford to lose in the search, but I had no choice. I gave one of the local deputies money, and he brought back thin burgers on stale buns for the officers and the unfortunates caught in our web. I couldn't eat. Somewhere, that morning, I'd lost my appetite. I couldn't imagine how the day could get any worse until I heard a thrashing overhead. I looked up and discovered, hovering above the terminal, a TV news helicopter.

"They've found us," I radioed to the captain.

"We know," he said. "The press conference starts at one P.M."

"Are you sure you want to do this?"

"Sarah, there's no other way."

Twenty-four

"This is the largest task force in Texas history," the captain said to the television cameras.

"Who's the target?" asked a reporter.

"While we can't comment at this time," he said, to a chorus of protests, "we can tell you that INS is involved and that this is a combined effort of many agencies. Our intent is to enforce our borders, to put teeth into the Homeland Security laws."

"This doesn't look like you're just rounding up illegals. This dragnet is a lot like the methods used to try to trap that railroad killer, Resendiz. Have we got another serial killer riding the trains? Is it true that you're looking for Lieutenant Armstrong's supposed serial killer?" a voice prodded.

Watching on the small television inside the main lobby, I knew before the camera revealed his face that the reporter would be Evan Matthews.

"As I said, we cannot comment on specifics at this time. All we can say is that this is a combined effort enlisting the aid of many agencies and that INS and Homeland Security are both actively involved. We should have more information for you at the end of the sweep."

"When will that be?" another reporter prodded.

"No comment," said the captain.

"Since the INS is involved, can we conclude that this search is targeted at apprehending aliens entering the country illegally and traveling via railroad?" another reporter asked. "And that they'll be deported out of the country."

"As I've said, I have no comment on specifics at this time. You can infer what you wish from the fact that the INS is an integral part of this operation."

"Is that really what all this is about?" Matthews shouted. "Or is that spin to cover up a massive manhunt for one man?"

"Again, no comment," the captain said.

"Just answer the question, Captain Williams," he said. "Should the people of Texas be on the lookout for a serial killer?"

Without answering, the captain turned and left the hastily erected lectern in the parking lot outside our Houston offices.

"Sometimes that Matthews guy gets things right. People should be warned," I muttered to no one in particular. I noticed an officer standing behind me at the doorway—munching on a candy bar—shrug.

Of course, the press attention hadn't come as a surprise. Everyone in charge acknowledged from the beginning that we couldn't keep the task force a secret, not an action this massive, one with so many agencies involved. Still, we'd hoped for more time, at least one full day, before the information flooded the television news. Scroggins's decision to call in Homeland Security and INS played right into the hands of the muckety-mucks at the central office. The captain had been instructed to say precisely nothing while insinuating we were involved in a sweep for illegals crossing the border. The biggest disappointment was what the press coverage would do to the manhunt. Whether or not Gabriel realized the effort was aimed at him, he'd be alerted to the existence of the search points. Sure, there was a chance he might not see the television and newspaper coverage, but not much of one. We already had evidence he read the newspapers: the newspaper clip he'd personally mailed to me at the office.

The afternoon wore on like the morning. The train station's lobby bustled with all the illegals, the vast majority young men. INS arrived and the agent in charge, Tim Preston, who looked more like an accountant than a law officer, worked through the paperwork with each of the detainees. After processing, they would all be fingerprinted, checked for outstanding warrants, and then sent back across the border, most to Mexico but others to Colombia, El Salvador, and Guatemala.

About four that afternoon, when I had a break in the action, I put a deputy in charge and did something I'd been considering all morning: I walked into the lobby and motioned for the back half of the line to follow me. Preston looked up, startled.

"Where are they going?" he asked.

"It's too crowded in here. This is a fire hazard," I explained. "I'm going to break them up into a couple of rooms and have them brought out when you're ready."

"Good idea." He nodded. "I'll let you know when to bring in the next batch."

"You bet," I said.

At the yard office storage room, nearly empty except for shelves of office supplies, I motioned and the first group filed past me, entering their temporary prison without protest or questions. Many had been through this drill before, and for them being detained was a minor inconvenience. Within weeks they'd cross the Rio Grande again and hop another train. A little more than half my charge of illegals secured, I stationed a deputy at the door and then continued on with the remainder of my procession to an empty office, furnished with a desk and a few chairs. Anticipating my orders, the remainder of the prisoners breezed past me, until I reached the end of the line, the final four would-be immigrants, a family with two small daughters, maybe five and eight. I motioned for them to wait outside the room, and they stopped, the children looking up at me, their eyes clouded with fear.

"Deputy Cox," I called out to one of the men nearby. "Secure these prisoners. I'm going to put this family in a separate room. Keep the children segregated from the rest of the population."

"Sure," said Cox, a plump deputy in his fifties. "Good idea, Lieutenant."

"*Señor y señora,*" I said to the family. In Spanish, I instructed them to bring their children and follow me. The youngest, a small girl with dark brown eyes rimmed by a startling fringe of long black lashes, wrapped her arms around her mother's leg, afraid to move. But the nervous woman pried her off and pulled her forward.

We'd found them in a boxcar, sleeping on the hard metal-and-wood floor, most likely exhausted from the heat. The interior of those cars, even on a day like this when the thermometer hadn't broken eighty, must have been nearly a hundred. I couldn't help but consider what would happen to them if we sent them back and they tried to reenter the States again in a few months, when summer was in full force. By then the heat inside the boxcars would be at least twenty degrees higher, too hot for anyone, especially a child, to survive for long. There was a strong probability that they'd die of heat stroke, like the eight unfortunate illegals whose lifeless bodies we'd carried out of boxcars, reeking of urine and sweat, the summer we searched for Resendiz.

To attract little attention, I brought them through a side door and, in the sunlight, escorted them to my Tahoe. When I opened the doors, the father looked at me, puzzled and wary, but he motioned for his wife and children to climb inside. He sat beside me as I drove. He looked old and tired, but I guessed he couldn't have been more than forty, his brow deeply furrowed from years of squinting in the sun, his hands thickly callused, and his expression weary.

As I drove, I glanced back at the mother in the rearview mirror. Her features wide and thick, her long black hair parted down the middle and pulled taut in a ponytail, she fussed over her little ones, pressing her finger to her lips, motioning for them to be quiet. She wore her panic openly on her face, reminding me of a red fox Bill and I once found while camping. Caught in a hunter's trap, it had gnawed halfway through its tethered leg in a vain attempt to break free. Bill tried to help, but terrified each time we approached, the animal bared its teeth and snapped. We abandoned it there, bleeding and helpless.

Minutes later, I pulled into a convenience store parking lot. I lowered the windows, turned off the Tahoe, took the keys, and ordered the family to wait. Inside the store, I hit the ATM for cash then piled up candy bars, sandwiches, and drinks at the cash register. They were still in the Tahoe when I returned. Even if he had been tempted, the father hadn't risked an escape attempt with his wife and daughters. I then drove ten minutes down the road to the edge of town. I pulled the car onto the shoulder, parked it, and took two twenty-dollar bills from my pocket, handing the money, along with the bag of food, to the father. I got out of the car and opened all four doors.

"You're free to leave," I told them in Spanish. They stared at me, the parents searching my face, unsure of my intentions. "Go, now, before someone sees. The next town is just down the road. Please, just be careful. Take care of your little girls."

A moment's hesitation and the mother began sobbing. The father shook my hand until I believed my old tennis elbow might act up. I pulled myself away, got in the truck, and drove off.

I'd been gone less than half an hour. Back at the yard office, no one noticed the family's disappearance, especially Preston whose line grew longer with each passing hour.

At six that evening, I'd had enough. Video footage of the task force dominated the news, and any element of surprise we'd once had was lost. I left Killdeer in the hands of a sergeant with the local sheriff's department and took the chopper back to Houston. At home, the corral elm tree blazed with lights, and Maggie waited when I walked through the door.

"Our picture's in the school newspaper. Strings's and mine," she said. "Look here."

I glanced at the edition of *The Armadillo* she held in her hands. It was four pages of computer paper stapled together with the school mascot, a smiling armadillo in a cowboy hat, hand-stamped at the top. Accompanying a short article written by one of the seventh-grade students on Maggie, Strings, and their projects, they'd run a photo of the kids grinning proudly, Strings pointing at his exhibit.

"That's wonderful, Magpie," I said. "You two are real celebrities."

"All we've really done is win our district," she said. "We have to go to regionals, then state, then nationals. Mrs. Hansen thinks at least one of us will probably make it through to the state level, but no one from our school has ever gone to nationals."

"However far you two go, it's great," I said. "Listen, I'm proud of both of you already."

With that, Maggie looked down at the newspaper again, and her enthusiasm waned. "Mom," she said, a little hesitant. "Dad would have been really proud of me, wouldn't he?"

For just a moment, I was startled, surprised that Maggie would even question how delighted Bill would be. "Of course, honey," I said. "You know Dad. He'd be smiling so big, his chest would be puffed out so far, Gram would be telling him to take a breath before he burst his buttons."

She laughed and I realized how long it had been since we'd been able to talk about Bill that way. Before he died, Mom, Maggie, and I loved to tease Bill. He called us silly girls and joked that if he didn't have us, who would keep him in line?

"Sometimes I'm really mad at Dad," Maggie said, then, and I saw tears in her eyes.

"Oh, Maggie, no," I said.

"I think sometimes he should have driven better, so he didn't crash into that truck," she whispered, looking up at me. "And then I feel bad, because I know it wasn't his fault. When the captain came to the house, he said that other driver never gave Dad a chance to get out of the way. So then I feel worse, because I know I shouldn't be mad at him. But I am."

"Your father wouldn't have left us for anything," I said, slipping my arms around her. *In a few years,* I thought, *I won't have to bend down to hug her. One day she'll probably have to lean down to hug me.* "Your father loved us as much as anyone can love. He never would have left us if he'd been given a choice. You have to believe that."

Maggie said nothing, so I went on. "I understand being upset. I am too. But don't be angry with Dad."

"I forget sometimes what he was like," she said, tears running down her cheeks. "I try to remember things we did together, but sometimes I can't."

I hugged her tighter and whispered, "I'll never let you forget your father. I remember him like he just left us yesterday. Remember at the softball games, how he'd run his hands through your hair and say he was rubbing you with luck? Then when you hit the ball, he'd whoop and holler, louder than any other parent in the stands."

Maggie nodded. "Yeah," she said. "I used to get really embarrassed sometimes, 'cause he was so loud."

"Remember how he laughed at me when I tried to cook?"

"He really laughed," Maggie said, wiping away a tear. "He said he was going to find out what Gram was cooking for dinner."

"He sure did, didn't he?" I said, hugging her tighter. I put my hand under her chin and tilted her face back, so I could look in her eyes. "Anytime you want, you just talk to me, and we'll remember together."

"Promise."

"Promise," I said. "Always."

Maggie's smile grew broad, and she hugged me back.

"You know, if only one of us makes it all the way to nationals, I hope it's Strings," she said, pulling away and brushing off the tears. "I want to go, but I think I'd like it even better if he did."

I've never been prouder of my daughter. I thought, *It was a lousy day, but this makes up for a lot.*

Yet even at that moment when things started to seem right again, I couldn't forget—Gabriel was still out there, maybe stalking his next victim, while the public went about their business, unwarned. And unless the captain had a change of heart, I had only one day left to stop him.

Twenty-five

It felt like *Groundhog Day*, that movie where Bill Murray portrays a TV-weatherman who keeps reliving the same day, over and over. The second morning in Killdeer, except for the fact that I'd had a few hours sleep and breakfast, wasn't any different from the first. Our only accomplishment: slowing the entire rail system in Texas to a crawl. At our little station alone, trains backed up fifty miles out of the terminal, waiting to be inspected.

Although the captain had called in reinforcements, it seemed hopeless. Even if Gabriel lived in a vacuum, if he'd missed the news reports on the task force, he'd figure something was up when the trains bottlenecked. The hilly terrain around Killdeer didn't have the woods to disappear into that, say, the piney woods of east Texas offered. But there were plenty of gullies and oak trees big enough to hide a man. Not to mention barns and stables. Or maybe he'd just hide out near the tracks, waiting to hop a train heading in the opposite direction.

Couple that dismal outlook with a gaggle of reporters milling outside the terminal and news choppers circling overhead, and we were just going through the motions, carrying on with what had become a charade because none of us really knew what else to do. Still, I figured we just needed the right break. The truth is, more of law enforcement than most police would like to admit boils down to luck. One of Bill's old stories was about John B. Armstrong, no relation, the ranger who arrested outlaw John Wesley Hardin, back in 1877. That time the luck was in the form of a suspender that caught on Hardin's gun when he tried to draw it. Those extra seconds gave Armstrong the opportunity to knock Hardin unconscious by walloping him over the head with his weapon. That's what we needed now, a good pair of suspenders to tie this Gabriel up long enough so we could catch him.

About then, I heard Captain Williams's voice on my radio.

"Sarah, David's apprehended a couple of gang members," he said. "He wants you in on the interrogation. He's got them in the lockup at the Dallas County jail. The chopper's waiting for you."

"Got it," I said, praying this was the break we'd all waited for. "I'm ready."

"You need to tell us everything you know about this Gabriel," David ordered the thug sitting before him. Pounding his fists on the jail's old wooden table until I thought it might crack in two, he threatened, "If you don't, you're withholding evidence, and that's a criminal offense. We're talking a multiple-murder investigation here. You want to spend the next dozen years or so in a Texas prison?"

When the man in front of him stayed mute, I took over. "Listen, we know you're not involved in these killings. We're not trying to implicate you in any way. All we need is a little information," I said. "Tell us what you know about this Gabriel and you can be on your way. We're not looking to tie you up over the drugs. Nobody here really cares about that."

"Unless he doesn't cooperate," David blustered. "Then this whole thing could take a real bad detour. You won't walk out of this jail by the door. You'll be driven out the back, in the jailhouse van."

"Agent Garrity, I'm sure he's a reasonable man. He doesn't want that to happen," I said, leaning forward. "Do you?"

The focus of our attention snickered. "Listen, you two assholes can play all the games you want. I'm not talking," said the tall young man with the long, greasy black hair who traveled the trains under the nickname Quaker. "I'm not telling you anything. I been through this before, lots of times, and nobody else has been able to turn me into a snitch, and you two won't either."

With that, he crossed his tattooed arms across his chest and stared at us, defiant.

We'd already run his fingerprints and knew Quaker was a minor criminal, mainly drug charges, whose real name was Billy Joe Bobbins from Little Rock, Arkansas. David spotted him and his traveling companion, another gang member, as soon as they were taken off the train. Both were dressed as we'd been told they would be, all in black. Quaker carried a backpack filled with dirty clothes, Xanax and Ecstasy pills, and a two-ounce bag of crystal meth.

"So, you're some kind of big man. Unbreakable," David said, the sarcasm dripping. "Well, we're real impressed, Billy Joe. The truth is that we meet hoodlums like you every day. You're ordinary, a small-time druggie."

"I may be a druggie, but I'm a druggie who has information you want," he said, smirking and showing off the silver cap over a front tooth. "And I'll burn in hell before I give it to you."

"Listen, asshole. I have no doubt you'll burn in hell. That day may come sooner rather than later if you don't cooperate," David said, grabbing Quaker. "Come on, get up."

"Hell, you found me with drugs. That's nothing," he said, jerking his arm away. "I can do that kind of time without breaking a sweat."

"But you're forgetting, Mr. Bobbins, or would you rather we call you Quaker?" I asked.

"You can call me whatever you want, I ain't doing real time for this. It's a penny-ante offense," he said. "Nickel and dime stuff."

"Now, see, that's where you're mistaken," I said. "You're in Texas, and we've got this little law in the state that's called the habitual offender act. Ever heard of it? You've got two felonies. One more conviction and it's three strikes, you're out. Sentence is a mandatory—and that's the key word here, Quaker, *mandatory*—twenty-five years in a Texas prison. You think about that, Quaker. You think about twenty-five years behind bars. Twenty-five Julys in a Texas prison cell without air-conditioning."

The kid glared at me, eyes wide, and I knew I'd hit my mark.

Wanting to give Quaker time to ponder his fate, David pulled him out of the chair, and then pushed him into an open holding cell, locking the door behind him.

"We'll be back," he said. "Meantime, enjoy your new quarters. Your cell in the Texas Department of Criminal Justice won't be this big, and you'll share it with three other inmates."

Across the hall we opened the door on another interview room where "Rusty" sat waiting in a cell. David unlocked the door and pulled him out by his arm, pushing him into a chair.

"You ready for a little talk now?" he asked.

"Sure. Anytime you are," he said. "I told you. I know nothing about this guy Gabriel, not a damn thing to help you."

Short, sullen, with straggly red hair, Rusty, we'd learned from his record, was a high school washout named Mike O'Brien from Madison, Wisconsin, who'd recently been released from an Ohio prison after serving eight years on a robbery conviction. Rusty and Quaker were buddies. The two men were found riding just two cars apart, on top of hopper cars, reclining on sheets of cardboard to keep from sinking in. We had an ace on Rusty. He'd been found with a 9mm, semiautomatic handgun in his duffle bag, a clear violation of his parole.

"I don't think Rusty wants back in prison . . . do you, Rusty?" David taunted.

"No, shit-for-brains. But I'm telling the truth. I've never met this psycho you're looking for. The most I've done is hear about him, that he's some kinda looney tunes, and that if you run into him, you hop off the train and wait for the next. If you stay in the car and fall asleep, what I hear is that you never wake up."

"What else have you heard?" I asked.

"Listen, I've got no love for this guy. I hated jail, and I wouldn't go back to protect my own mother," he said. "But you gotta believe me. I don't know shit about this guy. Just what I told you, and that people say he's easy to spot, stands out in a crowd."

"How?"

"His eyes," he said. "People say you'll know him by his eyes."

Our plan was to let Quaker stew for an hour and then go back at him, after he'd had time to fully appreciate the prospect of a sentence that would put him away until he was well into middle age. But Captain Williams called on my cell phone, and I knew immediately from the sound of his voice that my time was up and I wasn't in line for a reprieve.

"We made an agreement," he said.

"But—"

"You gave me your word, Sarah. Three days and you'd walk away.

Remember?" he said. When I didn't respond, he went on, "Besides, there's something else. You got another letter in today's mail. This Gabriel guy's focusing on you. You've become a liability to the investigation. The chopper is waiting. Garrity can handle things there. I want you in the office ASAP to turn over all your files on this case to Ferguson."

Twenty-six

The captain and Sheila stopped talking the moment I walked into the office. He looked tired and worried, but when he saw me, he smiled.

"This isn't your fault, Sarah," he said.

"No one would be able to tell that from the way I'm being treated," I said.

"Come on. Let's talk. My office."

Seated among his collection of ranger memorabilia, the frame full of aged badges, decades-old prints of our Stetson-wearing predecessors, he poured me a cup of thick black coffee. Bitter enough to have been made first thing that morning, it flowed warmly down my throat and gave me something to do with my hands. At the moment, I didn't feel totally in control.

"The situation, Sarah, isn't that I believe you're mishandling this case. Hell, you and Garrity have done a great job. Looks like you two were right about this guy all along," he said.

"Then why am I being punished?"

"It's not that you're being punished. It's that between Matthews's headlines and this guy's letters, attention's being diverted to you, instead of where it belongs, on the investigation." He hesitated and looked warily at me. "Plus, to be blunt, I'm concerned about this guy's interest in you. I don't want you visible in this investigation in any way. Heck, take some time off, a few days to spend with Maggie— you deserve it."

He picked up a plastic evidence sleeve from his desk and tossed it at me.

"Look at this," he said.

I'd almost forgotten that he'd mentioned another letter on the telephone, but there it was, just like the others, on ordinary white copy paper, penned by the same precise hand.

Man will never understand the will of God.
I cannot be judged by human standards.

"Looks like Gabriel's given up on the guys on the train and he's lecturing me," I said, fighting to keep my voice light and calm. "This is certainly nothing to worry about. He just wants to use his newfound fame as a soapbox. Besides, he's too smart to come after me. He can't take me by surprise, unarmed, the way he did Mary Gonzales."

"Maybe so, but you're missing the point," he said. "Whether you like it or not, this guy's focused on you, and I can't have that."

"So how do you propose catching him?"

"We're going to extend the train searches another forty-eight hours."

"That won't work."

"Why not?"

"This guy's not dumb. By now all the press has alerted him. He's not going to deliver himself into your hands. He enjoys what he's doing. He doesn't intend to stop."

"Then what's your suggestion?" he said. "Give me an alternative."

"It's time to go public," I said, seeing his face immediately harden. "This works twofold. We get people all over the state, all over the country, looking for this guy. Plus, we alert people to lock their doors and windows, to protect themselves."

"You understand the circumstances. We're under a gag order. We can't."

"Yes, we can," I said. "We just don't link him to the Lucas case, the only one involved in Judge McLamore's ruling. We say Gabriel's sought for questioning only on the Gonzales and Neal murders."

The captain hesitated, considering my proposal.

"I haven't told you, but I've agreed for a long time that we need to warn people about the danger, but the call isn't mine. This case has become a boondoggle at headquarters. Too many of the people at the top have an interest in how it turns out. Seems like the contingent that wants to see Priscilla Lucas guilty has been running the show," he admitted. "That said, I like your idea, and I'll run it past the bosses in Austin. In the meantime, I need assurance from you that whatever they decide you'll adhere to it. That you won't go public on your own."

When I didn't answer, he cautioned, "Sarah, so far you haven't mortally wounded your career. You do this without permission, and that's the result. Everything you've worked for, gone."

That afternoon, I turned over my files on the case to Lieutenant Dick Ferguson, explaining everything I knew so far. He seemed reluctant to take them. Ferguson, one of my favorite rangers, an old-timer who'd been with the department for nearly thirty years, understood that I felt as if I was handing over a part of myself, the part that made me feel valuable.

"We'll get this guy," he said.

"Do it quick, before he kills again," I said. "Because he will."

I also gave him my "To Do" list, parts of the investigation that I'd been too busy to follow up on. Number one on the list were bank statements and financials on the whole lot, including all the victims and their immediate families. We had them on Priscilla Lucas, but Scroggins and Nelson had never requested them for the rest, even though they'd assured me they would. Since the money motive—the Lucas/Knowles murders being a paid hit—still hadn't been entirely put to rest, I'd wanted to know everything I could about everyone's bank accounts. All we'd discovered in the past two weeks made me even more certain Priscilla Lucas wasn't involved. If this operation fell apart and we never found Gabriel, I wanted to do everything we could to make sure that she wasn't unjustly prosecuted.

My desk cleared, I was almost out the door when the phone rang. Laurie Thomas, from the National Center for Missing and Exploited Children, wanted to fill me in on the status of the investigation into Ben's death.

"The DNA's a match, and the Centerville police arrested the mom's boyfriend this morning," she said. "He confessed to the killing. He beat the boy with a pipe for wetting his pants. Get this. He says he didn't mean to hurt him. He disposed of the body outside Houston because he thought in a big city no one would spend much time investigating."

"Thanks, Laurie. You don't know how much I needed good news today."

"Glad I could accommodate," she said. "Hope whatever's gone wrong goes right."

I'd almost hung up the phone when I had a thought. "Laurie, can you age progress from a sketch—you know, a drawing?"

"It's not easy, harder than dealing with a photograph, but we've done it once or twice," she said.

"If your staff can predict what a child will look like as a teenager, can you take a sketch of a man, like a composite drawing from a criminal investigation, and regress it, reconstruct what the person probably looked like as, say, an adolescent?"

"I don't know why not," she said. "What do you have in mind?"

Twenty-seven

Mom didn't press when I walked in the door. She never asked why I was home unexpectedly for dinner. Guess she could tell it wasn't good news. Maggie and Strings were at his house doing homework, so the place was quiet. The aroma of roasting chicken hung in the air, and I tried to convince myself it wasn't the worst thing in the world to be free from the case. It was a hard sell.

At dinner, Maggie buzzed about plans for the next afternoon. Mom had promised to take her to the University of Houston to meet with Dr. Norton Mayer, an astronomy professor. Mrs. Hansen had made the arrangements, including an early dismissal to allow her to get there by two.

"I'm hoping he has some more ideas for me," Maggie said, very grown up. "He's going to show me the observatory, the telescope, and everything. Bet it makes my little telescope look like a stick."

"That's great, honey," I said, only half-listening.

"Mrs. Hansen says that Dr. Mayer was really impressed with Maggie's interest in singularity," said Mom proudly.

"Gram said she would bring me, because you're busy chasing that killer," Maggie said. I almost objected, since it appeared I'd be free for a few days, when I realized how excited Mom was about the event. Besides, it saved me from having to explain the reason I was free. "Couldn't Dr. Mayer see her after school? So she wouldn't miss her last class of the afternoon?"

"No. That's the only time he could fit Maggie in," Mom explained.

"So this is someone Mrs. Hansen knows?" I asked. "She's familiar with this man?"

"She's the one who set it up," Mom said. "She says he's well known in his field."

"He's a famous scientist and everything, Mom. I don't want to tell him I can't take off school to meet him. Besides, Mrs. Hansen says it's okay. She's even going to let Strings go with us," Maggie stressed. "I pulled some stuff up on the Internet about him. Dr. Mayer has published lots of articles on black holes."

"Very exciting," I said.

"I think I'd like to be an astronomer," Maggie mused. "Just like Dr. Mayer and write about things that people know are there but can't see."

I marveled at my daughter, who'd gone from accepting only what could be proven to exist to believing in heaven and celestial explosions that hadn't yet been documented with the most powerful telescopes.

"Then that's what you will be, Magpie. Someday, you'll be such a famous astronomer, I'll have to make an appointment to see you." Placing my fist next to my right ear, thumb and little finger extended, I said, in my best old-lady voice, "Hello. Is my daughter the famous star-gazer available? This is her mother. Does she have time to talk to me?"

Maggie giggled. "You can be totally dumb sometimes."

After dinner, I had a few things to clean up. I climbed the stairs to the workshop, where, as I'd hoped, I had a fax waiting from Laurie

Thomas. Though fuller and younger, the face was unmistakable, Gabriel as an adolescent. I scanned the new sketch into the computer and e-mailed it to Captain Williams at the office. On the cover sheet I typed: "since our guy's so young and he may have been riding the rails for a while, I thought a sketch of him at a younger age might help. This might be more the way people remember him."

Later, in my bedroom, I peeled off the shirt and slacks I'd worn all day and slipped on a robe. Down the hall a bathtub full of lavender-scented bubbles waited—Maggie's Mother's Day present from the year before—when the phone rang.

"I'm sorry, Sarah," David said. "I knew this was happening, but I really didn't believe it."

"Neither did I, right up until the moment the captain pulled me off the case I hoped he would back down. Guess not this time. Did you get anything interesting out of Quaker?"

David laughed.

"All that big, important information he had, the guy kept saying he didn't want to be a snitch, he had hardly anything," he said. "Figures, right?"

"Yeah, it does."

"He met Gabriel once. Says he looks like the guy in the sketch and that he scared the hell out of him. He knows nothing about him. Not his real name, not where he's from, zip."

"Couldn't tell you anything about what the guy's like?"

"Besides being scary, he said the guy has an accent."

"What kind?"

"A Southern drawl, like he grew up in Alabama or Mississippi."

"That's something, but not much to go on."

"Yeah, tell me about it," he said with a rueful chuckle. "Another road to nowhere."

There was an uncomfortable distance between us that I sensed meant more than just my being taken off the case.

"Sarah, we never talked about the other night," David said. "I don't want you to think . . ."

"I don't think anything right now, David. We've been caught in a whirlwind. I reached out for you, and I appreciate your being there for me," I said. "Beyond that, our lives are too chaotic right now to read any more into it."

"I guess you're right. But it's important that you know that I do care about you and that I'm there for you. Whenever you need me," he said. Then he laughed. "Just so you don't misinterpret, we're not talking just physically here, although I'm definitely there whenever you need a—"

"Thank you, David, that's comforting," I broke in, with a laugh. "Hey, you know, it's late and I'm exhausted. Maybe we'll talk tomorrow?"

"Sure," he said. "And maybe the tomorrow after that."

"Maybe," I agreed.

Moments after I'd hung up, the phone rang again. This time it was the captain. The powers-that-be in Austin had scrapped my suggestion. There'd be no public announcement.

"I don't agree with this decision, and I told them so," he said. "I'm sorry, Sarah. I know how strongly you feel about warning people."

I thanked him, mentioned the e-mail with the new composite I'd just sent, and then hung up.

After the captain's call, I soaked for a while in the bubble bath, the water by then cooled, never really relaxing. Afterward, I couldn't concentrate on the television screen. Giving up, I clicked it off and went downstairs, where Mom had water heating on the stove. She pulled out a second cup and plopped in a bag of chamomile tea. As we let it steep, she talked about the high school girl she'd hired to help with the horses after school, how she needed a few days off to visit colleges with her parents. Mom sounded sympathetic but worried about caring for the stock while she was gone. Then she talked about how one day I'd be taking Maggie off to look at colleges, just like this girl and her parents. I was only half-listening. I didn't notice at first that Mom had stopped chattering and instead stared at me.

"Sarah, what's wrong?"

That's when I told her everything. Some of it she'd read in the newspapers: the letters, the accusations that I'd been the leak in the investigation. None of that seemed to matter anymore. I'd once asked Priscilla Lucas's father, Bobby Barker, if he understood the bottom line. Somewhere, that night, I'd found my own bottom line, a point beyond which I couldn't be silent.

"I need to warn people, Mom," I said. "I can't live with myself if someone else dies, and I've kept my mouth shut."

"Well," Mom said, as she walked over and held me in her arms. "Then that's precisely what you need to do. Remember what I used to tell you as a girl, Sarah? When you had trouble at school or with a friend?"

I honestly didn't remember, so I just shook my head.

"I told you to focus on what's *really* important," she said. "That if you put your mind to it, you will always find the right path."

"But sometimes things aren't as simple as they were when I was a kid," I answered.

Mom put her hands on my shoulders and stepped back. She gave me one of those looks, a mixture of love and pride, I remembered from my youth. "That may be true," she said. "But you're a fine woman. You'll find your way."

With that, Mom picked up her teacup and left to watch her

Kathryn Casey

favorite program, *Iron Chef* on the Food Network. She'd heard the secret ingredient that night was clams. She was gone only a few moments when I grabbed the telephone and dialed information.

"I need the phone number for the *Galveston County Daily News*."

Twenty-eight

The restaurant was a dive, a dilapidated twenty-four-hour coffee shop on the southbound feeder of the Gulf Freeway. At nine that evening, the parking spaces were nearly all empty. The place smelled of mildew, and we were the only customers.

"So, what's the arrangement you're suggesting?" Matthews asked. "You want to go off the record?"

"No, you can quote me," I said, toying with my spoon in the cup of coffee the waitress had set before me. Like everything else in the place, the cloudy liquid in my cup appeared coated by a thin layer of grease.

The reporter pulled out a pack of cigarettes and looked at me. "Do you mind . . . ?"

"Not if they don't," I said, motioning toward the waitress.

Matthews shook his head. "It's why I like this place. They could care less. As you can see, they need the business," he said, lighting a cigarette and taking a long draw. He puffed a cloud of smoke, and then retrieved a bit of something off his tongue to flick into his coffee cup saucer.

"Those things will kill you, you know," I said.

"Yeah, probably," he said. "So, what's the catch?"

"We don't talk about the Lucas murders," I said. Before he could object, I continued. "You can infer anything you like, but I'm under a gag order, and I'm not going there. I am willing to tell you about the serial killer I've been chasing, the other murders he's suspected of, and the task force that's been searching the railroads the past two days."

"Go on."

"Then we're agreed. You will not ask me any questions about the Lucas killings, and you will not suggest in the article that I commented on them in any way. If you mention the Galveston murders at all, you will include the fact that I respected the judge's gag order and declined comment."

It was a loophole, one I hoped might save me from a stint in a jail cell for contempt of court and one that might, and this was a long shot, save my job.

Matthews hesitated, undoubtedly turning my offer over in his mind.

"You've got a deal," he then said, reaching in his back pocket and pulling out a thin reporter's notebook. "Let's get started."

Looking back, I'm sure I rambled. I talked for more than an hour. Without divulging the type of evidence that could become an issue in a courtroom, I described in general terms the events of the previous two weeks. Meanwhile, Matthews scribbled notes, pausing to light a new cigarette just before he stubbed out the butt of his last into the quickly overflowing ashtray. Occasionally he'd ask a question, but mainly he listened. I talked about Louise Fontenot, Mary Gonzales, and Dr. Neal. I explained how we'd used forensic evidence to tie Gabriel to the railroad, about the Freedom Fighters and the two-day search that had yielded little. When he asked, I verified that the INS connection was a ruse and that Gabriel was the target. I also detailed why I believed the search was doomed to failure.

"So, this Gabriel is a Resendiz copycat?" he asked.

"Yeah, in some ways he is, just smarter."

"Shit, Resendiz caused a near panic in this state," he said, tapping off an ash. "This is going to send people through the roof again, looking over their shoulders, afraid of their own shadows."

"I know," I said.

"They need to be warned though, so they can take precautions," he said, angry and I knew frustrated with all he'd been through trying to report on the investigation. "Why the cover-up? They don't want to jeopardize their case against Priscilla Lucas?"

"Like I said in the beginning of this conversation, I can't comment," I said. "But, now I've got a question for you."

"I can't tell you who my source is," he objected. "I'm grateful for the interview, but that's someplace *I* can't go."

"That's not my question. I already know Detective Nelson's your mole," I said. I paused and Matthews didn't object, but I wasn't sure I'd guessed right. He didn't react to Nelson's name, and I wondered if I'd been wrong. "You've been all over this story. You've had it right from the beginning. What I want to know is, why haven't you run the San Antonio composite?"

Matthews looked almost embarrassed, stared down at his cigarette and frowned. "The directive from your office said this guy may have been a witness in the Gonzales killing and was wanted for questioning. My editor, in his vast wisdom, went with the story about the murder and suspicions it was connected to the Lucas killings, but then, somehow, I still can't figure out how, decided not to run the composite. We were short of space that day. He wouldn't run the sketch without confirmation that this guy was a suspect in the island killings. No one at your office or the FBI would talk. Not even my source," he said. "Funny thing. At times, I've had a feeling my mole, as you called him, really didn't want this guy found."

Just what I'd suspected.

"Now," I said. "With what I've told you, will you run it?"

"Yeah, now I can run it."

With that, I took a copy of the new sketch out of my pocket.

"Then run this one, too," I said. "It's Gabriel as a kid. It could help get this guy caught and save some lives."

Matthews took the sketch. "Ordinary-looking bastard to be this evil."

"One more thing," I said. "If I'm not overstepping my bounds, I've got a suggestion for you."

"Shoot."

"Bad choice of words when you're dealing with a Texas Ranger," I said, chuckling. He laughed along with me, and I thought maybe Evan Matthews wasn't such a bad guy after all. "First, you have to warn people to lock their doors and windows, especially if they're living anywhere near a railroad track. Like I said, this is just like the Resendiz thing, and that's how this guy's been getting in, through open windows."

"No problem."

"Second, how about running profiles on the victims with your piece, especially Dr. Neal and Mary Gonzales? Your article will be about a serial killer who claims to be an instrument of God, punishing sinners. Mary and Dr. Neal were truly good people."

"I don't know . . ."

"Listen, Evan, we both want this guy caught, right?"

He didn't answer, but I went on as if he had. "A story on his victims, one that shows them for what they were, just good, ordinary people, will make him angry. We need him angry. That's when he'll make mistakes. Right now, he's just too damn careful. We need him rattled."

"I'll see what I can do."

"Make sure you describe this guy as he really is," I said, staring hard at him. "He's not an archangel. He's a sniveling coward who's killing for no reason other than to appease his own sick fantasy."

I got up to leave and said, "You can quote me on that."

In the car on the way home, I felt the weight of the last few days slip away. No matter what happened the next morning when the story broke, I knew I'd done the right thing, and I understood that I had no real choice. There was something else: recounting the past two weeks for Matthews had brought a lot of the investigation back into focus, including those first days. I dialed David on my cell phone, without looking at the clock.

"Yeah," he said, his voice hoarse from sleep.

"David, it's Sarah."

"What time is it?"

"Not too late," I said. "Listen, I want to head out early tomorrow morning and drive back to Bardwell. You up for it?"

"Why? We already—"

"No we didn't. We both planned to stay there longer. We cut the trip short to try to talk Judge McLamore out of signing the arrest warrant," I reminded him. "What if Miss Fontenot was his first victim? Maybe Gabriel knew she was the town gossip because he grew up in the Thicket."

"Yeah, but Quaker said our guy's Southern," David objected.

"Lots of East Texas folks talk with a little Louisiana in their voices," I pointed out. "It wouldn't be a stretch."

David was silent for a minute. "I'm supposed to be back out on the stakeout tomorrow."

"Do you really think that's the way you'll stop him?"

"Well," said David, cautiously. "Tell you what. Pick me up at five and have a Thermos of coffee with you. We'll be there when the sun comes up."

Twenty-nine

David was waiting on his front porch, a newspaper tucked under his arm, when I drove up at precisely five the next morning. He slipped into the passenger seat beside me, motioned away the Thermos I offered, and said, "I've already had a pot. My phone's been ringing since three. Did you see the Galveston newspaper? I ran out and picked one up this morning."

"No, but I brought apple crullers," I said, holding up the white paper sack. He waved it away, uninterested. "Apparently you've had breakfast, too?"

I claimed a cruller and took a bite, the sugar coating sticking to my lips. Knowing the furor I'd begun by talking to Matthews, before bed I'd taken the precaution of turning off my cell and leaving the ranch phone off the hook. In hindsight, it was an excellent decision.

"The captain, my boss at the Bureau, everyone's calling. You're in a mountain of trouble," David said, slapping the newspaper open on my lap. "Sarah, how could you have put your career on the line this way?"

The banner headline screamed:

RAILROAD KILLER COPYCAT ON RAMPAGE
TEXAS RANGER ADVISES: "LOCK YOUR DOORS AND WINDOWS."

The *Daily News* had my interview with Matthews front and center. As I skimmed the article, I couldn't help thinking how the story had undoubtedly thrown the newsroom into chaos. As I'd suspected he would, Matthews had called everyone reachable for comment, including psychiatrists who detailed the traits of such killers. The captain, probably roused out of a deep sleep, had choked out a "No comment."

The editors had devoted more than a quarter of the front page to the main piece. To my great satisfaction, the dominant images were the two sketches of Gabriel, side-by-side, front and center. My picture was tucked into the copy, a file photo taken at a drug-bust briefing I'd given a few years back, but in large block print they'd run my parting quote from the night before: Gabriel is "a sniveling coward, killing for no reason other than to appease his own sick fantasy."

Under a black-and-white shot of the outside of the Lucas family's Galveston beach house, the caption read: *Barred by a gag order, Lt. Armstrong refuses comment, but other sources speculate that the Galveston double murders may also be tied to the serial killer, who calls himself Gabriel.*

"You're smiling?" David said. "This makes you happy."

"It looks like a lot of folks didn't sleep well," I said. "And it looks like Matthews got it right."

On page four, the main article wrapped around ads for a local Internet service provider and one touting free interest and no payments for six months on waterbeds. They'd also run a spate of accompanying articles, quickly thrown together by other reporters, including a recap of the gruesome career of the Railroad Killer, Resendiz. I found what I was hoping for on page six, profiles of Gabriel's victims. In the photo that accompanied a piece on Dr. Neal, he examined a woman in the clinic where he volunteered. The article explained that the doctor had been instrumental not only in founding the much-needed facility but bringing in the federal and state funds necessary to keep it running. In the second paragraph, a young woman who'd survived cancer credited the doctor with saving her life. Near the end, a nurse speculated that without Dr. Neal the facility would be forced to close. "Our patients are poor, and they need this clinic. Where will they go?" she lamented. "How could anyone do this to a man who did nothing but good work for others?"

"Apparently, the killer mistakenly believed Dr. Neal performed abortions," the reporter wrote. "In fact, the doctor worked with infertile patients hoping to have children."

As happy as I was about the coverage of Dr. Neal's career, the next photo was the one that washed away any lingering doubts that I'd done the right thing. In a snapshot from the previous Christmas, Mary Gonzales stood before her family's small tree decorated with homemade ornaments, surrounded by her children. "Mother dreamed of America's promise for her children," the headline read. "She was a wonderful woman and a devoted mother," said the manager at the restaurant where Mary worked. "She worked hard and dedicated herself to improving her family's life."

I'd nearly forgotten he was there when David demanded, "Sarah, why?"

"I didn't have a choice," I said. "We had an obligation to warn people as soon as we were sure."

"But you know what this could mean for you," he said.

If I didn't, I soon found out. I'd turned my cell phone on only as I drove up to David's front door. Although it was barely sunrise, it rang. When I clicked on, the captain's voice left no room for misinterpretation. He was furious.

"I thought we agreed that you wouldn't do this," he said. "The governor, everyone in the department, is up in arms, asking how you could have gone public against explicit orders."

"I'm sorry this has caused a problem for you, Captain. That wasn't my intention. Believe me," I answered.

"Sarah, I have orders for you to report to my office today to turn in your badge. I'm instructed to tell you that you're suspended without pay until further notice, so that this matter can be fully investigated," he said.

"Captain, I'm not coming in. Not until tonight."

"You're disobeying another direct order?"

"Yes," I said. "I am."

"Sarah, I can't cover up for you. What will I tell headquarters?"

"I don't care. Tell them I refused. Tell them you couldn't reach me," I said, my heart pounding in my chest. "I'll have my badge on your desk before morning, but I can't come in now. It's just not an option."

"Where are you?"

"I have a few days off, remember?" I said. "I have a personal matter to take care of."

The captain was quiet, considering, and then said, "Garrity called in. He said he didn't feel well and wouldn't be at his checkpoint this morning. Is he with you?"

I looked over at David.

"I'll talk to him," he said, taking the phone.

"Captain, yes, I do understand," he said. I wished I could hear the captain's side of the conversation. I should have considered how asking David to come with me would affect his career. This was my war, not his. I hadn't been fair to him, I now realized.

"I'm acting on my own accord, and I'll accept responsibility," David said. He listened for a minute before he said, "I'm sorry you feel that way. I'll put Sarah back on."

"Captain, this is my decision. David had nothing to do with the article. He didn't even know about it until a reporter called early this morning," I protested. "He agreed to accompany me today at my request."

"You're both about to lose your jobs," said the captain, ignoring my explanation. Rather than angry, however, he now sounded resigned. "I won't say anything about Agent Garrity's involvement unless or until it becomes an issue."

"Thank you."

"What should I tell the governor, Sarah?"

"Tell him that this is about only one thing, saving lives," I said. "Tell him I'm sorry, but I had no real choice."

"Sarah."

"Yes, Captain."

"Be careful."

Thirty

The drive uneventful, we arrived in Bardwell before seven. We'd called ahead, and Sheriff Broussard waited for us at his office in the center of town.

"I didn't figure I'd see you two again," he said with a warm handshake and a smile. "Seemed like you'd moved on."

"We did, but we're back and we need your help," I said.

"Anything I can do."

"We need you to paper the town with these," David explained, handing him a stack of the flyers I'd made the night before, displaying both sketches.

"That looks like that poster your office sent us. I've got it up on the wall in my office," Broussard said, pointing at the original composite. "This the same guy as a kid?"

"Yeah, we had it age-regressed," I explained. "Sheriff, don't just post one in your office. We need you to make sure these are displayed in all the main spots in town. Hand them out on the street. As many people as possible need to see this flyer as quickly as possible."

"Hell, that's easy. I'll have the town papered with these by noon," said Broussard, looking over the drawings. "You think this kid killed old Miss Fontenot?"

"Yeah, we do," I said.

"He looks a little familiar, but I'm not sure why," said Broussard. "I'll think about it. How long you staying?"

"Until we've done all we can here," said David. "We're here to finish the canvass we started. We need someone to guide us through the Thicket, to help us find the places someone might hide, as well as to help us connect with anyone we missed interviewing the first time. Who knows the area better than anyone?"

"You gotta talk to Gus Warren," he said.

Half an hour later, Warren, the local mechanic, had wiped the black motor oil from his hands on a soiled rag and closed his car repair shop, and the three of us headed in my Tahoe down a country road that looked no bigger than a gravel driveway. The farther we drove the less sunlight fingered its way through the umbrella of trees: pines mixed with beech, magnolia, and oak, already unfolded into leaves the tender green of spring. Indian paintbrush speckled the roadside a bright orange. Had we been in the Thicket for another reason, I might have enjoyed the scenery.

"I can't promise you I know everybody, but I know quite a few folks living back here," he said. An avid outdoorsman, Warren had grown up in the Thicket and knew nearly every road that led to a fishing hole or a hunting blind. As I drove, in the backseat he and David divided a map of the surrounding area into six pie-shaped pieces. The first covered a slice of the forest north of town.

"Where to first?" asked David.

"Well, there's this couple name of Gibeteaux. They've been

around here longer than almost anybody. I thought we'd stop at their place first. They know quite a few people living in the Thicket. Thought they might recognize your guy."

"Good," I said. "Just point me in the right direction."

The road wound through the trees, many dying under thick coats of vines crawling up their trunks and Spanish moss hanging from their branches. Warren, clearly delighted with the prospect of an adventure, plotted in the backseat, talking with David, describing people he knew and places a criminal on the run could hide.

"Turn left, here," he said, pointing into an opening in the trees that led into a clearing. "That's their place back in the woods."

I pulled over, put the Tahoe into four-wheel drive, and then followed tire tracks between the trees and through low brush into a clearing. Straight ahead, on the porch of a double-wide trailer home surrounded by trees, an elderly man dressed in coveralls rocked on a chair. When he saw us, he jumped up and ran inside, emerging, moments later, followed by his wife and carrying a shotgun.

I pulled to a stop.

"Hey, Willie," Warren yelled out the window. "It's me, Gus, and I got a couple folks here to see you. A Texas Ranger and an honest-to-God FBI agent."

"That you, Gus?" the man said, popping his Caterpillar tractor bill cap back on his head as if that would give him a better look.

"Yeah, it's me all right."

"A ranger and an FBI agent, you gotta be pulling my leg."

"Nope, it's the real thing. They're looking for Miss Fontenot's murderer."

"Damn," he said, waving toward us. "I'll put this thing down, and you bring them in."

Up close, rust pocked the trailer's siding and much of the wood porch flirted with rot. Inside, family photos covered walls and tables in every style of dollar-store frame imaginable. We congregated around a worn aquamarine Formica kitchen table with matching vinyl chairs, and Edna Gibeteaux invited us to sit down.

"We need your help," I told them. "We're trying to find the person who killed Louise Fontenot."

"A Texas Ranger and an FBI guy come all the way out here to find out who killed Louise Fontenot?" Willie Gibeteaux scoffed. "That don't sound right. Must be more going on here than the killing of one old biddy."

"Willie, you stop that," his wife ordered, waving a crooked, arthritic finger. "Louise was a good woman. Why wouldn't they come here to help?"

"Well, we do have one other reason," confided David, conspiratorially drawing them in. "We believe this same person may have killed others."

"That the truth?" asked Willie, his eyes widening in wonder.

"Yeah, that's the truth," I answered.

We stayed nearly half an hour. The Gibeteauxs were good people, and they tried to help. They examined both composites and thought long and hard. Finally, they shook their heads.

"Maybe he looks a little familiar," said Willie, pointing at the composite of our suspect in his younger years. "But I can't say why. And I sure can't tell you who he is."

That settled, they gave us the names of others they hoped could help more, and then waved good-bye from the porch as we drove away. Disappointed, I knew we'd accomplished no more than supplying the couple with a bit of entertainment.

From the Gibeteaux place, Warren directed us through the Thicket to other trailers, shacks, and remote hunting and fishing camps along the river, more secluded than anything we'd seen so far, most without electricity or telephone. The folks we encountered offered no more answers than the Gibeteauxs, and we found no sign of anything amiss. No evidence of an intruder, a killer hiding on the run. Throughout the morning, I checked my cell phone, wanting to call Sheriff Broussard, to find out how he'd fared with the composite in town, but we'd traveled so deep into the Thicket the screen on the phone shone blank. Angry with myself that I hadn't asked the sheriff to lend us a radio, I realized we no longer had any connection with headquarters or, for that matter, the outside world. If we needed help, we had no way to get it. I said nothing. Instead, as Warren directed, I circled back, to begin yet another loop on a road as remote and inaccessible as the first.

Just before noon, we'd been at it for four and a half hours and we'd exhausted every possibility Gus Warren, the Gibeteauxs, any of those who'd tried to help us had supplied. We drove toward town to drop off our guide and begin the ride home. The morning had begun with hope but ended with frustration that hung between us like a curtain, stifling conversation. I knew what David had to be thinking, I'd brought him all this way, laid his career on the line, and we knew no more about Gabriel than we had when we'd left Houston. I thought about Maggie and Mom. How would I explain the suspension to them? When Bill died, I told myself I'd take care of Maggie for both of us. I promised myself that she would never suffer because she no longer had a father. Now I'd buried myself in my work and jeopardized my job, all for nothing.

"Of course, there's a bunch more places out in the Thicket," I heard Warren explaining to David. "Nobody knows who all is living out here. Some parts would take a boat to search. Gets swampy, and no way you can drive in. Most of the time the forest is too thick to see anything much from the air. Could take days, maybe even weeks to cover."

Weeks. I was lucky if I had hours.

With that dismal assessment, I noticed the service lines flash across the panel on my cell phone; it beeped and a series of messages popped onto the screen. Most were from Captain Williams and head-quarters. I knew he was under pressure to produce me, to answer for my wayward ways. Ignoring the others, I focused on a call at the very bottom of the list.

"Where the hell you been?" asked Sheriff Brousssard.

"Out of range," I said. "What's up?"

"We may have a hit for you over at J. P.'s joint. You know? The bar on the outskirts of town."

Thirty-one

We dropped Gus Warren at his garage and arrived at J. P.'s just after noon. The place was populated with a few women but mainly men wearing cowboy boots and blue jeans, sleeveless T-shirts and plaid cotton shirts with snap-down pockets, most limp and stained with sweat. Sheriff Broussard led us to the bar, where J. P. stood jawing with a cache of paying customers.

"J. P.'s got someone he wants you two to meet," Broussard said.

With that, the proprietor motioned us forward and introduced us to one of his patrons, W. O. Harris, a man so old his hands looked as gnarled as the thick black branches of the ancient live oaks surrounding the joint.

"Well, J. P. here showed me that picture of that boy. He told me what you two was asking for, and I got some questions. Give me the right answers, and I might have a name for you," he said, his short gray beard flapping with each syllable.

"What questions?" David asked.

"Ain't no way this freak is ever gonna know I was the one who first said his name?"

"No way," said David. "My word on it."

"No way this old man's ever gonna have to testify against no one. 'Cause if that takes place a bad case of that amnesia stuff might just hit this old man and he won't remember, not one thing."

"I can't answer that until I know what you've got to tell us," David replied, looking sympathetic but stern.

"But we understand," I said, ignoring a look from David that radioed be-careful-what-you-promise. "Agent Garrity and I know that a man with amnesia probably won't be much good to us on the stand."

The old man assessed me. He surveyed David. He scanned Sheriff Broussard's blank face.

I knew he wanted to talk.

"Hell," he said. "That being the case, I suggest you look for a boy, about twenty, maybe twenty-one. I can't say as I've seen the kid in years, but that drawing of yours, the younger one, sure does remind me of Doyle Tyler."

"Who is he?" I asked.

"He lived back in the Thicket with his mother, a pretty woman considering that she used to make money by supplying what a man needs to some of the old boys in town," J. P. interjected. "No one ever saw much of that boy after the time he turned a teenager or so. Never did come to town much. He and his momma didn't much care for people."

"He was a strange one," flapped W. O. "Let's say, I used to avail myself of his mother's charms at times, when my old lady was out of sorts. You know?"

"Sure," said David.

"Thelma Tyler was an odd woman," he explained. "She wasn't like a normal person in her profession."

"Explain that," I said.

"Well, her daddy was a preacher, not formal educated but kind of his own religion, real fire and brimstone, talked in tongues and laid on hands to heal the sick. He held services in the front room of the house for some of the folk living out in the Thicket. Her momma died when Thelma was a little one. Her daddy raised her after that, and they lived a real solitary life out there, living off the land, him making a little with his preaching. Then the daddy disappeared, when she must'a been about fourteen or so. Just up and left when he felt a calling to preach the gospel in other parts, the way she told it. That point on, Thelma made her living on her back. But that girl had her daddy in her. All the while a man was cranking away, she was spouting Bible verses, just like her old man on the pulpit. Some of the boys in town didn't care for it much. Said it hindered the natural flow of things, if you know what I mean. They stopped coming around. Me, it never bothered. Don't much believe in all that religion mumbo jumbo."

"Who's the boy's father?" I asked.

"Don't rightly know," said W. O. with a shrug. "Thelma never said, that I know of. But she had him not long after her daddy disappeared. Some in town always figured, isolated like she was, that Doyle's most likely daddy was . . ."

"Say it," I said.

"Some always figured Thelma's daddy wasn't living what he was preaching, and that he fathered the boy," he said. "But that's only gossip. Don't believe no one really knows for sure."

"Tell us about Doyle," David prodded.

"Well, that kid was smart as a whip, but doing some very peculiar things, even when he was a little one," he explained, shaking his head in disbelief. "One day I walked up on him skinning a possum."

"Why's that odd?" I said.

"Damn thing was still alive," he said, shaking his old head.

David shot me a glance, and I could feel the fine hair on my arms stand up, as if from static electricity.

"That poor thing wailed like a sinner on judgment day. I asked that boy, he was maybe eight then, why he was doing that to that poor animal. I never liked possum much, but some things you just don't do. He never said a word, just looked at me with those eyes, those hateful eyes, ice-cold blue eyes. I just shrugged it off. Left to go see his momma, which was what had brought me out there in the first place."

"Tell us more," I asked.

"The last time I saw Doyle, he looked like that sketch you got there. He might'a been twelve or thirteen. After that, when I did go see his momma, which weren't too often, mainly because my years were coming on and my manly needs weren't as strong, the boy was never around. When I asked about him one time, Thelma said he was living out in the Thicket. He hardly ever came 'round, even to the house. Strange kid."

"And what happened to them, to Doyle and his mother?" asked David.

"'Round 'bout two years ago Thelma stopped catering to the local men. Her religion got real strong," Harris explained. "Last time I went to see her, she told me she was hearing the call herself, just like her daddy. She said she was devoting her life to God and that she needed to start over, someplace different. Guess that's what happened. Never saw her again."

"And Doyle?"

"Don't know. He might'a gone with her. Or, it could be that he's still out there somewhere, living off the Thicket," Harris said. With a chuckle, he added, "Guess that's a question you two big-time police will have to answer."

"We need to go out to the house, to see where they lived," David said, an edge of excitement in his voice. "How long will it take to get a search warrant, Sheriff?"

"One thing about little towns like this one. Not a lot of red tape," Broussard answered. "I can have one for you in ten minutes. This time of day the judge is easy to find. He's eating lunch in his office."

That settled, David turned back to the old man. "We'd like you to take us, Mr. Harris."

"Guess I could, but I'd prefer not to."

"Why not?"

Harris shook his head as if David had taken leave of his senses.

"It really ain't too far from town. You used to be able to drive right up to the place, but we had a hellacious storm little more than a year ago. Trees down all over. No one living there so nobody's been around to clean up. Now, the only way there's on foot," he said. "Plus, that woods is full of critters, hogs, wild cats, not to mention cottonmouths and rattlers. Never had much love for snakes, which is one reason I settled here in town. Besides, I've claimed this here bar stool and my ass weren't planning to leave it the rest of the day, except to relieve myself, and then I'm just going as far as that there men's room."

"Mr. Harris," I said, softly. "There's something you've got to understand. Doyle Tyler isn't just a suspect in Miss Fontenot's murder. We believe he's responsible for the murders of at least five people, one a young mother who left little children behind."

Harris looked at me and gave me a wizened grimace. "I know what you're doing, making me sympathetic and all."

"That's exactly what I'm trying to do. There are a lot of families suffering because of this man," I said. "And if we don't stop him, there'll be more. Because this boy, as you call him, isn't going to stop killing."

Harris thought for a moment, and then nodded. "All right. Guess I gotta do it. I'll meet you out front in ten minutes. No bathrooms in the Thicket. I suggest you do your business here before we leave. These days, it takes me a while to do mine, 'cause of age, you know."

Thirty-two

In the bright midday sun, W. O. Harris's skin had a gray-yellow cast not apparent in the dim light of the bar; it that reminded me of cigarette smoke and liver disease. He took David's place in the Tahoe's front passenger seat and directed me to back up and turn right onto the main road. We wound through the town, past the sheriff's office and turned left onto a narrow back road just past the Cut and Curl narrow back beauty parlor, then drove ten minutes east, where the houses ended and the pavement was replaced by gravel that pinged the SUV's undercarriage. As we traveled deeper into the Thicket, we passed narrow dirt roads that trailed into the forest. Some we'd traversed just hours earlier with Gus Warren.

In the backseat, David stared silently into the woods. I knew he had to be considering the uncertainty of what lay ahead. Was Doyle Tyler Gabriel? Would we find him waiting for us in the Thicket? I had that familiar gnawing in my gut I get when we're closing in on a suspect, and I guessed David had it too. But what if we were wrong? What if Doyle Tyler had nothing to do with the murders, beyond the unfortunate circumstance of resembling the killer? Lost in thought, I almost missed the turn when W. O. motioned to the left. I steered off the gravel and, as the old man directed, parked at the entrance to what appeared to have once been a dirt road, blocked by fallen trees and claimed by high grass.

"That's what that storm did. A bunch of tornadoes whipped through, bringing trees down all over the place. Unless you're fixing to move these here trees, this is where we start walking. Hope you're up for it," said W. O., as we all climbed out of the SUV.

"How far is it?" David asked, staring into the woods.

"The most a couple of miles, but you should've worn boots, like your lady friend here," he said, glancing down at David's tennis shoes. Spitting the runoff from his tobacco chew onto the ground, he smiled, his decaying teeth coated with thick brown saliva, and raised his right foot to display his own tattered lizard-skin boots. "Like I said, there's critters you don't want to step on out here."

I didn't have an extra pair of boots for David in the Tahoe, but I unlocked the metal locker in the back and pulled out two Kevlar vests, a twelve-gauge Remington shotgun with a twenty-one-inch barrel, basically a riot gun, that I handed to David and a .30 caliber Remington semiautomatic rifle for myself. We both had our pistols in our belts. Whether we stepped on an unfriendly snake or met up with Doyle Tyler, we were prepared.

Our vests on, we hiked what remained of the overgrown dirt road for twenty minutes or more, W. O. in the lead, with David stepping over fallen branches. Every few minutes, I felt for my pistol, just for security's sake. On one side of the road, rickety poles with electrical lines ran overhead. Around us, the woods grew dense. The temperature felt ten degrees cooler than in town, and the pine-scented air filled my lungs with a heavy dose of oxygen. Sunlight dappled a mat of ferns, pine straw, and fallen leaves. The only sounds were those of courting insects, the breeze ruffling through trees, and the crush of our own footsteps.

Not far ahead, a wide swath of sunlight.

"Almost there," flapped W. O.

Moments later, at the edge of a clearing, we stopped. Two hundred feet ahead stood a dilapidated, weather-worn cabin, large sections of its wood siding rotted away. A front porch ran the length of the small wooden structure. An ancient tree crumpled one corner of the cabin, its trunk still attached to a knotted ball of roots heaved from the ground, and a thick branch pierced the roof. On the only section spared by the tree limb, someone, perhaps decades earlier, had built a makeshift steeple, topped by a cross.

"Must'a been that storm I mentioned," wheezed W. O., sizing up the damaged cabin and scratching his head, his breathing labored from the walk. "Place looked bad before but never this bad."

"What a lonely place," I said.

"For me and you, yeah. But not for Thelma. She loved it. Never liked neighbors or seemed to have the need of other folk, just her and the boy. She used to say the best thing about living out here is that no one bothers you. You get to live like you're the only people on earth, with no one but God to answer to."

David wasn't listening, his eyes narrowing as he scanned the clearing, five acres or more, around the cabin. He was worried. Without cover, we would be easy targets. A gun wasn't Doyle Tyler's preferred weapon, but he'd used one in Galveston. We could be walking into a trap.

"Wait here," I ordered the old man, as David and I stepped forward.

"Don't worry about me," he said, slipping his hand inside his jacket pocket and retrieving a .38. "I always carry it with me. Snakes."

"If you see the kid, don't shoot unless you have to," David ordered.

"Hell," scoffed W. O., "I'm too old to worry about being a hero. Leave that to you two. I see that boy coming at me with anything but an olive branch in his hand, he better have said his prayers, because he's meeting his maker."

With that, David and I warily worked our way toward the cabin. I focused on the woods, scanning the trees, searching for movement, anything that appeared out of place, a futile effort at best. The forest offered abundant opportunities to hide. Behind a tree trunk or with his belly pressed flat against the earth, Doyle would be nearly invisible.

David led the way, holding up his shotgun and keeping his focus on the cabin, as I rotated side to side, aiming my rifle at shadows. Something slithered away from our approaching footsteps, under the thick coat of ferns that covered the ground. A hawk flew silently overhead, the only sound the rhythmic thudding of its muscular wings against a pale blue, nearly cloudless sky.

When we reached the battered log cabin, David nodded toward the front door, and I cautiously took the five steps up onto the porch, its boards ulcerated with rot, the once rust-colored paint buckled and peeling. I positioned myself at the front door, listening intently for any sign someone might be waiting for us inside. Footsteps. A voice. I heard only silence from the cabin and the sounds of the forest around me.

David left me standing guard, as he circled to the back of the house. My heart threatened to drill a hole through my chest as I waited, silent, alert, surveying the woods with my rifle scope as a guide and listening at the cabin door until I heard David shout, "Now."

At that moment, I became instantly calm. I turned the handle; the door was unlocked, and I pushed through into the cabin.

"Police," David shouted. "We have a search warrant. Come out with your hands up."

His only answer was silence.

Once inside, we rushed to the center of the room, then stood back-to-back, shuffling in a circle, our weapons targeting the walls, as if partners in some awful dance. My mind registered snapshots, a spray of light flooding through the jagged opening surrounding the tree limb, a sink black with mildew, battered kitchen cabinets, a table with two ladder-back chairs, and what appeared to be the remains of a broken third chair leaning against a wall. A fireplace and a stack of wood. A television with a shattered screen. A small corner altar had a cross anchored to a post behind it.

I heard a sound and swiveled, aiming my rifle at the tail-end of a cat-size rat vanishing into a hole left by a missing chunk of wall.

Satisfied the main room was clear, we cautiously made our way to a closed door next to the soot-black stone fireplace. David swung the door open and we entered the cabin's only bedroom. A scratched and tarnished metal frame held a sagging mattress.

"Look," David said, nodding toward the wall.

Above the bed, another bloody cross.

We circulated through the room, guns drawn, my pulse quickening.

Thelma Tyler's clothes, housedresses, jeans, and blouses worn to threads, hung on a rusted metal rack. The dresser drawers yawned open, the top one containing a few careworn yet neatly folded negligees and lace undergarments, tools of her trade. I zeroed in on a faded color photograph, on top of the dresser in a black plastic frame, of a plump young woman with an anxious smile, wearing a wide-brimmed straw hat and a beige cotton dress. Next to her stood a small boy, no more than seven or eight, with an empty expression and a mop of pin-straight blond hair.

The bedroom secured, David nodded toward two doors leading off to the right.

The first was the bathroom, so small the corroded sink, toilet, and shower left barely enough room to stand. Behind the second door we found what could have been a closet, had most of the floor not been consumed by a tattered blue-and-white-striped stained mattress. Abandoned boy's clothing and frayed, soiled schoolbooks lay scattered beside it. The low ceiling and sloped walls made it impossible to stand upright once inside.

"I saw a shed around back," David said.

We left through the back door and made our way to the shed, again watching the forest, knowing it was possible we were being observed in return. I saw W. O. Harris in the distance, still clutching his .38.

At the shed door, I put down the rifle and held my .45 in one hand, the doorknob with the other.

"I'll stay here," David said.

I nodded. With both of us inside, we would have been easy targets, like killing livestock in a pen.

I turned the knob and eased inside. The only window was thick with filth and covered by a frayed cotton curtain. Coming out of the bright sunlight, at first I saw only darkness. As my eyes adjusted, I detected a glint of metal. My heart lunged and I swiveled, expecting Doyle Tyler to spring at me, brandishing his knife. Then I realized the glare reflected off the walls, covered with chains, saws, hammers, and a sickle, all dangling from hooks. My eyes swept the shed, not knowing exactly what I was looking for. In one corner I saw the skeleton of a fourth kitchen chair, broken, lying in a heap little bigger than kindling. In another, a large cardboard box. Wiping away layers of grime with a handful of brown leaves I grabbed off the floor, I read the top and sides. The box had once held a twenty-four-inch RCA color television, most likely the one inside the cabin, its screen reduced to shards of glass, as if someone had kicked it in.

Pushing against the box, I felt weight shift inside.

"I found something," I called out to David.

"What?"

"Probably nothing, but give me a minute."

Someone had tied the box shut with a thin rope, the kind used for hanging laundry. I took out my pocketknife, flipped open the blade, and sliced back and forth twice. The rope, rotted and weak, easily severed. I edged it away, careful not to disturb the two knots that held it together. They could end up in a courtroom someday, evidence in a trial. I felt certain they were the same as the slipknot the killer used around Annmarie Knowles's neck.

The rope pushed to the side, four strips of silver duct tape bound the carton shut. I yanked off two, enough to open one side of the box, but an inner flap blocked my way, so I ripped off the remaining two. I eased open the box and uncovered a layer of dried pine straw. The faint smell of something rotting filled the shed. I gingerly pushed the straw aside, uncovering a shiny, black plastic garbage bag. Not wanting to disturb the green wire tie at the top, where fingerprints would most likely be found, I again used my knife, slicing through the bag. With the blade's first puncture, the cabin filled with a heavy, unmistakable stench. My stomach roiled, and when I breathed in, it felt as if the noxious odor coated my throat, tongue, and teeth.

A surge of nausea made my body tremble.

Certain I knew what waited inside, I stretched open the black plastic, exposing one fragile, leathery human hand, its fingernails painted the deep blue-red of blood as it makes its way to the heart.

I walked outside, took a deep breath of fresh air, filled my mouth with saliva and spit, and then turned to David.

"My guess is that we've found Thelma Tyler."

Thirty-three

The body was mummified.

In death, the woman's skin had cured translucent amber brown. Decomposition tightened her muscles and tendons, until they pulled as taut as expanded rubber bands, locking her joints. The orbits of her eyes empty hollows, the brown roots of her dyed blond hair still anchored in a cheap plastic barrette. Wearing a silky red camisole and panties, she'd been bound at wrists and ankles, cinched together with rope discolored by the seepage of bodily fluids. Inside the box, her body had been neatly folded into a fetal position, knees pulled up and her chin tucked against her chest. From the side, I saw the edge of a gaping wound at the base of her throat.

Minutes after discovering the body, I contacted the captain, who called the department higher-ups. An hour later, DPS helicopters began landing in the field beside the cabin. The scene soon swarmed with FBI agents and my fellow rangers, most pulled off the train searches, and a DPS crime-scene unit there to process the cabin and confiscate evidence. Along with Doyle Tyler's discarded schoolbooks, they bagged dishes, clothes, and a hairbrush to send to the lab, in hopes of uncovering clues, including DNA.

While David and I watched, two men readied what remained of the woman for transport. With no local medical examiner capable of handling the examination, the captain made arrangements to send the body to the coroner in Houston. The rest of the unwrapping would take place at the county morgue, where conditions could be controlled. They'd already sealed the box in sterile, white trace-element sheets, to prevent any evidence from being lost during the trip. I had no doubt we'd verify that the corpse was what little remained of Gabriel's mother.

Meanwhile, W. O. Harris sat back, eyes wide and just a little sad.

"Yeah, Thelma looked great in that red getup," I heard him tell an FBI agent who scrawled his every word into a notebook. "True, that woman wasn't a saint, but I gotta think she deserved better than that. Can't understand how any boy can do that to his very own mother."

At two-thirty that afternoon, the sun hung high overhead and glared relentlessly down upon the scene at the cabin. One team of lab techs concentrated on the house, while another scrutinized the shed, including firewood stacked and leaning against the back wall. This was just the beginning. The lab guys would be here for days, examining, inspecting. Including the woman found at the cabin, we now had six murder cases, plus the probable killings of no one knew how many unfortunate illegals on the trains, hanging in the balance.

As I watched a deputy carefully pull away the first piece of firewood, Sheriff Broussard bumped me on the radio. I'd asked him to use his contacts in Bardwell to find out anything else he could about Doyle Tyler, aka Gabriel. Townsfolk, he said, described the boy as a loner, a sullen child who faded into the shadows, easily overlooked. In school, his grades were average, Cs and the rare B, but more than one teacher sensed a keen intelligence. Some said they'd attempted to break through the wall the boy had around his emotions. All eventually gave up, their intentions thwarted by his persistent silence.

From an early age, small and spare, he'd been a frequent target for schoolyard bullies. That ended at the age of ten, when he retaliated against one young tyrant. Half the bully's size, Tyler left the playground thug with three broken ribs and a gash from a knife across his cheek. After that, the other boys left Tyler alone. The following year, he virtually disappeared. According to school records, the boy simply stopped showing up. The local sheriff at the time, Broussard's predecessor, remembered once traveling out to Thelma Tyler's house with the mission of bringing her son back to school.

"The sheriff had a spat with her, told her he didn't care how she made her money, but she was going to educate the kid," said Broussard. "She said she saw no reason the boy needed to know any more than she could teach him and claimed she didn't know where Doyle was anyway, said he spent most of his time in the Thicket. For a few years after that, hardly anyone saw the boy, unless they came upon him unexpectedly in the woods. When someone did, he never talked, just stared at them until they got spooked and left. That point on, it's like Doyle Tyler ceased to exist. No driver's license, no work records, nothing. Can't tell you where he's been for the last eight years. Guess he must'a lived out there with his momma, but nobody I talked to remembers seeing him."

After I thanked the sheriff and hung up, I did something I'd wanted to do since I first noticed the photograph on Thelma Tyler's dresser. Wearing evidence gloves, I carefully removed it from the frame and scanned it into my laptop. With the photo on the screen, I cropped in around Doyle's young face until everything else disappeared. I then moved the image onto the left half of the screen. On the right side, I pulled up the sketch of Gabriel as a boy. My fingers sprinting across the keyboard, I played with the two images until they became similar in size, then I superimposed the sketch over the photo, easing it into place, lining up the corners of the eyes and the unusually high cheekbones. I clicked on the photo two more times, to blow it up, just a bit, until it filled the outline of the sketch. My body shivered, as if chilled by an undetected breeze. The two faces were a close match, their bone structures eerily similar.

Finished, I bagged both the photograph and the frame to turn over to forensics, just as David returned from taking a phone call.

"The captain just got a report from the lab. Some of the fingerprints they've collected from the house and e-mailed in are consistent with the San Antonio fragment and identical with the one from Dr. Neal's back window. Did you notice that the knots on the box and the bindings on this body match those used in the other murders?"

"Yeah, I noticed," I said.

With that, we both sank into silence, watching the activity surrounding us, lost in our own thoughts.

"So this is how you grow a Doyle Tyler?" I finally asked. "Are we supposed to feel sorry for this kid?"

"No," said David. "We're not."

I wasn't willing to leave it at that.

"So from the mattress, we surmise he lived in the closet, slept in there, probably listened to everything going on in the other room while his mother bedded down the locals for money and spouted Bible verses. But is that enough?" I asked. "What transformed the child in the picture into a psychopath, obsessed with torture and murder?"

"You can quote the same studies I can," he said, frowning, his eyes carrying the sadness of having seen too much suffering. "Abuse, physical, sexual, verbal, emotional, usually factor in. But that can't be all. Otherwise, why do some kids live through indescribable hell and grow up to be normal, functioning adults? And what about serial killers who aren't abused as children? What happens to them? Maybe someday, along with defective genes for cancer and heart disease, they'll identify one that predisposes children to grow into monsters."

"Do you think he'll come back here?" I asked.

"No," David said. "My guess is he's happy to be rid of this place and all it represents."

"But he's been here, recently," I said.

"How do you know?"

"When I went back into the kitchen, I looked around. I found an empty pint-size milk carton in the trash," I explained. "The expiration date isn't until next week."

Just then, one of the crew dismantling the woodpile called out, "Lieutenant Armstrong. Agent Garrity. Over here. We found something."

A group crowded around the man, but as David and I approached, they opened their ranks, making a path for us to walk through. There, crouched on the ground, was a deputy holding a paper grocery sack in one hand and a fistful of newspaper clips in the other.

"We found them inside the bag, hidden behind the woodpile," he said.

On top was the *Galveston County Daily News* photo, taken as I left the scene of the Mary Gonzales murder. That wasn't surprising, but as the deputy quickly paged through the pile, he uncovered every article that had run on the killings. The last clip on the stack was Dr. Neal's obituary, three columns wide, listing his many affiliations and awards. The only articles missing were those that had just run that morning, the interview I'd given to Evan Matthews and the profiles of the victims. Wherever he was now, I was sure Doyle Tyler had already read them. *He must be furious*, I thought.

"That's not everything," said the deputy. "There's one more."

Something about the way the officer looked at me telegraphed that this would not be good news.

"We found this," he said, handing me a soiled sheet of computer paper.

At first, I simply stared at it, trying to understand how I could be holding a copy of the photo and article about Maggie and Strings from the school newspaper. That wasn't possible. Doyle Tyler could never have found it. How could he? It was a school newspaper, handed out only to students in Maggie's middle school. Then, my pulse drumming ever harder and a shadow of dread descending upon me, I noticed the school district's Web site address printed across the top. *No*, I thought. *They wouldn't . . . ?* But they had. The main office had recycled *The Armadillo* photo and article, using them in an online newsletter. My hands began to shake when I realized that I must have been distracted the night Maggie showed me the article and the photo. Why hadn't I noticed before that my face was visible in the background?

"Oh, God, no. . . ." I said, my head reeling, as if I'd sustained a hard physical blow. "David, no."

Thirty-four

M om would have called if there was a problem. Maggie's not due to get out of school for ten minutes. She's safe there," I said, as David and I ran toward one of the helicopters parked in the clearing. Every word stumbled off my lips. I felt as if I were moving in slow motion, trapped in a bizarre dimension where seconds became minutes, and minutes lingered like hours. All the while, inside my head, a terrified voice screamed "No" over and over, growing louder and louder, until I barely recognized my own, still remarkably calm voice say, "I'll have headquarters connect me with the school, and Mrs. Hansen will keep her until we arrive. It'll be all right, David. You'll see. It'll be all right."

At the chopper, David pulled back the door and we jumped in. My heart pounding, I didn't realize at first that we were the only ones inside. No pilot. I had to keep reminding myself that, as unreal as it felt, this wasn't a movie, where a wild-eyed guy in a leather jacket invariably stood ready to whisk us to Houston in the span of a few frames of celluloid. We had an hour's flight ahead of us.

While I struggled to remain calm, David stuck his head out the door and shouted toward the men still milling around the shed, "Where's the pilot?"

"Sorenson. Now. They need the chopper," someone yelled, and a man loped toward us. The engine geared up and the blades churned, at first slowly and then building speed. We were airborne, on our way to Houston, when David radioed the captain.

"Why does Sarah need to talk to Maggie's teacher?" he demanded. "What's wrong?"

"Not now," David ordered. "Just patch us through."

Seconds later, as the helicopter cut across the sky over the top of the forest, the school receptionist's familiar voice crackled through on the speaker.

"This is Mrs. Armstrong, Maggie's mother," I explained, shouting over the noise of the engine and the blades sweeping overhead. "I need to talk to Mrs. Hansen. It's an emergency."

"Mrs. Armstrong?"

"Put me through to Mrs. Hansen, now," I shouted, a ragged edge of hysteria creeping into my voice. "This is important."

"Mrs. Armstrong? How nice of you to call. My, it's loud wherever you are," said Mrs. Hansen, cheerfully. "Hold on a minute, would you?" Without waiting for an answer, she turned her attention to a student.

"Mrs. Hansen, please . . ." I yelled into the radio.

She didn't respond. Instead, I heard her say, "Todd, I told you that you had to have that paper in by last Thursday, not this Thursday; now please sit down at your desk and wait. I said we'd discuss this after dismissal. Right now, I have a phone call to take care of."

See, everything's all right. They're still in session, I thought. *Maggie's safe.*

"Mrs. Armstrong, what can I do for you?" Mrs. Hansen said, rather breathlessly. "You've caught me at a busy time of the school day."

"The children are still there."

"Yes. Of course."

"That's great," I said, relief flooding through me. "Mrs. Hansen, I need to have you keep Maggie with you, supervised, until I get there. I'll be there in . . ." I looked at the pilot who mouthed "forty-five minutes."

"I'll be there in less than an hour to pick her up. Don't let her leave with anyone. Don't let her out of your sight. In fact, I'll have Tomball P.D. send squad cars to surround the school, to stand guard until we get there."

She hesitated a moment, then said, "But Maggie's not here, Mrs. Armstrong."

How could that be? I thought. *That just can't be.*

"You just said the children are still in school," I shouted, the terror I'd tried to suppress rising in my chest.

"Don't you remember? Your mother picked up Maggie and Frederick nearly an hour ago."

"Mom and Strings?"

"To go to the University of Houston. Surely you remember. To meet with Dr. Mayer at the university."

No, I thought. *Please, no.*

"Mrs. Hansen, this is important. How well do you know Dr. Mayer?"

"Only by reputation."

"You've never met him?"

"No. But he called yesterday and inquired about Maggie. Said he'd heard about her project, and that's such a great honor, you know he's—"

"So, a man called you, introduced himself as Dr. Mayer, and asked about Maggie?"

"Yes, he heard about the Science Fair and said he was excited about her project. He seemed anxious to have you bring her to the university to meet with him. He said he wanted to congratulate you on your work."

"My work?"

"I assumed he meant in raising such a fine daughter."

Stunned, I said nothing.

Mrs. Hansen stammered. "But don't feel bad. I'm sure Dr. Mayer didn't mind that your mother and Frederick went along instead. After all, it was Maggie, not you, he really wanted to meet."

Dreading to hear the answer I felt sure would come, I asked, "So, you never talked with this man until yesterday, and except for what he told you on the telephone, you have no way to be sure the person who called you was actually Dr. Mayer?"

"Well," Mrs. Hansen stammered, "I guess. But why would anyone else call about Maggie's science project? Who would . . . ? Is something wrong?"

"How long ago did you say they left?"

"Maybe forty-five minutes. Mrs. Armstrong, I'm so sorry, if there's—"

There's still time to stop them. Mom always drives slowly, and with a little congestion downtown, it could easily take her that long to get to the university. I clicked off the radio connection with the school. Immediately, the captain's voice filled the chopper. He'd been listening. "Sarah, what's wrong?"

"Captain Williams, have them connect me with Mom's cell phone," I said, rattling off the number. "Now."

The telephone rang, and rang, and rang, and rang.

"No answer, Sarah. Tell me what's wrong."

"Captain, please, try one more time. Mom always has her cell phone with her," I pleaded. "Please, try again."

This time someone clicked on after the third ring, but no one spoke.

"Mom, is that you?"

Again silence.

"Is Maggie there? Strings? Where are you?"

The voice that spoke next was low and flat, with just the shadow of an East Texas drawl.

"You were supposed to bring her," he said. "Why didn't you come? Aren't you a good mother? You left your child unattended."

"Doyle, please . . ."

"Doyle?"

Pulling myself together, I started again. "I meant Gabriel. Am I talking to Gabriel?"

"Yes, Sarah," he answered. "You are."

"Wonderful. That's good. I'm so glad we can finally talk and get to know each other. I've wanted to meet you," I said, fighting to keep my voice level and light. "We both know that you don't want Maggie and the others. They're children, an old woman. We both know you really were hoping for me, weren't you?"

"But you're not here," he answered. "And they are."

"For the sake of God," I pleaded. "Please . . ."

"Yes, for the sake of God," he answered, his voice cool, calm. "For the sake of God, I'll wait for you. But not long."

"Thank—"

"You have one hour to get here. If you arrive on time, you can join me, and your family will go free. I'll let them go."

"Gabriel—"

"But if you're not here on time, Sarah, your daughter and the others will take your place."

The thought of the children and Mom at the mercy of that monster horrified me. Yet I needed time, time to get there, time to gather help and form a plan. I had no illusions that turning myself over to a madman would ensure anyone's safety. If I did as Gabriel wanted, what would prevent him from killing us all? Annmarie Knowles caught his eye, yet when he had the opportunity, he killed Edward Lucas.

"Please, Gabriel. I'm in East Texas. I've just gotten into a heli-copter to come to Houston. We're just getting ready to take off. I'm sure you can hear the racket, so you know that's true. It'll take two hours for us to land. One hour is . . . it's impossible."

Silence. When he spoke again, he said, "You've been to the Thicket."

"I—"

"That's why you know his name."

"Whose name?"

"The boy's name."

Square one and I'd already blundered, blurting out his real name. I should have known better. Gabriel could never accept any connec-tion with someone like Doyle Tyler.

"Yes, I've been to the Thicket. We're just leaving. That's why I can't be there in an hour."

"He doesn't exist anymore, you know," the voice said.

"Doyle doesn't exist?"

"That's right. He's gone."

"I'm glad you told me, Gabriel. I'd like you to tell me more," I said. "I want to understand."

"That's good, Sarah," he said. Then, after a hesitation, "I assume you met his mother?"

He's testing, I thought. *He wants to know if I'll tell him the truth.*

"Yes, we found her."

"Ah, you know it all then. Terrible, perverted person she was, yet to be killed by one's own son . . ."

"Gabriel—"

"Now you know everything. You've discovered all the boy's secrets."

But what about Maggie, Mom, and Strings, I wanted to scream. What about them?

"Gabriel, please, I'll be there—don't hurt anyone. Two hours and

I'll be there. I'll do anything you want. Absolutely anything. You have my promise. My word."

Only silence, a long, empty, horrid silence. Then his voice again, quiet yet churlish: "I'll wait ninety minutes, Sarah. It is, of course, you that I've been sent for, not the children and the old woman," he said. "But, Sarah, if you're not here when the time's up, I won't wait a minute longer."

Don't think about what he's capable of now, I told myself. *Focus. Focus on finding a way to stop him.*

"Gabriel, I need to talk to my mother," I said.

Again only silence.

"I'm sure you'd never lie to me, but you're asking me to turn my-self over to you. It's not unreasonable to want to talk to them, to know you really have them and that they're still alive," I said, strain-ing to sound as respectful and calm as possible. "I just need to be sure, before I come to you."

Dead air hung between us. Then, a voice resembling Mom's but different, pitted with fear.

"Sarah, it's me, dear. We're here with this gentleman. Mr. Gabriel."

"Are you all right? The children?"

"So far, but—"

Mom's voice vanished and again Gabriel spoke. "Ninety minutes, Sarah, starting now. You'd better hurry."

"Where are you?" I said. "How will I find you?"

"I'm disappointed, Lieutenant. Up until now you've been so smart, haven't you? Figuring everything out. If anyone did, I thought you understood my mission. Then I saw the article. Those hateful things you said. . . ."

"Gabriel, I didn't understand. I'm sorry."

"How fitting for you to come to be with me now, when it's com-ing to an end."

"Coming to an end?"

"Yes."

No, I thought. *Please, this isn't happening. It's not real.* "You're at the university, Gabriel?"

"Very good, Sarah. Very good."

"But where? Please. Tell me, where."

Again a maddening silence. I wanted to scream, to curse, to sob wildly, and to hide. Instead, I waited. "Gabriel, please, if you want me to come to you, you have to tell me where you are," I pleaded.

"You already know."

"Help me, Gabriel. Please. Help me come to you."

"One minute gone. Eighty-nine minutes left. No more. But I'll give you a clue," he said. I could almost picture him smiling. "It's a place with a view of the heavens."

Thirty-five

The pilot put the helicopter down in a lot south of downtown Houston. The captain waited, accompanied by a squad of HPD officers, who escorted us to the university in a motorcade of unmarked, white Crown Vics, no sirens, only flashing lights. We drove between the marble obelisk split in two, one on either side of the thoroughfare, like sentries guarding the edge of the University of Houston campus. On the grounds, I passed buildings I knew from my years as a student, yet I felt no interest in the surroundings, my mind filled with thoughts of Maggie, Mom, and Strings.

God, I silently prayed. *I've already lost so much. I'll promise you anything. Just please, please protect them.* Then, just in case, *Bill, if you're up there and you can hear me, please help!*

We pulled up next to a beige brick building with columns of smoky dark windows I recognized as SR1, Science and Research Building One, and ran through the courtyard toward the center entrance. The azaleas bloomed bright pink, but the rows of crepe myrtles remained barren from the winter, their naked trunks protruding from the ground like spears. The last thing I passed before I

jerked the door open and ran inside was a sculpture of a woman per-
petually caught inside two open squares.

Inside SR1's marble-paneled lobby, students and professors were
quietly and efficiently evacuating. No screaming or shouting. The officers had the scene under control, escorting groups in orderly lines.

"We have all the civilians exiting through the east doors. Gabriel
shouldn't be able to see anything out of the ordinary," explained the
captain. "We're keeping everything very quiet. We don't want him
to know we're here. And we especially don't want him to know that
you've arrived."

"Are we sure that's where he is, and that he has Mom and the
children with him?" I asked.

"All four of them were seen on the sixth floor, walking toward
the stairway that leads to the observatory," he said. My heart sank
when he added, "It's likely Gabriel made up some con, like being a
student assigned to take them to see Dr. Mayer, to get the children
and your mother to go with him. At that point, they didn't appear
frightened. In fact, they walked past a professor who said they all appeared happy. Maggie was laughing."

My thoughts flashed back to Maggie and Mom at the dinner
table, so excited, talking about their trip to the university. Maggie
bubbled with enthusiasm. And Strings, that dear sweet child, with
his rebellious streak. Why hadn't I gone with them?

Just then, a diminutive man, bald with a well-trimmed salt-and-
pepper goatee, wearing round glasses and a spotless white lab coat,
exited an elevator and bustled toward us. "I'm Dr. Norton Mayer,"
he said, pumping my hand and appearing highly agitated. "I told the
police. I know nothing about this man who has your family. I've
never seen him. I didn't invite your daughter here to the university.
Why, I—"

"It's all right, Dr. Mayer," I said. "I know this has nothing to do
with you. This man just used your name to lure them here."

"That's what I told that FBI agent," he said, incredulously. "How could anyone believe I was involved, after all—"

"What FBI agent?" I interrupted.

"I believe his name is Scroggins," said the doctor. "Horrible man. Why he as much as suggested that I was somehow involved in all this. I've never in my life . . ."

I felt sickened when I realized that Scroggins had arrived and already insinuated himself into the situation.

"Please, Professor, don't let it bother you," said David, who'd been standing behind me. "I'm sure Agent Scroggins was simply ruling out that possibility. We have no reason to believe you're involved in any way."

"Well then, as I was telling that disagreeable man, I am eager to help," he said. "I know the observatory better than anyone. I've held classes there for nearly thirty years and helped design the facility."

"Then come with us," said the captain, who held open an elevator door.

Nearly all the players in the drama of the past two weeks had already gathered when we arrived at the fourth-floor physics department offices—two floors below the observatory—hastily commandeered to be used as a temporary command center. The reception area resembled most academic offices, piled high with papers and books. The walls were covered in framed posters of milestones in the history of physics and tacked-up notices of changes in room assignments. Scroggins sat half-on half-off the corner of a cheap brown metal-and-Formica desk, as cocky as ever, and accompanied by two men and a woman I pegged as members of an FBI SWAT team. Detective Nelson had tagged along, probably to gloat, I assumed. But then I noticed he'd lost his swagger. Even more red-faced than usual, he looked perplexed when I walked into the room, as if he couldn't decide whether to hate or pity me.

Then I noticed Captain Jim Perkins, head of Houston P.D.'s SWAT and hostage negotiation teams, my first good news. Jim had been one of Bill's best friends for more than a decade, and our families were so close that I'd stood up as his daughter's godmother at her baptism five years earlier.

"Thanks for coming, Jim," I said.

He slipped his arms around me. His badge pinched my cheek, but I didn't pull back. "When I heard, they couldn't keep me away," he whispered. "Don't worry. We'll get them out."

Embarrassed, I brushed away a tear.

With every ounce of the little self-control I retained, I squared my shoulders and surveyed the officers gathered before me. "If Gabriel lives up to our agreement, we've got half an hour to get my family out alive," I said. "How do we make this happen?"

"It's our opinion, at the Bureau, that this man won't kill your family," said Scroggins, walking around the room, tapping a pointer he'd lifted from one of the desks. I'd been listening to his pronouncements and staring at my watch for nearly ninety seconds with no hint of what he intended. Now it appeared he planned to tell me. "Lieutenant, it's you he really wants, and he'll wait for you. Our tactic is to keep promising you but not produce you," he explained. "We want to wear him down, wait until he's tired, hungry, and then negotiate to gain release of the hostages."

I couldn't believe what I was hearing.

"He will kill them," I said, bridling in crushing frustration. "The man you're talking about is a psychopath who has killed at least six people. He loves nothing better than torturing and murdering. And now, he's suicidal. He knows his run is over, that he'll never leave this building alive and a free man. What he's done here, Agent Scroggins, is to orchestrate his own suicide, a dramatic finale. He intends to go out in a blaze of glory, but not alone. If we do nothing but talk, in precisely twenty-eight minutes, my mother, my daughter, and an innocent young boy will all die truly horrible deaths."

"That's not true, Lieutenant," Scroggins insisted. "You're too close to this and not looking at it rationally."

Was he right? Could I be wrong?

"What do you think, David?" I asked.

Glaring at Scroggins from across the room, David said, "I agree with Sarah. We cannot assume Gabriel will not kill his hostages. This is a highly motivated killer who has expressed what could reasonably be taken for suicidal intentions. We need to act as quickly as possible."

"I don't agree," said Scroggins. "I'm telling you—"

Ignoring him, I turned to Jim Perkins.

"Jim, what are our options," I said. "How will your team proceed?"

"As I explained to Agent Scroggins before you arrived," he replied, "if our SWAT team runs this scene, we do it with no interference from his men. I've already stationed officers around the building perimeter, outside the observatory door, and snipers on the rooftops of every adjacent building. I have a helicopter with a decoy on its way, so we can have it land on the grounds outside as a diversion, to stage your arrival. A specialist is ready to infiltrate the observatory with a pinhole tandem microphone and camera device to establish surveillance, as soon as he gets the order."

"What are you waiting for?" I asked.

"Assurance that we're in charge, Sarah," he said, motioning at Scroggins. "Currently, we've been ordered to stand down."

"I told you, Perkins, you don't need cameras and microphones.

It's never getting to that point." Scroggins bristled. "As for who's in charge, the FBI is in control of this scene. That means, as the senior agent, that I'm in charge, and there's no way in hell I'm letting you burst in and get innocent people killed. We'll negotiate those hostages out of there. We're not forcing entry."

"Who put you in command?" I questioned, my anger rising to the surface.

"When the FBI is on a scene, we run the show," Scroggins said, a thin coat of sweat glistening on his forehead, and his voice thick with resentment. "If Captain Perkins wants to hang around to see how it's done, well, that's up to him. But I'm calling the shots."

I couldn't take it any longer.

"Your services are no longer needed here," I snapped at Scroggins. "Get out."

"Sarah, we might need their help," David objected. Except to answer my direct question, he'd hung back, listening. I didn't know what he was thinking. Maybe he thought this was my fault, that I'd put my family in danger. Maybe he was right. "Let's scope this situation out first, before we start sending people away."

"No," I said, inwardly wondering if I was making the right decision. Yet my gut screamed one thing: something had to be done and it had to be done fast. "I want Scroggins and his men out of here, now."

"That's not your decision, Lieutenant," Scroggins shot back, anger spilling out with every word. "Your position in this room is that of a concerned relative of the hostages. Nothing more. On this case, you have no stature as a law officer."

"Captain," I said, turning to my boss, who leaned against the wall near the door. "They can't do that. Can they?"

"Well, Sarah . . ."

"I'm telling you, this is the way it is," said Scroggins, so haughtily his entourage, milling about the room, looked uneasy.

"Ted, we need to listen to the lieutenant. It's her—" Nelson ventured.

"Listen, you damn redneck, sit down and shut up," Scroggins barked. He then turned to his men. "Now, I want a phone line directly hooked up to—"

"Captain," I said again, a lump of bile swelling in my chest. "Isn't it true that the FBI is on this scene at our department's invitation?"

"Technically . . ."

"Well then, fire them."

"You sure, Sarah?"

"Yeah," I said, swallowing hard. "I'm sure."

Eyes narrowed, Captain Williams said, "Agent Scroggins, your services and those of your men are no longer required. Please leave the scene."

"You can't . . ." Scroggins blustered. "Washington will hear . . ."

"Go ahead, call D.C.," the captain said, frowning. "But in the meantime, get the hell out."

Scroggins glared at me but didn't argue.

"Thanks, Captain," I said. I was about to turn toward Jim Perkins, when I thought better of it. I wanted one more shot at Scroggins, who was angrily stalking toward the door.

"By the way, did you leak the information on this case to the press to set me up to take the fall when your case against Priscilla Lucas fell through? Is that why you did it?" I shouted.

Scroggins turned back to face me, his face contorted with anger. He said nothing, but I knew without question, I'd been right. David must have reached the same conclusion because he said, fuming, "Ted, leave. Get out of here before I throw you out."

Dr. Mayer, who'd been silent yet looking rather pleased throughout the entire exchange, smirked at Scroggins and observed, "Looks like you're just in the way here, Agent Scroggins."

After shooting the professor a smoldering gaze, Scroggins turned on his heels and stormed from the room, followed by his minions. Nelson hung back.

"I'd like to help," he said. "In any way I can."

"I'd appreciate that," I said. Then I turned to Jim. "Okay, how long before you have surveillance, and how do we get inside?"

"Sarah, just a minute," he said, motioning to one of his men. "Anderson."

"Yes, Captain Perkins."

"Get that camera positioned and functioning; you've got three minutes."

"Yes, sir."

"Sarah, this is what I've got in mind . . ."

Thirty-six

The situation was a difficult one. The building we were in, SR1, was the tallest on this section of the campus, ruling out any possibility that snipers would have a shot at taking Gabriel out. The gunmen were stationed merely as a backup, to prevent his escape if he attempted to run from the building.

Pushing books, papers, a telephone, and everything else aside, Jim unrolled a blueprint of SR1 on a desk. He explained that the observatory consisted of a rectangular room capped by a thirteen-foot dome. Perched on the roof at the west end of the building, the facility's sole entrance was accessed via a special sixth-floor stairway. A fire door positioned at the top of the stairs led directly into the observatory, while a second door, positioned off the same landing, led to the roof.

"How does the observatory door lock?" I asked Dr. Mayer.

"With a key from the outside, but it also has a bolt-lock mechanism on the inside. The students use the telescope to take photographs, and then develop their film inside the observatory," he said. "Bolting the door from the inside prevents it from being opened, admitting light, and ruining their film."

As Jim described it, the observatory had three openings and, therefore, three possible points of entry: the first, the fire door; the second, two sliding panels, or shutters, in the dome itself that, when fully opened, measured forty-eight-inches wide. They formed the observatory's aperture, the opening through which students pointed the telescope to view the moon and stars.

"The only way to control the aperture, the rotation of the dome, and the telescope itself is through a small control panel attached to the telescope," explained Dr. Mayer.

"Our office pulled a satellite photo of the campus and it appears that the shutters are currently open approximately eighteen inches, and the aperture is pointed west," Jim said.

The observatory, not attached to the building's heating and air-conditioning systems, had no vents in the walls or the floor. The floor itself was a solid concrete slab, but the walls were a less-substantial construction, concrete block. The third and final opening in the structure consisted of an eighteen-by-twenty-four-inch hole housing an air-conditioning unit.

"That's where Anderson is inserting the camera. He's snaking it through the unit's filter until it's flush with the lower grate. It should be well camouflaged. Gabriel won't be able to detect its presence," Jim assured us. "The good news is that the upper dome is fiberglass, easily penetrated. But then there's the bad news: the entire observatory is surrounded by a gravel rooftop, making it likely our guys' movements would be audible from inside."

To muffle any noise and prevent Gabriel from discovering their presence, Jim's men were carefully laying a special insulation material over the gravel. The first area they'd covered, from the door to the air conditioner, was already being used by Officer Anderson to quiet his footsteps as he inched his way around the perimeter of the dome to install the camera.

"Anderson's in," someone yelled, and we hurried to the adjoining office, where a laptop computer manned by an operator had already been set up. At first an image flickered, then swam across the screen as the tiny camera made its way through the final layers of the air conditioner's filter and stopped just behind the mesh that covered the lower third of the unit. When the camera settled into place, the computer operator keyed in instructions and a clearer black-and-white image filled the screen. The wide-angle lens gave an elongated view of the inside of a dim room. I saw desks and chairs, dusty book-shelves, a framed photo of the moon on the wall, photographic en-largers, and in the very center, on a tall black pedestal, a large white-barreled telescope pointed toward a shaft of light, the dome's opening.

"Where are they?" I said, frantically scanning the screen.

"There," said David, pointing at an object protruding from a far wall.

"He's got them locked in the equipment storage locker," said Dr. Mayer. "But I only see two people. A boy and a woman."

Even through the distortion of the camera, I could see the images of Mom and Strings locked inside what appeared to be a wire-mesh cage. I could hear muffled voices.

"Turn up the volume," Jim ordered.

The operator clicked on an icon and voices came through, loud and clear.

"Well, you're eventually just going to have to let us go," Mom could be heard arguing. "You can't keep us here. Why would you do that? We haven't done anything. We haven't hurt anyone. They're just children."

"I told you to shut up, old woman," Gabriel ordered, from some-where off-camera.

Strings cut in, "You shouldn't talk to Mrs. Potts that way."

"Be quiet," Gabriel shouted.

They're alive, I thought. *But where is Maggie? Where is she?*

"Jim, I don't see Maggie," I said.

Just then, I heard her voice. "You know, my gram is a really good person, and you're not being nice to her," she said, her voice strained by fear. "No matter what you say about being on some stupid mission and not really wanting to kill people, you're just a stupid killer."

"Shut up!" Gabriel shrieked. "Now!"

"There she is," Jim said, pointing to a small figure on a stepladder, near the base of the telescope.

"Oh, God, David, he's got her tied up," I said, as the camera zoomed in. Gabriel had used what looked to be electrical cord to tie the equipment locker shut and to bind Maggie's arms and legs to the ladder's frame. "He's going to kill Maggie."

"Sarah, stop," David ordered. But I saw my own terror reflected in his face.

"I need a schematic of this room," Jim ordered the operator. "We've got eighteen minutes before the hour's up. I need to know everything that's in that room, down to the smallest detail, in three. Now, do it."

As the computer tech and an assistant turned their attention to Jim's order, Dr. Mayer asked the question I'd been thinking, "Where's this bad guy? I don't see him."

We watched the screen for long moments, listening to the conversation inside, the camera adjusting and readjusting to every possible angle, zooming in and then pulling back until a figure emerged from the shadows, a lean, rigid young man with shoulder-length blond hair, dressed all in black. He looked in the direction of the air conditioner.

"He's seen the camera," I said, just as Gabriel walked toward us and stopped, within inches of the air conditioner. He looked directly into the lens, and I stared into the eyes so many had seen just moments before their deaths, the same eyes that had terrified Lily Salas. They were penetrating and empty.

"Do we need to pull the camera out before he makes it?" David asked.

"No, give him a minute. This thing's really small and it shouldn't be visible. Just hold on," said Jim, as on the screen Gabriel reached up toward the camera. He seemed to be twisting something.

"He's trying to turn on the air conditioner. It doesn't work," Dr. Mayer said, with a shrug. "I've been complaining to maintenance about it for weeks. A little uncomfortable in there now, but in a couple of months, once summer starts, it will be absolutely intolerable."

Apparently giving up, Gabriel walked away.

Moments later, Jim drew our attention back to the desk where the computer operator and an assistant were putting the finishing touches on a schematic of the room.

"This is the way the inside lays out. You've got the telescope in the center. One hostage is tied to the stepladder attached to it; the other two are in the cage at the southeast corner," the technician explained. "Now, lining the north and east walls are desks, computers, and some photographic equipment. The room's only telephone is in the northwest corner."

"Have we found any weapons?" Jim asked. Then, turning to me, he added, "What does this guy use?"

"His preferred weapon is a hunting knife," I said, trying not to think about how the hostages they referred to were people I loved. "When he takes the knife out, that's an indication that he's getting ready . . ."

My voice faltered and David jumped in. "That's an indication he's getting ready to act," he said. "But he has used a gun. In the Galveston double murder. So he's not averse to changing his MO."

"We may have a gun over here. We can see something on top of this desk, near the telephone," the technician said, pointing to a corner of the diagram opposite the door. "It looks like a semiautomatic pistol."

"No knife?" Jim asked.

"Haven't seen one yet."

"He'd have it close to him," I explained, working hard to get the words out. "Maybe even on him. It has a special significance for him."

David slipped his arm around my shoulders, and I momentarily thought about how easy it would be to just let go, to fall apart. Behind me I could hear Strings's voice coming over the speakers.

"My dad's a pastor in a church, and he says you've got God all wrong," he lectured. "My dad says God doesn't send people out to kill other people. And those weren't bad people you killed. That woman even had little kids."

"I told you to shut up," Gabriel yelled, seething. In an instant, he'd grabbed a computer keyboard, yanked it loose, and flung it toward Mom and Strings, where it smashed against the metal locker and shattered.

"Children, that's enough," Mom warned, clearly terrified. "Let's not upset Mr. Gabriel anymore."

On the screen, Gabriel checked his watch. I looked down at mine. We now had exactly twelve minutes.

"We need to set a charge, right here," Jim said, drawing my attention from the computer screen back to the schematic of the observatory. He was pointing at the northwest corner. "An explosion with enough force to blow a hole through the concrete block."

"Why there?" Dr. Mayer asked.

"Because that's the farthest distance from the hostages. That's the safest point, and that's where—"

"I'm sorry, but you can't do that," Dr. Mayer insisted. "Captain Perkins, you'll have to find another place for your explosion."

"What's wrong?" I demanded. "We're running out of time."

"There's a lab underneath that section of the observatory that stores radioactive material. A colleague of mine has been doing some rather exciting research on, well, you don't need to know all that," the professor remarked. "The impact of an explosion directly overhead could crack the containment unit and release the radioactivity into the air."

"What are we talking about here?" I demanded. "How much radioactivity?"

"We're not talking Chernobyl, but we're talking enough to make a lot of people very sick, anyone within a half-mile of this building, including the hostages and your own officers," he said, looking again toward Jim. "There has to be another way."

"That's our best chance, the least likely location to endanger the hostages, plus . . ." said Jim.

"Can we move this radioactive material you're talking about?" I asked the professor.

"Well, we'd have to bring up a hand truck and some equipment. It would take a little while."

"How long?"

"Ten minutes."

"We don't have ten minutes—can you do it in five?" I demanded.

"Maybe . . ."

"Can we spare that much time?" I asked Jim.

"Barely," he answered.

"Get started, Professor," I ordered.

The old man turned toward his lab assistant, who'd been leaning against the door frame listening. "Jerome, get it done, now. Don't wait for maintenance. Do it yourself."

"Martinez, pull some men to assist," Jim shouted toward one of his officers. "And get the explosives team working on setting the charge."

"I'll help with the hand truck," Detective Nelson offered.

Jim looked at me and I nodded. "Sure," I said. "Thanks."

Nelson and the other men ran out, and I turned back to Jim to ask, "How do we keep Gabriel from killing everyone when he realizes we're forcing entry?"

"That's what I was trying to explain. We lure him over here," he said, pointing to the diagram and again indicating the observatory's northwest corner. "Close to the site of the charge. If we set up the explosion correctly, we should be able to direct the force toward him. It will be enough to at least stun him, if not injure him. There's a possibility, depending on his distance from the wall at the moment of impact, that the explosion could even kill him. The charge goes off and four of my men will immediately enter through the opening in the wall, find Gabriel, and secure the safety of the hostages."

"This all sounds fine, but how do we get Gabriel to cooperate?" David asked.

"We . . ."

"The telephone," I said, interrupting Jim. "I call him on the observatory telephone."

"Yes. That's what I was trying to explain to you. That's where the telephone's located, hardwired into the wall," said Jim. "We'll land the helicopter outside on the grass, where he can see it. Then we'll have the decoy run toward the building. When the phone rings, he'll assume it's Sarah, that she's just arrived and needs to talk to him about letting her into the observatory. While he's in position, at the desk, we set off the charge."

"What if the phone rings and he doesn't pick it up?" David asked.

"Then, we detonate anyway and hope we get to him before he has time to hurt Mrs. Potts and the children," Jim said.

"If this doesn't come together in time, Jim, if everything's not in place in nine minutes," I said, glancing down at my watch, "I want it understood that I'm doing what this guy wants, I'm going in, with or without your men."

"Sarah, you can't . . ."

"Jim, there's no argument, that's—"

"I'm not sure you have even that much time, Lieutenant. You may have a complication," Dr. Mayer interrupted, a look of deep concern on his face as he stared at the laptop screen.

"What?" Jim asked.

"Look," he said.

In the observatory, Mom and Strings remained silent in their storage-locker prison, as Gabriel paced back and forth in front of the telescope, staring up toward the skies. *He's looking for the helicopter, for me*, I thought. *He's eager for me to arrive.* He glanced again at his watch. Then I saw him slip a hand inside his jacket and run it toward the small of his back.

"He's checking for his knife," I said, with a shudder. "He's thinking about what he's going to . . ."

"Yes, I suppose he is," said the professor. "But there's something else. Look again."

I saw nothing, except that for some reason, the picture was growing brighter. "Did he turn on a light?" I asked.

"That's the afternoon sun beginning to line up with the aperture in the dome," explained Dr. Mayer. "But that's not all I'm talking about. Look at your daughter."

There, toward the center of the screen, Maggie could be seen, still tied to the stepladder. But something was different. She'd shifted her weight to one side and leaned backward, toward the pedestal that supported the telescope. Somehow she'd worked one hand free, and she held a rectangular object, the size of a pocket calculator, attached to the base of the telescope. She was pushing buttons.

"What's she doing?" I asked.

"Captain Perkins, I suggest you get your men ready as quickly as possible," Dr Mayer said to Jim. "If I'm right about the path of the sun this time of year, and I believe I am, in about six minutes, you're going to have chaos inside that observatory."

Thirty-seven

E xactly four minutes later, the last details were falling into place. Officer Larson, Jerome the lab assistant, Detective Nelson, and a handful of others had maneuvered a large lead container on a hand truck to the other side of the building, removing the complication of the radioactive materials. The explosives were in position, taped to the observatory wall. Two of Jim's best men waited twenty feet away, around a corner and protected from the brunt of the blast, ready to enter. The size of the explosion, according to the team's expert, was more than ample to blow a door-size hole through the cement block wall.

David and I stood behind the SWAT officers, next in line to follow them in. I'd wanted to go in first, but Jim insisted he wanted his men in the lead, insurance in case Gabriel survived the blast. Standing behind me, Nelson waited with the second wave, four officers who'd enter once the smoke began to clear. Nearby Jim and the captain monitored the activities inside the observatory on the laptop. Occasionally, I glanced at the screen. Gabriel was growing impatient, pacing, no doubt anticipating the minutest details of what he believed lay ahead, how he would punish and then kill me.

To my great relief, his obsession with me distracted him from Mom and the children. But I wasn't fooled into believing that his disinterest suggested any hope that he might agree to set them free. They were part of his game now. We all were.

With her captor preoccupied, Maggie cautiously proceeded with her own plan. As we watched on the computer screen, she repositioned the telescope toward the opening in the dome. Earlier, Dr. Mayer explained that he believed she was easing the barrel into position to aim the lens directly at the sun.

"That girl of yours is bright. Although the telescope may not appear flammable, many of its components will burn. In a matter of seconds, the sunlight will smolder the epoxy anchoring the mirrors. As the heat builds, the vinyl housing will ignite," he said. "We'll have flames. At the very least, the place will fill with a thick smoke and trigger the fire alarms throughout the entire building."

"Maggie's had experience," I told him. "Her first telescope caught fire when she took the shaded lens off and left it pointed at the sun."

"Ah," the professor said.

We had no way to communicate with Maggie, to let her know we were waiting just outside. Jim, unhappy with the complication of a fire, was determined to use the turn of events to our advantage, timing the explosion to coincide with the fire alarm. "The bastard won't know what's hit him," he said. "If we're lucky, it'll happen so fast, he won't have time to reach for that gun."

Still, Jim worried about the diminished visibility inside the observatory. He'd given strict orders; no one was to fire until sure of the

target. In the smoke, it would be easy to mistakenly kill another officer or one of the hostages.

Suddenly, overhead, we heard the beating of helicopter blades
against the stagnant late-afternoon air. Jim had planned every detail
meticulously, including ordering the pilot to line up the 'copter with
the opening in the observatory aperture, ensuring that Gabriel
would see it. Inside, a policewoman, wearing a dark blond wig, played
me. From a distance, I thought, even a friend could be fooled by the
resemblance.

As soon as the 'copter landed in a grassy courtyard, the decoy
jumped out and ran toward the building, holding a cell phone to her
ear, and Jim motioned in my direction. I hit the send button on my
cell phone and heard the observatory phone ring, once, twice, three
times. No answer.

"Let it ring," Jim whispered.

I waited, still no answer.

On the computer screen, Gabriel held Mom's cell phone, obviously wondering why I would call the observatory instead. He hit a
button. But we'd already planned for that reaction. The cell phone
wasn't functioning. David had contacted the company and had its
access turned off. I let the observatory phone continue ringing until
Gabriel finally picked up.

"I'm on my way. I should be there in just a minute. I'm waiting
for the elevator," I said. "When will you let Mom and the children
go?"

"What happened to your mother's phone?" Gabriel demanded.

"I don't know. It's not working," I said. "How will you let me in
and release Mom and the kids?"

"When you come into the observatory, I'll let them go," he said.
"You're going to have to trust me."

On the computer screen, a thin cloud of smoke trailed from the telescope's base. Jim motioned to the officer in charge of the detonation to get ready.

Sure, I thought. *Trust you?* But I answered, "That sounds fine. Just stay on the telephone and I'll let you know when I'm at the door. Do you want me to knock when I get there? Are you ready to let me in?"

"Yes," Gabriel said. "Yes, I'm ready. Just knock and—"

At that moment, the telescope erupted in flames and the shrill cry of the fire alarm sounded throughout the building. Jim signaled and instantaneously the explosion tore through the wall, hurling a thick cloud of debris. The telephone went dead.

"God, please," I whispered. "Please protect them."

Jim's officers stampeded through the jagged gap in the wall, with David and me following. Inside, the dust and rubble from the explosion—combined with the thick, black, sooty smoke from the telescope—burned my eyes and nostrils. One SWAT officer searched for Gabriel under the debris, while the others fanned out into the room, disappearing in the dense smoke and dust. Meanwhile, David moved in with a fire extinguisher, and I felt the whoosh of the carbon dioxide rush past me, as I groped along the wall. I walked toward the heat of the burning telescope, thinking only of finding Maggie and the others alive. Finally, I bumped into a steel frame, the telescope's stepladder. Empty.

He has Maggie? Oh, God, no.

Fighting back utter panic, I continued feeling my way, searching for Mom and Strings. I knew I'd reached my destination when my hands brushed the wire grid of the locker. I worked my way toward the door and found someone struggling to open it. I moved back, lifted my gun, and pointed it at the figure, still hidden in the smoky haze.

"Step back," I shouted, over the blare of the fire alarm.

"Mom?" Maggie cried. "It's me, Mom. Don't shoot me."

She rushed forward and grabbed me.

"Sarah, we're inside this cage thing. Let us out," my mother screamed.

I pushed Maggie behind me and against the wall and pulled out my pocketknife, then cut through the plastic-wrapped electrical cord tying the locker door shut, as I heard scuffling and voices behind me. When the door swung open, I pushed Maggie inside. Until we had Gabriel, she'd be safer in there, where he couldn't get to her.

"Sarah. Behind you," Mom screamed

I turned toward a figure emerging from the smoke, but, my eyes burning from the smoke, I couldn't see a face. Then, something else. Steel? A knife?

Instinct lined up my shot, and I fired before I realized I'd pulled the trigger, silently praying that I'd shot Gabriel and not David or one of the SWAT officers. Through the smoke, the figure stumbled forward, and I saw his thin face, his long blond hair. He fell backward against the telescope.

"Not the way you pictured it?" I shouted.

Scowling at me with contempt, Gabriel pushed off the ladder, back onto his feet, still holding his knife.

"Mom," Maggie screamed, and I thought about my daughter behind me, watching, and I hesitated.

"You won't kill me in front of your little girl," Gabriel taunted, holding the hunting knife with its long thin blade and rushing toward me.

"Don't count on it," I said, my finger on the trigger. I lined up my shot, his face in my sites, just as a blast rang out from the clearing haze. Someone else had fired.

With a look of surprise, Gabriel turned on his heel, dropped his knife, and fell.

Detective Nelson ran toward me and saw Gabriel's body writhing on the floor. Remarkably, the kid wasn't dead, and he hadn't given up. He grabbed for his knife, inches from his fingertips. Without hesitation, Nelson fired into the monster's skull.

Nelson gazed down at the kid, still pointing his gun at the now-motionless body. I tried to say "Thank you." But when I opened my lips, nothing came out.

"Get them out of here. Now!" David ordered, as he ran up, positioning his body next to Nelson's, between the equipment locker holding Mom and the kids and the dead or dying man on the floor. A SWAT officer rushed forward and pushed me out of the way, while another bent down to check Gabriel for a pulse.

Nelson flung open the locker door and pulled Mom, Maggie, and Strings out, then shoved all four of us through the observatory toward the door and out onto the landing at the top of the stairs, urging us down the stairs and into the hallway, where scores of Jim's waiting officers rushed past into the observatory.

"He's dead," someone shouted from inside the observatory. "We got him."

When Maggie heard the officer's words, she threw her arms around me, sobbing. Crying, Mom hugged us both, and then turned to comfort Strings, but he'd have none of it.

"I'm okay, Mrs. Potts," he said, wide-eyed. "Wow, now that was way cool."

Still standing at the top of the steps, Nelson held a handkerchief to his eyes, rubbing off the soot and smoke, and I shouted "Thank you." He nodded and gave a small wave in return.

"I was so scared," Maggie sobbed. "I thought if I started a fire, the alarm would go off and people would come. I figured that Gabriel guy would run away before you got there. He was going to hurt you and I think all of us. He was telling you he'd let us go, but I didn't think he would. And I didn't want you . . ."

"I know, honey, I know. It's okay now," I said, holding her tight and combing my fingers through her hair. I kissed her softly on the top of her head. "You were so brave. You did a wonderful thing, helping us like that. And Gabriel is gone. He'll never hurt anyone ever again."

Epilogue

I'm looking for Doyle Tyler. Where have they got him?" I asked.

It was the following morning and I was in the lobby of the Harris County Medical Examiner's Building, also known as the county morgue.

"Room five," the receptionist said, checking her computer. "Looks like they've already started cutting."

On a stainless-steel coroner's table, Tyler looked small and common. His hands were delicate and fine; his face, with his eyes closed, rather ordinary. The only mark on him, with the exception of the three gunshot wounds, was an amateurish tattoo over his heart, a knife dripping blood, superimposed over a cross. As I stared down at his cold naked body, I willed myself not to remember the young boy in the photograph. Maybe someday I'd be able to sort through the past few weeks with a cooler head, even gain some semblance of professional objectivity, instead of rage.

One of the assistant coroners, Dr. Joseph Fernandez, a round, thick-necked man, who on his days off wore a black leather jacket and rode with a motorcycle club, had already sliced through Tyler's chest and abdomen in a "Y," from the shoulders to pubic bone, and opened him up. "The subject is Doyle Tyler of Bardwell, Texas, twenty-one years old. Caucasian. Mr. Tyler has a thin build, five-foot-eleven inches tall and weighing one hundred thirty-five pounds," he said into a tape recorder.

I walked out the door. I'd accomplished what I'd come for. If she ever asked, I wanted to be able to tell Maggie that I had seen Gabriel dead. I never wanted her to worry about him again. Never, not for a moment, did I want her to imagine that there was any chance he'd be back.

Later that afternoon I sat in my office behind my desk, clearing up paperwork. I had a few things to tie up before my leave began, two months off to contemplate my future. It was the captain's idea, and this time I hadn't argued. Right now, I wasn't capable of making any decisions, especially whether I would return to the rangers or look for a new career.

From the moment I'd walked in the office that morning, I'd noticed eyes turning toward me. Sheila's, the captain's, my fellow rangers'. Every time they glanced in my direction, they quickly turned away. I knew what they were thinking, not so much whether I'd be back but whether Maggie and I would be all right. No one came right out and asked. They danced around it, like when the captain ventured, "Guess you might need some time off to get things straightened out at home." I just nodded. I wasn't up to talking yet. It was all too fresh. Besides, although he'd apologized for the suspension, it left a bad taste in my mouth.

Maybe that would go away. Maybe it wouldn't.

If anyone had asked outright, I would have admitted I didn't know how Maggie and I were *really* doing.

Maggie's outward strength surprised me. That morning she'd dressed for school as if nothing out of the ordinary had happened. Certain she needed time to come to terms with all that we'd been through, knowing I did, I convinced her to stay home with Mom for a day. Tonight, after dinner, we'd discuss the future. Mrs. Hansen had recommended a counselor, and I'd already called for appointments for both of us. I couldn't sidestep our pain any longer. No matter how long it took, I was determined that we'd heal from the horror of the past year.

On the other hand, Mom appeared to be recovering quickly.

In typical fashion, she'd worked out her anxieties in the kitchen. We weren't home fifteen minutes when she had the counters loaded with ingredients. She whipped up fresh lemon squares, to the delight of a platoon of officers who'd accompanied us to take our statements. And Strings? He was back in school, I had no doubt, boasting to every kid in the class about the experience. Before we'd even left the scene, I heard him ask David if he'd come to school to answer questions about how real-live FBI agents work. David agreed, contingent on Mrs. Hansen's okay.

"Someone here to see you."

I looked up and the captain stood at my office door.

"I'm not much up for company," I said.

"It's Priscilla Lucas."

I nodded, he left, and moments later she entered the room, accompanied by her father.

"I just wanted to thank you," she said, holding out her hand.

I shook it and said, "You could have avoided a lot of pain and saved a lot of people mountains of work if you'd just been truthful with the officers working this case."

"I couldn't . . ."

"Why did you give Annmarie Knowles the hundred grand?" I asked. She looked stunned, and I asked again. "Priscilla, you *owe* me an explanation."

"You gave the money to that woman, Edward's girlfriend?" said her father. Turning to me, he asked, "Are you sure?"

"Yes, I had the bank records for everyone involved in this case subpoenaed," I explained. "The same day your daughter withdrew the money from the bank, Ms. Knowles made a deposit, for the identical sum, in cash."

Turning back to Priscilla, I said, "You're not going to tell me that's some kind of bizarre coincidence, are you?"

"If I tell you why I paid her," she said, her voice tentative, "I need your assurance that the information will never be made public. Edward's family has vowed to fight for custody of the children, and they wouldn't hesitate to use it against me."

"This is no longer a murder investigation," I explained. "You've been cleared of any involvement, so there's no need for what you tell me to ever leave this room. But I want to know. I deserve an answer."

"Sarah, I . . ." she said, hesitating. "Frankly, this is hard to talk about."

"Do it anyway," I said.

She swallowed hard and looked at her father. "I wanted out of the marriage, and I knew Edward would never agree to a divorce, not unless he was, how can I say this, distracted."

"And you paid Annmarie to be that distraction?"

"Yes," she said, glancing at her father out of the corner of her eye. "Annmarie agreed to romance Edward. Part of our agreement was that she would convince him to agree to the divorce and to not fight for the children."

Rather than shocked, Barker looked intrigued.

"Pris, I didn't think you had it in you," the old man said, with a grin I can only describe as parental pride. "That man had been riding roughshod over you for so many years . . ."

"It wasn't something I wanted to do, but I saw no other way," she stammered.

"Annmarie took the money and then . . . ?" I prodded.

"She took the money and then, the following day, refused to help me. That's why we argued at her condo the night before their murders," Priscilla said. "Edward had suddenly proposed. She'd already said yes. He told her the children were part of the deal. Annmarie said she'd fallen in love with Edward, and, looking back now, she may have been telling the truth. When he was courting, my late husband could be quite charming. At the time, I didn't believe her. I accused her of double-crossing me to get Edward's money and the social position such a marriage would guarantee her. Whatever her motivation, Annmarie feared Edward would drop her if she challenged his plans. She may have been right. It was risky crossing Edward. I myself rarely had the courage to do it."

"So that's it?" I said. "The whole story?"

"That's it," Priscilla said, looking relieved to have finally explained her role. "And, again, I want to thank you. I can't help thinking about how this might have turned out."

"Next time," I said, "forget all the intrigue and just hire a good divorce attorney."

Priscilla laughed. "Believe me, there will be no next time. I intend to live a quiet, even boring life from this day forward."

"You know, that doesn't sound bad," I said.

"So, Sarah, what's the plan?" David asked when he walked me to my car late that afternoon. "You coming back or is Texas losing a great ranger?"

"Haven't a clue," I said. "Right now I'm not thinking past tomorrow afternoon."

"What happens tomorrow afternoon?"

"Maggie and I have a date at the Galleria ice rink," I said.

"Ah, she mentioned that you'd promised," he said. "May I join you?"

I thought for a moment. It was tempting. I would have liked to spend time with him, away from the office, if for nothing else just to talk. But, instead, I shook my head. "David, I'm sorry," I said. "This is a mother-and-daughter event."

He smiled, and then slipped his hand onto my shoulder. "Okay. I understand," he said, but his eyes looked troubled. "Now, what about us?"

"You're really interested?" I asked, making no move to pull away.

"Very interested," he said, without hesitation. "Probably, more than you realize."

"Well, I don't know what about us. I'm sorry. I can't think about us now. Not yet. I don't even know about myself yet. I have some work to do to figure out where I'm going, what I do next," I said, being as honest as I could at that moment, with so much of the future yet to be decided. "And then there's Maggie. Without Bill, after all that's happened, for a while she's going to need me more than ever."

"So you want time to sort through a few things? I can live with that," he said, running his hand over my arm. "How much time?"

"I don't know," I admitted. "I can't make any guarantees."

David frowned, but nodded. "Okay. One day at a time."

With that, I turned to leave, but then thought better of it. "Just one more thing?"

"Sure," David said. "Anything."

There was something I wanted to do. I wrapped one arm around his shoulder, the other firmly around his neck, and pulled him toward me. It was without a doubt the longest, wettest kiss I'd ever planted on a man in my life. I breathed in and inhaled him, holding him close and wishing for so much more. When it was over, I took a step back and smiled at him, shooting for casual, hoping he couldn't feel my heart race.

"That's not fair," he scolded, catching his breath. "You can't do that and leave."

"Just a little something to remember me by for the time being," I said, smiling and pulling open the Tahoe's door.

David laughed. "You are cruel, Sarah."

"Maybe," I said. "I just needed one for the road."

David's smile disappeared and his eyes narrowed. "I don't like the sound of that," he said.

"If we hook up again, maybe we could try a more leisurely pace?" I said, with a smile. "Maybe dinner and a movie?"

"Ah, a real date," he agreed, his voice calmer but still hesitant. "I'd like that."

With that, I slid inside the Tahoe and pulled the door shut. Moments later I'd eased into reverse and backed out of my parking slot.

Earlier, Mom had called to say that she had a pork loin and oven-browned potatoes roasting and that at my daughter's request we'd dine *al fresco*, at a picnic table Maggie set up beneath the corral elm tree. I didn't have to ask why. Maggie wanted Bill to see us, to know that we were okay. Not knowing what the rules are in heaven, I couldn't help praying that God would give him permission to visit us under the Christmas light stars.

At the street, I glanced in my rearview mirror. David hadn't moved. Arms folded, he watched as I merged into traffic and drove away.

Acknowledgments

A big thank you to all of the following:

To my agents, Jane Dystel and Miriam Goderich, of Dystel & Goderich, for employing their many talents on my behalf.

To my St. Martin's editors: Jason Pinter, who gave Sarah, Maggie, Strings, and Nora a wonderful home, and Daniela Rapp, who guided *Singularity* to completion.

To Philip Spitzer, who encouraged me to write fiction.

I'm grateful to my manuscript readers: Mary Kay Zanoni, Kate Shadid, Shana Aborn, Terry Bachman, Ann Tavernini, Elaine Larson, Jan Shadid, Claire Cassidy, Patti Dath, and Sue Vandegrift. Special thanks to Sandy Sheehy and Ken Hammond for their suggestions and perceptive comments.

For sharing his expertise: Harris County Assistant District Attorney Edward Porter.

At the Texas Rangers: Chief Earl Pearson, Sgt. Marie Aldridge, and Sgt. Drew Carter.

At Houston P.D., Captain Michael Walker, and at the Harris County Sheriff's office, crime scene specialist Gail Mills.

Acknowledgments

In the plastics industry: Blackwell Plastics, Michael Lastovica, Paula Harvey, Greg Warkoski, Pam Robinson, and Mark Lee.

For their insights into the minds of psychopaths and the role of profilers: *CourtTV*'s Dayle Hinman and Florida Department of Law Enforcement's Leslie D'Ambrosia.

Railroad men: Ed Handley, Bill Farrell, and Robert Ray.

For her adept research assistance: Patti Dath.

At the FBI: Julie Miller and Tom Knowles.

At the University of Houston: Ray Rottman and Jennifer Davis.

And, as always, my heartfelt appreciation to my family and friends. You're treasured more than you know.